THE RESCUE NURSE

A MICHAEL GRIMM NOVEL, BOOK 1

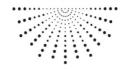

J. PHILIP HORNE

For news of upcoming works,
please join Mr. Horne's email list at
www.jphiliphorne.com
or visit him at facebook.com/jphiliphorne

Cover by J. Philip Horne

ISBN: 9798614763169 (paperback)

For Walker Dollahon
a muse to all who know
the word quirky
is a compliment

by unanticipated
twists and turns
this story traces back to you

CONTENTS

Prologue   1
Chapter 1   3
Chapter 2   17
Chapter 3   29
Chapter 4   37
Chapter 5   43
Chapter 6   51
Chapter 7   65
Chapter 8   77
Chapter 9   87
Chapter 10   101
Chapter 11   107
Chapter 12   117
Chapter 13   129
Chapter 14   143
Chapter 15   155
Chapter 16   163
Chapter 17   173
Chapter 18   183
Chapter 19   189
Chapter 20   203
Chapter 21   213
Chapter 22   221
Chapter 23   231
Chapter 24   241
Chapter 25   251

Also by J. Philip Horne   263
About the Author   264

PROLOGUE

*L*inda Greenblatt took a tentative sip of her coffee. Her nose scrunched up. Still too hot.

The phone rang. She sighed and set her mug down. Pulling on the headset, she punched the answer button.

"Rescue Nurses Worldwide. How can we help you get safely home?"

Silence. Perhaps a faint hiss on the line. Linda's eyebrows pulled together.

"Rescue Nurses Worldwide. Hello? How can we help you get safely home?"

"I need..." The female voice sounded thin, and Linda didn't think it was due to a bad connection. "I need help. To travel to Montreal."

Solid English, but an accent. Eastern European?

"Yes, ma'am," Linda said. "It's what we do. We get people safely home. Where are you now?"

"Rome."

Huh. Maybe an Italian accent.

"And are you injured, ma'am?"

1

"I need a rescue nurse."

Linda's eyebrows pulled back together. "Yes, ma'am. You've called the right place. Are you injured?"

"I need a peejay. With combat experience."

"A pee-what? Combat experience? Ma'am, we provide all the planning and support needed to get you safely home on a commercial airline when injured. We'll even maximize your insurance coverage. Is that what you need?"

"I need a PJ. Air Force Pararescue. I need one with combat experience. I've heard your company can help."

How's PJ an acronym for pararescue? This woman makes no sense.

"Ma'am," Linda said. "Do you need medical support and accompaniment to get home on a commercial flight?"

"Talk to your supervisor. I'll call back in an hour. Tell them I'll pay whatever is needed. Ten times your normal rate. Anything."

The line went dead.

CHAPTER ONE

*M*ichael Grimm took a long pull from his water glass, eyeing the man across the table. He swished the water in his mouth for a moment before swallowing, grimaced, and put his glass down hard enough to slosh some water out.

"Just spit it out," Michael said.

Jeffrey Smith's mouth quirked up on one side. Restless memories surged forward, and Michael blinked slowly, clearing the vision of Jeffrey, face dirty under a combat helmet, standing over a wrecked, bloody body.

"You've got a problem with commitment," Jeffrey said.

"What the hell does that mean?" Michael shifted in his chair. "I was faithful to Bethany. I didn't divorce her, she divorced me, and you sure as hell know I had reasons to."

Jeffrey's smirk transformed into a real smile. "Oh, I know. It's who you are. Loyal. Faithful." He waved a hand vaguely in the air above his burger. "It was the same with Ann before her, right? That's the problem."

Michael glanced at his own half-eaten burger, reached for it, but changed his mind. "How's that a problem with commitment?"

Jeffrey's chair scraped back a couple inches as he shifted forward, elbows on the table, the smile gone. "You commit to anything and everything. You commit fully. You tie yourself to people, to women, who are just, you know. Bitches."

The familiar pain constricted Michael's throat. Deep breathe. He felt the tickle of rage on the back of his neck, a rising heat. He fought it with a practiced suppression. "Little soon, don't you think? The divorce finalized like, what, two hours ago?"

"Sorry, buddy." Jeffrey sat back and took a bite of his burger. "I'm here for you, right?" The words barely fit around the food being pulverized in his mouth. "Sat with you through the whole damn thing. But my flight leaves in a couple hours. Now or never, you know? Anyway, you've known it was coming for months, right? Look, I'm sorry. You know I am. But you've got to make a change, or you'll just do it again."

Michael's mouth hardened in a tight line. "That's bullshit. Who are you to lecture me on commitment?"

Jeffrey shrugged. "Make it about me if you want, but I'm not gonna stand by while you do this shit again."

Michael sat back and took another deep, calming breath. He looked over Jeffrey's shoulder at a TV hanging above the bar. Some news story involving lots of ambulances. His neck had cooled off. "You're right. Sorry."

Jeffrey half-stood to reach across the table and slap him on the shoulder. He sat back down and popped the rest of his burger into his mouth. He tried to speak, started to choke, coughed weakly, and held a hand up to reassure Michael he was okay.

"Listen." He forced the word around the food. "Just talk to someone, okay? Before you, I don't know, go and marry again. Me. One of the guys. Hell, you've got a pastor, right?"

"Yeah, I've got a pastor," Michael said. He looked Jeffrey in the eye. "You guys know I had to get out, right?"

Jeffrey shook his head. "You were the best of us. Angel of death incarnate. Marines wouldn't have screwed you over."

Michael shrugged. "Rescuing people's more my thing. Shooting them, not so much. It was my own fault how it ended."

Jeffrey wiped his hands on his napkin and looked him in the eye. "General discharge? And you had to fight for it? No, you got screwed over." He waved the words away. "Doesn't matter now. But listen. You and I both know, sometimes, the way you help someone"—he held up an imaginary gun, took aim at Michael, pulled the trigger—"is by shooting someone else."

Michael glanced one last time in the rearview mirror and watched Jeffrey disappear through the doors of the terminal. His eyes flicked to his side mirror before he gave the little Honda some gas and pulled away from the curb. Lanes twisted among orange cones and temporary fences as he headed for the airport exit.

Different every fu— freakin' time I come here. Always building something new.

Michael shook his head as he accelerated onto the main road out of the airport. A few hours with a Marine buddy and he was already getting loose with his tongue.

"Shit!" Michael braked and swerved toward the shoulder as

a large SUV drifted into his lane. He rode the horn for a moment but gave up as the vehicle continued over and pulled ahead of him.

Michael had told Ed he'd need the whole day off, but now that the divorce was done, his newish one-bedroom apartment had no appeal. He exited the airport and swung onto the highway. He'd head to the worksite.

Traffic was light. Michael flipped on the radio and listened to a few songs before turning it back off. He fished his phone out of his pocket, flicked his eyes down to the screen, sucked in air. Bethany sat at the top of the speed dial list.

Not now. Not going to think about it.

He punched the second speed dial. Ed picked up on the third ring.

"Michael? Ain't you off today? What's up?"

"Hey Ed. Hold on." Michael switched the phone to his other hand, took a glance at the side mirror, and changed lanes. "I need to work today. Sweat it off. I'm on the way over. Making good time."

"You weren't called, were you?"

"About what?"

"No work today," Ed said. "City shut us down. I'm in a line downtown filing a form with some asshole city clerk who's probably younger than my kids."

Michael frowned. "You got nothing for me? I'm telling you, I need to work it off."

"I got nothing. Go hit the gym. Beat the shit out of some rich kids. They'll love you for it. Cause that totally makes sense."

"Come on, Ed."

"I'm messin' with ya. Hey, you hung with Jeffrey, didn't you?"

"Yeah, just dropped him off to catch a flight."

6

"Huh." Ed went silent for a moment. "He doing alright?"

Michael's mind flashed back over their conversations. He grimaced. He'd never asked Jeffrey how he was doing. What an asshole. What a complete and utter—

"He's doing great, I think." Michael saw the exit for his gym, hesitated, then swerved into the exit lane. "Natural born salesman, right?"

"Hell yeah, he is. Not like us. But we do okay, don't we?"

"Thanks to you," Michael said. "Between the construction and the rescue nurse gig you found for me. The ends are meeting, even if the belt's a little tight."

Ed let out a long, low chuckle. "Still messes with my mind to hear you called a nurse. You, the most efficient—" The line went silent for a moment, then Ed's voice came through muffled, indistinct.

Michael's mouth pulled in a hard line. His wife had left him, but the past clung to him like a jealous lover.

"Hey," Ed said. "Gotta go. My turn to beg for a signature."

"Alright. Guess I'll hit the gym."

"Take no prisoners," Ed said and hung up.

"No prisoners," Michael said to the empty car. He took a couple turns and pulled into a cramped parking lot.

Pappa Sal's Gym stood defiantly among worn out store fronts, office buildings, and restaurants on a street that had not yet experienced the gentrification sweeping other parts of the city. Pappa Sal was long gone, but his son Patrick had managed to transform the boxing club into an underground hot spot with young professionals who wanted to play MMA. Patrick had a soft spot for ex-military, and it was a good thing. Membership came at a premium, and Michael Grimm was not up to paying a premium for anything. He grabbed his gym bag out of the trunk and headed in.

The smells hit him as he stepped through the door, layered

7

like an archeological dig. Strata of sweat, oil, polish, and cleaners, some ancient, others still emanating from their sources. Oiled workout gear, polished wood racks and bars along the walls, and men breaking each other down.

Michael smiled. A good smell. Like coming home. His eyes unfocused for a moment, the poem forming in his mind.

oil and wood
sweat and steel
bag and mat
balm to heal

His smile broadened as his eyes snapped back into focus. He shook his head and chuckled.

Just terrible. More dangerous than my fists. But weirdly helpful.

Two boxing rings dominated the middle of the large space. Both were occupied by combatants, padded up but hitting and kicking each other with enough ferocity to test the limits of the safety gear. All around the perimeter men worked alone, in pairs, or small groups. They lifted, pulled, pushed, jumped, stretched, spotted, trained.

Michael cut across the left side of the gym toward the locker room. Guys nodded, smiled, held their fists out for him to bump along the way. Definitely a better home than that sterile apartment he'd moved into the previous month.

Most of the young men at the gym lived in a crust of society that Michael had only witnessed from far below. He was grateful for them. If Patrick didn't do a booming business with young rich guys from the financial district, he wouldn't have been able to afford charity cases like Michael.

They were good kids, most of them. Almost family. And they liked to take a beating. Made no sense. Maybe they'd grown up watching *Fight Club*. They liked it, and Michael delivered, like a violent mother hen. He was bigger than most of them, and stronger than all but the roided out guys. But more than that, Michael had a knack for violence. Always had.

Michael found himself standing stock still, staring at his open locker. Why did he like it? Hadn't he left the Marines to get away from it?

No, he'd left the Marines to get away from the killing, the war, the rage. He could live with enjoying violence in the safe confines of a gym. His moment of angst resolved, he scrambled into his workout clothes, grabbed his protective gear, and headed into the gym.

Michael stood in the corner near the lockers and surveyed the huge room. He had a lot to burn off today. Probably best to head straight to the rings.

A smallish guy sidled up and stood beside him for a moment, watching the gym. What was his name? Jim? George?

"Hey, Michael."

"Hey, man." So lame. Jonas? Jerry?

"This is gonna sound like a bad movie, but there's these twins that showed up today. Black belts in some martial art. Total pricks. Been beating on our people. Real ugly."

Our people. The regulars. Michael's people. His neck prickled.

"Where?"

The kid pointed. Josiah. That was it. "Far side of ring two."

"They fight together, Josiah?"

"They've both done a couple solos, and then they just tore up Frank and Gerald in a pairs. Frank should be at the hospital by now getting his nose fixed."

Michael bumped Josiah's shoulder with his fist. "They may have picked the wrong day to mess with me. I'm on it."

"Sorry, Michael."

Michael turned toward him. "What do you mean?"

Josiah kept his gaze forward, toward the rings. "The divorce. It was today, right?"

"You guys know?"

He shrugged. "Word gets around. We're family, right?"

Michael nodded. His throat felt tight. He forced the word out. "Family."

He strode across the gym and cut around ring two. He felt eyes latch onto him as he walked. The two guys in the ring broke off from sparring and looked at him. Michael nodded to them and got a look at their faces behind the headgear. Sam and Kevin. Hedge fund traders. Good kids. Lots of energy. Terrible fighters.

He saw the twins lounging in the dim corner. They sat side by side on a bench. One had a phone out, showing the other a video, both laughing.

Michael stepped up in front of them. The heat had enveloped his neck, but his throat had opened back up. "Hey. You gentlemen got another fight in you today?"

Two pairs of eyes swiveled up and locked onto his. Definitely twins. The laughter trailed off.

"Watching a funny video?" he asked.

"Oh yeah," the one on the left holding the phone said. "I filmed Dan in his first match. Opponent was a loser. We'd heard this place was legit."

Dan stood and shook his head. "Not legit. Right, Don?"

Don stood, shook his head. "Not legit."

They were both thick through the torso, had longish arms, substantial legs. They may have given up a couple inches on Michael but had to be about six feet tall. Built to fight.

"Man," Michael said. "I hate to hear that. Tell you what, why don't you hand your phone to someone so we can record one more video."

"You wanna fight one of us?" Dan asked. "Don't need someone else to film it. There's two of us."

"I was thinking I'd spar you both."

Dan and Don glanced at each other for a moment. "Pairs?"

Michael shrugged. "For you. I don't have a twin, so I'll have to make do by myself." He gave them his best grin. "Up for it?"

They looked at him for a moment. Don's eyes narrowed, but Dan grinned.

"Hell yeah!" Dan said.

It took a few minutes for Michael and the twins to gear up. He took his time and worked through his stretches while putting on his head guard, wraps, gloves, and shin instep guards. Tried to breathe out the heat. Sweat beaded on his forehead.

Control. Control, dammit!

By the time he grabbed a rope and pulled himself into the ring, the twins were waiting for him. Michael glanced around. The gym had gone quiet. The men had arranged themselves in a loose circle around the ring. He nodded. They were hoping for payback. Michael planned to deliver. The heat was a fire, held at bay by a thin line of self-control.

He looked back at the twins and stepped toward the center of the ring. "Shall we?"

There was no pause. No hesitation. They split to both sides of him. Dan on the left, Don on the right. Or was it the other way? Didn't matter. He had a fifty-fifty chance of being right, and Michael had always liked to put a name to people he fought.

Dan took two quick steps and launched himself at Michael with some sort of flying kick. Don was on the move as well, but Michael had surged toward Dan the moment he took his first step. Michael's elbow came down hard to meet Dan's shin, blocking the kick, sending him spinning to the mat, howling in pain.

Michael followed his elbow down, lashing a foot backwards as he rolled to the mat, Don's punch glancing harmlessly off the curve of his back. His heel sunk into Don's solar plexus.

So predictable.

He did a quick kip-up as Don stumbled backwards clutching his gut and collapsed. Dan was back up, but he wasn't trying any more flying leaps.

Dan circled, throwing punches and kicks, not engaging. It felt weak, ineffectual. Michael realized he was buying time to get Don back in the fight. He'd assumed they'd fold under a little pressure, but they were engaged, fighting smart. Maybe complete assholes, but dangerous assholes. Behind Dan, Michael saw Don grab a rope and haul himself to his feet.

He let go. Felt the heat burn away his anger, his hurt. Saw his vision constrict to his two opponents while opening up to every movement in the gym. Heard Don's ragged breathing. Smelled the oil, the wood, the steel.

Time to finish it.

An hour later, Michael tossed his gym bag into the trunk, got in his car, and headed for his apartment. The workout had been medicine to his soul. The divorce had loomed like towering, dark clouds on the horizon for so long it had proved a relief to have the storm break. Where he'd expected the agony of rejection to grow and consume him, instead he found a budding peace.

Except for the part where he'd let himself go.

They're gonna be okay. Held back just enough.

Twenty minutes later, he pulled through a rolling gate into the apartment parking lot. He popped the trunk as he stepped out of the car, grabbed his gym bag, closed the trunk lid.

Michael took the stairs two at a time, up two flights. As he slid his key into the lock on his door, his neighbor two doors down came out of her apartment and headed toward the stairs. Toward him.

He'd seen her before, but only from a distance. Across the parking lot, or just disappearing into her apartment.

Michael left the keys in the lock and turned toward her. "Hi. I'm Michael. Michael Grimm." He glanced at his apartment door, then back to her. "Your new neighbor."

She smiled halfheartedly as she kept to the far side of the walkway. Eight kinds of cute in that smile. Fine looking woman. Really fine. Maybe mid-twenties. She stopped across from him at the top of the stairs. "I'm Sherry."

Sherry. Sherry. Remember someone's name for once. Sherry.

Michael stuck out his hand. She jerked back like it was a live snake. He rotated it, checked the back. Dried blood. Probably from one of the twins. Why'd he always come home to shower? Why couldn't he clean up at the gym like everyone else?

He let the hand drop. "Sorry. Just came from the gym."

She cocked her head to the side. "My spinning classes don't leave me covered in blood." A ghost of a smile played across her lips.

"Oh, yeah, not that kind of gym. More MMA than aerobics."

"Okay. My new neighbor is an MMA fighter?"

Sherry. Sherry. Good. Didn't lose it.

"No, I just use it to clear my head."

"Your blood?" Sherry asked.

"What?"

"The blood." She pointed. "On your hand. Is it yours?"

"Oh!" Michael grinned. He could be so damn slow when talking to pretty women. "No, it's from Dan or Don."

"Wait, you can't remember his name, or there are, like, multiple candidates for the blood?"

"Identical twins. New guys. Couldn't tell them apart. Anyway, they beat up some of our regulars pretty badly. I was helping them, uh, learn manners."

Idiot! What the hell are you saying?

"You just got them in line? To teach them manners?" Sherry had her smile back, this time in full effect.

"No, they sparred as a pair with me." He shrugged. "Honestly, they were pretty good. Black belts in some martial art, I think."

Sherry's smile faded. "You're not BSing, are you? I'm pretty good at spotting BS."

Michael shrugged. "No BS here. Why?"

She shook her head. "Nothing." She pointed back to her apartment door. "I'm at the far end." Her finger shifted to the door one over. "Liza's between us." Her hand dropped to her side. "I guess it's your job to guard the stairs, being closest and all."

Michael smiled. "You bet. Seriously."

"And what do you do for a living, Michael?"

"Spent some years in the military," he said. "Marines. Then Air Force Pararescue. Didn't end very well."

"Wait," she said. "What was the second one?"

"The PJs. We ran rescue operations into less-than-friendly places. Render medical aid in hostile situations while getting people out. That sort of thing."

"Okay. That's pretty amazing," Sherry said. "And now?"

"Now I'm working construction and taking jobs as a rescue nurse on occasion."

Sherry's eyebrows pulled together a bit. "Wait. That's different than the PJs? A rescue what?"

Michael smiled. "Very different. A rescue nurse. Odd name, huh?"

She nodded. "What does a rescue nurse do?"

Michael shrugged. "Not as much as I'd hoped. We cover logistics and medical aid to get someone home who's injured overseas."

"That's pretty cool! How many times have you done it?"

"Four, so far. I just fill in when they have too many jobs going. It actually pays better to be the extra. How about you?"

"Freelance photographer." Sherry frowned for a moment, then smiled. "It's aspirational. For now, I survive by waitressing. Speaking of which, I've got to go work the dinner shift."

Michael nodded. "Cool. What restaurant?"

"Amore Mio."

"Oh." He smiled. "Don't think you'll have me as a customer anytime soon."

"Totally understand," Sherry said. "It's pricey. Great tips, though. Okay, see you around."

Michael nodded his farewell and turned back to the door as she headed down the stairs.

Sherry. Sherry. What was the other girl's name? Liza. That's it. Liza. Sherry and Liza.

Michael stepped through the doorway. The sense of peace he'd felt driving from the gym wavered, then shattered. His apartment was barren, lifeless. He might as well have been just out of high school, trying to strike out on his own. Except he wasn't. He was nearly twice as old, and alone again.

A mismatched thrift store couch and coffee table were the

only furniture in the living room. Michael collapsed on the couch and curled up into the fetal position. The emotion leached out of him. The euphoria of fighting, the sensation of being alive. The small lightning flickering through him at meeting someone new. Someone attractive. It all bled out into the empty room.

About an hour later, he drifted off to sleep.

CHAPTER TWO

*M*ichael's eyes snapped open. He cataloged his senses. Late afternoon sunlight leaking between the curtains. Subdued noises of apartment life. The dingy, hand-me-down smell of the couch. No movement. No threat. His phone buzzed.

He must have woken between rings. He swung his feet off the couch, sat up, and pulled his phone out of its pocket. The caller ID read RESCUE NURSES WORLDWIDE. He hit accept and put the phone to his ear.

"This is Michael."

"Michael, it's Joann. We need to talk. Can you take a moment?"

He rubbed his eye. "Sure, Joann. What's up?"

"Well, first off, I'm going to call you right back."

Michael shook his head. "Not following you, Joann."

Silence. Michael pulled the phone from his ear for a quick glance. The call had ended. "What the hell?"

The phone buzzed. The screen displayed NO CALLER ID.

Michael cocked an eyebrow. "So that's how we're gonna play this."

He hesitated a second, punched the answer button. "Hello?"

"It's Joann. Sorry about that. Feeling cautious."

"Good to know," Michael said. "Why?"

"We had an unusual call this morning. A woman who needs transport from Rome to Montreal."

A thought struck him. "Are you on a burner?"

"Michael, we're talking about a lady who needs transport."

Michael could be patient. "The phone, Joann. Is it a burner?"

"Does it really matter?" Her voice seemed more tired than tense. Michael waited. "Yes, it's a burner."

Michael nodded. "Okay, good. Wanted the context. So. A woman needs transport from Rome to Montreal. Sounds normal, but there's more to this or you wouldn't be going backchannel. Let's hear it."

He could hear her faint breathing over the line. "She requested a PJ if we had one. With combat experience."

Michael sat up straight. "Okay, that's getting unusual. So that's me, right?"

"It's why I called," she said.

"But there's more. Let's hear it."

Joann sighed. "She listed some things the rescue nurse needs to bring to Rome. Lots of medical supplies. IVs. Blood for a transfusion. That sort of thing."

"Oh," Michael said. "That's... let me ignore the fact you're on a burner and play this straight. I mean, sure, I can handle it, but if she needs a transfusion, she shouldn't be calling in help from another continent. And circling back to the fact you have a burner ready to go, and she called for you—"

"Michael," Joann said, cutting off his words, "listen to me for a sec, okay?"

"Yeah." Michael rubbed his forehead and sat back on the couch. "I'm listening."

"We get calls sometimes. Stuff that goes way beyond the normal service. We don't do them. Not through the company."

"Okay," Michael said. "Keep going."

"We don't do them through the company, but I have an arrangement with the owners to quarterback such situations as an individual consultant and still have access to our infrastructure. And we have quite a bit of capability that goes beyond the normal needs of a rescue nurse, okay? The people who need such help are willing to pay extraordinary amounts of money. And word gets around that we can help. You following?"

"Well, you had me at 'extraordinary amounts of money' but keep going."

"Let's spell it out. Today's client offered an immediate transfer of funds to front all costs, fifty thousand when we have a nurse onsite with her, another fifty thousand when she gets to Montreal."

"That's..." His voice trailed off, his eyebrows pulled together. He tried again. "That's a crazy amount of money. But there's got to be a reason, right?"

Joann paused again. "You know what I know. But yeah, the medical care needed, the whole situation, this one's going to be dangerous. I've worked some crazy ones, but this one looks intense. But your background says you do dangerous well. To be honest, it's the main reason I hired you. If you sign on to this, I'll do the initial transfer to make sure her account is actually funded. I'll wire you what you need. We'll split the proceeds at the end three ways. Me and the RNW owners will split half.

You'll get the other half. I'll quarterback the whole thing, handle logistics. You handle the work on the ground."

"Wait," Michael said. His heart was racing. His mind felt sluggish. "That's fifty grand for me, right?"

"Yes."

Fifty grand could buy a whole new beginning. It wouldn't fix his heart, but it would probably take care of most everything else. Why would anyone pay that much? Had to be a freaked-out mess on the ground. He tried to look at all the angles.

Fifty grand
new beginning in hand
and for the danger
it's no stranger

"Michael? Still with me?"

He shook his head to clear it. Stupid poems. "Yeah. Sorry. Listen, I can't just buy blood and fly to Italy with it in my luggage."

"No, you can't," Joann said. "That falls under logistics. I've developed a bit of a network for items that are hard to acquire."

Michael worked his neck. He felt taut. That moment of anticipation before all hell broke loose. He grinned. Made him feel alive.

"Learn something new every day, Joann. I'm impressed."

In his mind's eye, he saw himself being who he was meant to be. A rescuer. He'd had the gig of his dreams as a PJ, before it'd all gone to hell.

"And?" she said.

"And I'm all in."

"Excellent. I'm going to get to work, starting with the funding. I've got it set up. Hitting send now. If this goes through, I'll send instructions along shortly, along with some release papers you'll need to sign, okay? You're going to need to go shopping tonight and leave for Italy tomorrow."

"Tomorrow," Michael repeated.

"That work for you?"

"For fifty grand? Lots of things work for me for fifty grand. Look, you give me the support needed, I'll get her to Montreal, period."

"Good to hear. And the transfer went through. We're funded. I'm going to wire you some money to cover the shopping and incidentals. Look for an email. Won't look like it's from me, but hopefully no one else will be giving you shopping lists tonight. We'll talk soon."

"How do I call you?" he asked.

"You don't."

Joann's shopping list was a mix of normal and crazy. Weatherproof duffel bags? Normal. All sorts of travel supplies, toiletries, energy and protein bars, dried fruit, and the like? Normal, if a bit detailed. A bunch of black athletic clothing for himself? Crazy. Who the hell required their rescue nurse to wear all black athletic clothing? Feminine hygiene products? Awkward, but normal. Matching clothing down to the underwear for a woman approximately 5'7", 135 pounds, C cup? Even if it wasn't crazy, how was he supposed to know what to buy?

He was down to the woman's clothing and had about thirty-five minutes until the store closed for the night. Michael stood in the midst of women's athletic apparel and wasn't sure what to do. In his limited experience, the sizing on women's clothing was next to useless.

Michael needed a stand-in. A model. He glanced around, saw a blue-shirt at five o'clock. He cut through the racks of clothing and hit the aisle near her as she turned to walk the other way.

"Ma'am?"

She kept walking.

"Ma'am?" Louder this time, a bit of command in his voice.

The woman stopped and turned toward him.

"How can I help you?" she asked, a polite smile etched on her face.

"I need some help buying clothes that will fit a woman. 5'7". 135 pounds. Athletic build." He held his hands up and pantomimed. "C cup." His hands dropped to his sides.

The woman's smile faded, and her head turned a bit to the side, her eyes still on him. "Not sure how I can help with that."

Michael flicked his eyes over her short, somewhat round frame. "Do you have anyone working here who comes close? I just need someone who can give me some level of confidence in the fit."

She eyed him, then shrugged. "I'm guessing Sheila will do. Give me a sec."

She took a step to the side of the aisle and lifted her walkie talkie to her mouth. "Sheila to women's athletic, Sheila to women's athletic" crackled over the PA.

Michael gave her a nod and smiled. She just looked at him. It was a stare that filled up the awkward silence between them with an almost physical discomfort.

"What's up?"

Michael turned to find a woman who looked to be an athletic five-and-a-half feet tall standing behind him.

"Sheila?" Michael asked.

"That's me."

Michael pivoted to thank the first woman, but she was already down the aisle about twenty feet and moving fast. He turned back to Sheila.

"I need to buy some clothing for a woman."

Must I always sound like an ass with the ladies?

"Great. I think we've got some." Sheila held a hand out toward the racks of women's clothing beside them.

"Right. I need to confirm the fit. She's 5'7", 135 pounds, C cup."

Sheila's face scrunched up. "Okay, so you want me to...?"

"Make sure I get stuff that will fit her. Price isn't an issue. Just quality and fit. Here's the list of what I need."

Michael pulled his phone out and held it out to Sheila to read the list in Joann's email. She skimmed down it and looked up at him.

"You know that list makes it even weirder, right? All black?"

Michael shrugged. "Can you get it? Before this place closes?"

Sheila took another look at the list. She shrugged. "I can try. But I'm not trying on the bras and panties, and I'm not modeling any of it for you."

> *bras and panties*
> *never create*
> *right words spoken*
> *on a first date*

Michael smiled and nodded. "Good enough for me. Want me to wait up front?"

"No, I need the list. Just making sure we're on the same page."

Michael nodded. "Absolutely."

Sheila went to work, and thirty-five minutes later Michael walked out of the store with several hundred dollars worth of clothing that he added to the shopping bags filling his trunk.

Once he was in the driver's seat, he cranked the car and headed for his apartment. His phone rang. *No Caller ID.* Michael stared at it for a moment, shook his head, picked up the call.

"Little creepy," he said, "you calling me right when I'm back in my car."

"Not really," Joann said. "Retail's retail. I figured the stores had just closed. You get it all?"

"All of it."

"Okay, good. I'm emailing you your flight info. Flights were tough. No idea why. You'll connect through Toronto with one hell of a layover. I picked up a business class seat for you. You won't land in Rome until the following morning. Let's hope she's still around for you to help. You need to be at the airport tomorrow morning first thing."

Michael nodded. "I can make that work. And the medical stuff?"

"I'll have a driver for you in Rome with the supplies, and a couple other things."

"A couple other things?" Michael switched the phone to his other ear so he could hit the turn signal. "What couple things?"

"Papers. A false identity."

"Like, a passport?"

"Like a passport," Joann said. "It's all about minimizing risks. You'll do the deal as Thomas Paine, fly to Montreal with her, then go back, pick up your real identity, and fly home. Michael Grimm won't travel to Montreal with some injured woman. Thomas Paine will."

Michael nodded. "You can do that?"

"I have connections," Joann said.

"Resourceful," Michael said. "And pragmatic. I think we're going to work well together. So once I'm in Rome, how do I get ahold of you?"

"The driver will have it set up for you. Just be on that flight."

Once home, Michael hauled his purchases upstairs in a single trip, bags hanging from both arms and hands, a final one held in his teeth. He dumped them in front of his door to unlock it, then took two quick trips to relocate the bags into his living room.

The barren room sucked at him, tried to leach away his new-found sense of purpose, but his hands stayed busy, and his mind clear. Unwrapping, removing tags, folding, rolling, packing. The duffel bag was stuffed full in minutes, and Michael sat back on his heels. His stomach growled.

He glanced at his watch. His mouth twisted, a crazy notion taking shape.

I'm such a fool. She's probably ten years younger than me.

He got up, locked the apartment, and drove to Amore Mio. The crowd in the restaurant was thin at 9:40 PM, though the bar was still packed.

"A table in Sherry's section, please."

The hostess gave him a smile that didn't seem to reach her eyes and studied her seating chart for a moment, then grabbed a menu and waved him to follow. She led him to a small table next to a window.

"Michael?"

Michael looked up from the menu. Sherry was staring at him, her eyes pulled narrow, the corner of her mouth twitching toward a smile.

So, confused, but not disappointed. Not a bad start.

Her pale blonde hair was pulled back in a ponytail. Michael liked ponytails. He smiled.

"Hey, Sherry."

She smiled back, but Michael saw the edge of concern in a

tightness around her eyes. "I thought you couldn't afford my illustrious employer."

"I couldn't. Now I can. Got a big rescue nurse job right after we spoke. It involved"—he signed quotation marks—"significant funding for incidentals." Michael shrugged. "Figured if I was going to drop a tip using someone else's money, might as well keep it in circulation on our wing of the third floor."

"I like the way you think." Her smile blossomed. "Where you going to do your rescue nurse stuff?"

Michael decided a half-truth was in order. "Rome to pick up the patient, then back to the States."

"Wow!" Sherry said. "I think I'm jealous."

"Well, if you ignore the rest of my life and only pick out the word 'Rome', then yeah, I get that. So, what's good on this menu?"

A little over an hour later, Michael drove home, full of food that had cost more than his furniture, his head a little foggy from the wine. He hadn't seen much of Sherry, but he'd seen enough to figure he'd lucked out having her in an apartment two-doors down.

Ten hours after that, he punched the button on his arm rest to recline his seat as the plane reached cruising altitude. The chair didn't budge. A moment later, he figured out the pressure he felt on the back of his legs was part of the seat. He lifted his legs, hit the button, pushed back. The seat went back and a leg rest swung up.

This thing probably cost more than my car.

He pulled out his phone, connected to the complementary wifi, and sent Ed a text explaining his absence. That done, he closed his eyes and tried to fall asleep. Restless thoughts of Bethany struggled against him.

Then Jeffrey showed up, like his mind was some sort of clown car, full of hard memories and hard rebukes. Would loyalty and love never be enough? Was Jeffrey right? Would he do it again?

Michael shifted, found a more comfortable position. He needed this job. He needed... what?

I need to save someone.

CHAPTER THREE

*M*ichael stood next to the steel baggage carousel and scanned the bustling crowds of Fiumicino Airport. He spotted a shortish man, dark hair tucked under a black baseball cap, white placard held up displaying the name "T. PAINE". The man drifted through the crowd toward the baggage carousel, his eyes roaming until they found Michael's.

Michael gave him a small nod. The man tucked the placard under one arm and cut through the crowd toward him. Michael turned back to the carousel just in time to snag his large, black duffel. He hauled it up and slung it over the shoulder opposite his backpack.

"Mr. Paine?"

Michael turned back to the man, now a foot away, intruding into his personal space. He stood several inches shorter than Michael, about average compared to the other men milling around. He wore a white dress shirt buttoned all the way up, tucked into bluejeans, with brown leather shoes.

"You are Mr. Paine?" he asked again with a thick Italian accent.

"I am if you have my stuff. Am I that easy to spot?"

He cracked a small smile. "The description I was given was sufficient. Big man. Brown hair. Black clothes. Plus the papers. Your picture is on them. This way, please."

Michael put a hand on the man's shoulder as he tried to turn away. "Do you have a name?"

"Yes, but you can call me Leonardo." He winked, turned, and started working his way through the crowd.

Michael followed, muttering apologies as first the duffel and then his backpack bumped people. They made it to an exit and stood waiting for a shuttle. The weather was a close approximation to glorious perfection. Maybe mid-50s with a bright, midmorning sun. April had never been better.

He pulled his sunglasses out of the front pocket of his lightweight black running jacket, put them on, and followed Leonardo onto a shuttle that pulled up in front of them. A few minutes later, they exited the shuttle and walked out into a short-term parking lot. They stopped at the back of a red Fiat 500X. Leonardo glanced around and opened the rear hatch.

"You have a spare duffel?"

"Yep." Michael set down his duffel, unlocked the zippers, and pulled a folded up, matching duffel out of it.

Leonardo started handing Michael large parcels wrapped in brown paper out of the back of the car. Michael frowned at the first one, turning it slowly over. He found a small, three-digit number written near one corner.

"I have an envelope with your papers," Leonardo said. "It has a list of supplies labeled by number, yes?"

Michael nodded. He packed the parcels in the duffel, and estimated it was about three-fourths full when he tucked the last one in.

Leonardo handed him a bulky manila folder. "Papers, phone, currency."

Michael stood and lifted the new duffel, placing it on the folded down rear seats. It was unwieldy and heavy. He was pretty sure two of the large packages had been bottled water, and there had to have been various fluids and dry ice. He set his other duffel beside it and closed the hatch.

"Let's get moving." Michael held up the manila folder. "I'll look it over on the drive."

Leonardo smiled and nodded. They got in and Michael shifted his seat back as far as it would go. He squeezed his backpack between his feet, then tugged open the envelope as Leonardo drove for the exit. He pulled out a paper with a list of items, each next to a three-digit code. IV gear, saline, an IO drill, pain killers, antibiotics, sutures, forceps, blood, the works.

Michael frowned. "Joann checked the blood type?"

"Sí. All set up. Miss Joann always gives good directions."

So this really isn't Joann's first rodeo.

Michael smiled. Professional support. High risk. Improvisation in unknown territory. Just what he needed to keep his mind off the divorce.

He reached back into the envelope and pulled out a passport and a Nebraska driver's license. Thomas Paine, American citizen. They looked perfect. Michael reached back into the folder and retrieved two flat, bound stacks of euros. A lot of euros. He unzipped a pocket on his pants leg and jammed in the money, then pulled his wallet and passport out of a zippered pocket on the other leg. He removed his driver's license and credit cards and slid them with his passport into the manila folder. He slipped the new driver's license into his wallet and put it with the fake passport back in the pocket.

"Phone?" Michael asked.

Leonardo squinted for a moment, then broke into a grin. "Ah!"

He slipped a hand into his back pocket, tugged something

out, and handed Michael a new iPhone. A yellow sticky note had the word TPA1N3 written in bold letters. Leonardo reached over and tapped the note.

"Passcode, yes? You set up the finger reader if you want."

"And how do I call Joann?" Michael asked.

"Ah!" Leonardo tapped his head with a finger and smiled. "It is an app. You enter the password, it makes the secure call over IP."

"And the password?"

"Yes, the password. No spaces, last letter of each word capital, yes? You use a phrase. Call Joann from Rome like this."

Michael took a slow breath. "Like what? What's the password phrase?"

Leonardo stabbed the air with a pointing finger. "Ha! No, you see, it is the phrase. Call Joann from Rome like this."

"Got it. Call Joann from Rome like this. And no spaces, only the last letter of each word capitalized?"

Leonardo smiled. "You have it."

Michael retrieved his phone from a pocket, powered it off, and slipped the new phone into its place. He dropped his phone into the envelope with the rest and waved it at Leonardo.

"I'll put this in the duffel once we arrive."

Leonardo shook his head and stuck out a hand. "You give it to me, yes? I keep and give back when I return you to airport."

Michael held the envelope, processed the situation. What would be the point of a false identity if his real IDs were a few feet away in his luggage?

Leonardo glanced at him and smiled. "It is okay. You call Joann, yes? Confirm instructions? Test the app?"

Michael shook his head and handed over the envelope. It disappeared under the front seat.

"How do I contact you when I'm ready to head back?"

"You call Joann. She call me."

Michael nodded. "So where are we going?"

"Small hotel," Leonardo said. "Near San Luigi dei Francesi."

As though that means anything to me.

"How far?"

"Thirty kilometers."

Thirty klicks. Not too far.

"And after that?" Michael asked.

Leonardo shrugged. "You give your name. You check in. After that, I do not know."

"Huh. Joann said you'd have directions for me."

"Miss Joann, she said I give you the parcels, I drop you at the hotel, and I am done. You go inside. Ah! You ask for room 122. After that?" He shrugged again.

"Okay, good enough. So how much money was that?" Michael patted the pocket holding the euros.

Leonardo's eyes flicked over toward the motion. "You live like, ah, like movie star for a week. Or you live poor for a year."

Michael nodded and grinned. He leaned back in the car seat and watched the scenery gradually change from bustling, developed pseudo-rural to full-blown city. Old-world city.

> *green spring meets city*
> *of autumn, ancient beauty*
> *birthplace of the west*

He frowned. Did 'ancient' have two or three syllables? It had better be two or his haiku didn't work.

About forty minutes after leaving the airport they pulled up in front of the hotel. Weathered. Ancient. Some ornate stonework on the third story roofline. Michael double-strapped his backpack, slung one duffel bag over each shoulder, and headed in after giving Leonardo a firm handshake.

The hotel lobby resembled the outside. Old and substantial, full of wood and stone and other heavy materials. It was empty. He walked up to the front desk and rang a small bell. An elderly, dark-haired woman scurried up from a back room.

"Come posso aiutarti?"

"Do you speak English?" Michael asked. He'd set up a translation app on his phone but hadn't checked the new one yet and didn't want to fumble around with it right then.

She shrugged. "Little."

"Room 122." Michael spotted a notepad and pen on the side of the desk and wrote "122" on it.

Her weathered eyes squinted, and she nodded. She hustled back through the doorway behind the counter and popped back out a moment later. She thrust a key toward him and pointed toward a wooden stairway to the side of the lobby.

"First floor," she said, and jabbed a finger toward the staircase again.

"First floor?" Michael pointed the floor all around him.

"No." She pointed to the stairs. "First floor." She pointed to the floor. *"Piano terra."*

Michael shrugged and smiled. "Do I need to pay or anything?"

The woman smiled and bobbed her head.

She's got no clue what I'm saying.

He nodded his thanks, grabbed his bags, and headed for the stairs. The wooden steps had shallow troughs worn in them. Michael found his feet pulled toward them, falling in line with the countless footfalls that had come before as he ascended.

At the top of the stairs, a small landing split into two short hallways. He glanced at the nearest door numbers and took the hall straight ahead, which started with room 120. He'd heard something about this before, that Europe numbered their floors differently. The second door on the left was 122. He set down his bags and slipped the key into the deadbolt. It clicked open after a moment's hesitation.

The room was large and fancy without being cluttered. Everything from the old-school four-poster bed to the curtains were detailed and textured, whether in materials, carvings, or patterns. It should have been too much. It should have clashed, but whoever had put it together clearly had an eye for daring detail. Michael grabbed his bags and headed in, flipping the door shut behind him with his foot.

A flashing light caught Michael's eye. On a small bedside table carved to look like a tomato vine sat a white phone with pulsating red light on its face. Voicemail.

Michael dumped his luggage on the floor, crossed over to the phone, and sat down on the edge of the bed to study it. How was he supposed to listen to his message? Then he saw it. The flashing light was a button.

He went back to his backpack and retrieved a pen and small pad of paper. Setting the pad beside the phone on the table, Michael picked up the handset and punched the flashing button.

A robotic Italian voice greeted him with a question. He had no idea what it had asked so he waited. After a moment of silence, it beeped, the red light stopped flashing, and a woman's voice spoke softly into his ear. She sounded exhausted and out of breath.

Mr. Paine, please follow these instructions precisely. Leave the hotel tonight at one in the morning. Be discreet. Your instinct will be to check the route during daylight, but I ask you to not be seen. Discretion is critical. Exit the hotel through the back door off the kitchen and turn to the right. Follow the alley past two cross streets then turn left at the third, another alley. Enter the third door on the left. There will be stairs immediately to the right. Go up three flights then enter the hall. Enter the second door on the right. Bring everything with you. Don't check out. Delete this message.

Michael finished scribbling his notes as the robotic Italian voice listed options. He hung up and pulled out the new phone. Unlocking it, he found it had the default apps plus an app titled IPSecCall. He opened a browser and looked up the Italian words for 'delete', 'remove', and 'recycle', along with the first ten numbers. Armed with the new words, he retrieved the voice-mail once more, then pressed three to delete the message after listening to the options.

He stared at his notepad. What did it mean? The hotel, the voicemail, sneaking around at night dressed in all black. Whoever his client was, she did not want to be traced. She was injured, seriously injured if the supplies he was bringing were any indication. And all this was going down in Rome.

"Shit." The word popped out as his mind worked through the most likely scenarios. "I'm getting tangled up with the mob."

CHAPTER FOUR

*T*he list was straight-forward.
Shower.
Dress.
Pack and repack.
Eat.
Sleep.
Maybe some weapons.

Michael started with the shower. The shower head had been installed by a plumber who hated tall men, but he soldiered on. After getting dressed in another identical black outfit, he repacked everything to distribute the weight evenly between the two duffel bags. The paper with his notes from the voicemail went into the pocket with the euros.

He glanced at his watch. It was 1:12 PM local time. He grabbed the hotel room key and headed out to find some lunch. He stepped out of the hotel into the cramped and busy street. Cars and pedestrians brushed by each other. Nothing seemed to run in a straight line.

Michael merged in with the flow of people walking by and

found a corner cafe half a klick up the street. He stumbled and motioned his way through a lunch that was superb. Some sort of lamb dish with capers and a sauce. The table wine met his basic standard of not tasting like vinegar.

Capers caper to and fro
While why wine whines I'll never know

He shook his head and grimaced. That couplet didn't even make sense. It was time to scrounge up a weapon. He paid, left what he hoped was a generous tip, and headed up the street in search of inspiration.

Michael found it about two klicks further on in the form of a small plumbing supply store. He bought two 60 cm pipes made of heavy, blackened steel, and a couple large rolls of sturdy, black duct tape. Twenty-five minutes later he was back in his hotel room.

With the pipes laid out on the bed, he went to work with the duct tape. It took three tries, but half an hour later he had a working harness he could strap around his leg just above his knee and just below his crotch that held a pipe securely along the outside of his leg up to his hip.

Michael practiced whipping the pipe out of the harness with each hand. The draw from the same side was awkward but effective. The cross-body draw was an abject failure. The pipe tangled in the harness every time. He tore away a portion of the harness, taped it up with a slight variation, and tested it again. It wasn't great, but he got an effective draw with either hand.

Laying the test harness out on the bed, he fashioned four new pairs of harnesses, with each pair of harnesses constructed to be the mirror image of each other. He packed three of the pairs in a duffel and left the last pair out with the pipes.

When he'd listened to the voicemail, his first instinct had been to reconnoiter the route, but she'd specifically called that out as a bad idea. It seemed crazy to walk it blind at night, but she knew the situation, and he didn't. Was she competent and trustworthy? He had no real proof, but his instincts said she was. He decided to follow her guidance.

Better catch some sleep. Need to be sharp tonight.

Michael laid out his black leather gloves with the pipes, kicked off his shoes, and crawled into bed. He set an alarm for midnight. One thing he'd learned how to do as a Marine was sleep. Normal people didn't think of sleep as a skill, but he knew better. In the unique calm found in the eye of a storm, with chaos raging all around, it took a certain practiced perspective to immediately drop off to sleep.

Michael's eyes flicked open, his hand moving of its own accord to silence the alarm beeping on his watch. He glanced down at it. Midnight. One hour until he hit the point of no return.

He got up and fished a protein bar out of his backpack where he'd packed it earlier in the day. Sitting on the edge of the bed, he chewed methodically while sipping from one of the complimentary bottles of water he'd found in the bathroom.

Was it really the point of no return? Michael could feel it in his gut. A palpable sense of danger. A nagging instinct that he was walking into a trap. He brushed the crumbs off his hands and started in on some stretches.

He'd learned the true depths of his capacity for violence in the bloody alleys and buildings of the al-Naziza district during the second battle of Fallujah. He'd also learned how much he hated it. The memories always lurked, reminding him what true madness felt like. So why did tonight weigh so heavily on him? He'd never felt fear tug at his will before, pulling him away from a mission.

You've never gone out on a mission alone. You've never fought simply to get paid.

Was that it? He'd always followed orders, always believed in the mission, but in the immediacy of a firefight, it had come down to fighting for his fireteam. It had never been about the paycheck, and he'd never gone at it alone.

Michael shook his head, willing his mind to focus. He had no reason to believe it was a trap. He didn't know if the mob was involved. What he did know was that a woman was probably dying and needed his help. And that he'd be paid fifty grand. It had to be enough.

He rose, hit the restroom one last time, then geared up with his duct tape harnesses, pipes, and gloves. His watch displayed 12:47 AM. Close enough. Michael double-strapped the backpack, slung a duffel bag over each shoulder, and headed out the door.

The lobby was deserted. Shadows played in the slice of light emanating from the partially open door behind the front counter. He stepped softly across the wood floors, passed through the small dining area, and pushed through the staff door to the kitchen. A single light gleamed off the silvery surfaces of counters, sinks, and ovens.

Michael navigated the narrow spaces to a short, dark hall at the back. A few strides further on stood a heavy-looking exterior door. He gently pushed it open and glanced outside. Utter darkness. The sliver of light from the kitchen fell across three short steps down to the alley, but that was all he could see.

He slipped out down the steps and eased the door closed behind him. Air must have been pushing out of the hotel with him, because the moment the door shut, he smelled the sharp sting of rotting vegetables and other putrid trash. The air felt heavier, and clouds obscured the night sky. To his right, dim light spilled into the alley from a street a few dozen paces away.

Michael stepped to the side of the stairs and backed up against the wall of the hotel. He waited, letting his eyes adjust to the darkness. The shadowy outlines of dumpsters and trash cans slowly materialized

Time to move.

He headed to his right, toward the light of the cross street. Eyes closed to slits to protect his night vision, he gave a quick glance each way and cut across the empty street, plunging into the darkness of the next alley.

The next cross street was alive with sound and activity. Michael studied it from the deep shadows of the alley. There were bars and cafes lining the street, and a mix of couples and groups wandered about. He waited for a lull in the foot traffic, then put his head down and walked purposefully across to the adjoining alley.

Either his eyes had taken in too much light, or the alley was even darker than the others. Michael squatted, set both duffels down, and pulled off his backpack. He retrieved a headlamp from the top compartment, strapped it on his head, rose and put his gear back in place. With a flick of a switch the head-lamp emitted a dim, reddish light.

It was enough. He could see the contours of trashcans and refuse. He headed forward a couple dozen paces and saw an alley branching off to the left. Michael turned into the cramped space and reached out, brushing an elbow along the walls on each side, confirming that it was no wider than a narrow hall-way. He glanced up and saw a sliver of night sky between the looming buildings four stories up. He passed a door, then another, and stopped in front of the third.

Michael took a deep breath. Adjusted his gloves. Double-checked each pipe. Shifted the duffel bags. They were heavy, the straps digging into his shoulders. He reached out, took the door handle, and gave it a turn. It hesitated, then squeaked around and the door pushed open.

The alley had been dark, but the cramped vestibule he stepped into was pitch black apart from the red light of the headlamp. He swung the door closed behind him and glanced around. A door to his left, stairs to the right. He took the stairs two at a time to a landing with another door and a switchback with the stairs continuing up.

Michael stopped for a moment and leaned his ear against the door. Silent, which made sense. Even if there were people on the floor, it was the middle of the night. He headed up the next two flights of stairs. At the top, he put an ear against the door. Absolute silence. It opened noiselessly and he stepped into a narrow hall that barely fit him and the duffel bags.

The stairwell door was near the end of a long hall. To his left, a blank wall formed one end of the hall. Michael figured it was the exterior wall facing the alley. At the far end of the hall a narrow window leaked a bit of light in from the busy street below with its cafes and bars. He reached up and flicked off his headlamp as he stepped forward, placing his feet with care, minimizing the noise. Past a door on the left, a door on the right, another door on the left, to the second door on the right.

Michael grasped the doorknob, turned it, and pushed the door open. Dim light. A cot, lengthwise to the doorway in the middle of the room maybe four paces away with a woman slumped on it. A gun aimed directly at him.

ichael jerked to the side of the doorway, put his back against the wall. He took a deep breath, closed his eyes, and replayed what he'd seen. She'd had a suppressed handgun laying across her stomach pointed at the door. There'd been a second gun gripped in her other hand, resting near her hip, also suppressed. But her face. She hadn't moved. Had her eyes even been open?

Michael slowly lowered the duffel bags to the floor, then eased off his backpack. He stepped away from the wall, staying to the side of the door, tensed, and leapt. He flew through the doorway at an angle, landed in a shoulder roll, and came to his feet in a crouch, ready to move. She lay motionless on the cot.

The smell of blood and urine assailed him. Empty water bottles and what looked like energy bar wrappers lay haphazardly around the cot. A lightweight black jacket lay in a heap next to the cot with a weapons harness on top of it.

He crossed to her and seized both handguns simultaneously, pointing them toward the far wall as he gently tugged them out of her hands. He needed to check his patient, but his eyes were drawn to the handguns. Berettas, 9mm, modified. Matte black with Vertec grips and G-style decockers. They showed hints of use, a scuff here, a faint scratch there.

Your patient may already be dead and you're admiring her hardware. Idiot.

He shook his head and slid the guns along the wood floor toward a small table against the side wall. It held the single lamp shedding light into the room. His fingers were probing for a pulse on her neck before the guns had come to a rest. It was there, faint, fluttering, fast. Her breathing was shallow and quick.

when conscious thought
avails us naught
our bodies fight
to stall the night

Yeah, she's clinging to life, but not by much.

Michael retrieved his baggage from the hallway and closed the door. He surveyed the room. A small kitchenette stood in the corner to his right. There was the table with the lamp along that wall, and a door on the wall to his left.

He needed light, but there was no light fixture or switch on the wall that he could see. Only the lamp. Michael dragged the cot over to the table. He looked down at her and assessed. The dark canvas of the cot was slick with congealing blood underneath her. A lot of blood. Looking closely, he saw the small tears in her black shirt, crusted with blood. Entry wounds. Her dark, loose curls were matted to her face and formed a halo under her head. Her skin had the pallor of blood loss and was cool to the touch. Her face was striking, even beautiful, though marred by a rather prominent, straight nose and a jaw that was perhaps too strong.

And all her features wore the anguish and aging of severe injury.

He moved with quiet precision, studying his inventory sheet and opening packages to lay out what he'd likely need on the floor. He scrubbed his hands with a sanitizing foam and retrieved a pair of scissors. Carefully, slowly, he cut open her shirt from the waist to the neck, then out to the arms. The shirt clung to the skin but came away with gentle tugs. She was fit, well-formed.

There were four entry wounds. Upper left hip, left waist, right shoulder and left lat up near her armpit. They looked like 9mm or .40 caliber wounds, but he couldn't get a good read on it because they'd been glued shut. Michael rubbed his hands with more sanitizer, then picked at one and pulled off a small flake. Dermabond, or some other field glue.

He cut away her pants and checked her legs, inspected her scalp, probed her joints and bones. He didn't find any other injuries. Finally, he rolled her up unto her side. Her skin tugged at the canvas cot, glued to it with thick, congealed blood. A small bottle of Dermabond was stuck to her back. All three entry wounds on her left side had a paired exit wound, raw and starting to leak fresh blood, though the flow was thick and slow. The backside of her right shoulder was whole.

Michael realized she'd purposefully lay in her own blood, hoping the clotting and pressure would help seal up the exit wounds since she couldn't reach them with the glue—a rough but practical approach that had probably kept her alive. Michael tugged the Dermabond bottle free and tossed it aside.

He let her gently slump onto her back and evaluated the veins in her arms. He couldn't find anything to work with for an IV, so he settled on an IO. He unfolded a small tripod and placed it on the table above her to hold the bags with fluids and antibiotics. Another hit from the sanitizer, and he prepped her shoulder with antiseptic wipes. With practiced movements he located the humeral insertion point on her left shoulder and drilled into the bone with the intraosseous insertion drill. He repeated the process on her right shoulder, a couple inches from the entry wound, and attached the tubing.

Once the IOs were in place and the fluids were working their way into her, Michael rolled her back onto her side, manipulating her shoulder to keep the IO insertion point clear. One by one, he washed the exit wounds with sterile, bottled water and sewed her up as best he could. He'd always been average at sutures, and she'd have more scarring than probably needed to prove it. Putting her once more on her back, he retrieved a small container of petroleum jelly and smeared each of the entry wounds with it. He waited for the jelly to work on the adhesive for a couple minutes, then began picking at the wound on her right shoulder.

The glue released bit by bit until the wound was fully reopened. After a quick wash with water, Michael went fishing in the bullet hole with a pair of forceps and large tweezers. He found the slug in under a minute lodged up near her shoulder joint, extracted it, and was thrilled to see it was intact. More water. More sutures. On to the next entry wound.

Thirty minutes later, he sat back on his heels and stretched his neck in slow circles. All in all, her wounds were remarkably minor given she'd been tapped four times in the torso. If not for the blood loss, Michael was pretty sure she would have made it on her own. With the blood loss, he was surprised she'd lasted this long. But the color of her skin, the whites of her eyes, everything pointed to her major organs all being intact and functioning.

Michael got up and went to see what he could use to clean her up. The door on the far wall opened into a bedroom that held two twin beds. A bit of light followed him through the door from the lamp, enough to see there were two more doors off the bedroom, and a gym bag sticking out from under the bed on the left. He glanced back toward his patient, and then to the beds.

The cot gave her better odds of clotting and coverage of the entrance. Clever lady.

The first door in the bedroom was a closet with a pull string light that lit up to reveal stacks of blankets, sheets, and towels. The second door was a bathroom, also blessed with a pull string light, empty but for a small bag holding some soaps, shampoos, and toilet paper.

He flipped the hot water on in the sink and left it running while he went to the bedroom and lifted the mattress from one of the beds. It was a tight fit through the doorway, but he squeezed through and dropped it on the floor near the cot. He glanced at her as he stood and found the barrel of a gun pointed directly at him.

She was flat on her back in the cot, just as he had left her, but held one of her Barettas in her right hand, bracing it across her body. The tip of the suppresser was dead steady, aimed at his center of mass. Her head was tilted toward him, eyes cracked open.

"Who?" Her voice sounded brittle and breathy.

Michael held his hands out, palms facing her. "Your rescue nurse."

She nodded and closed her eyes. Michael stepped to the side of the line of fire, stepped over to her, and once again disarmed her. She was unconscious. His anger flared at his own stupidity—he'd disarmed her then pushed her cot right next to the guns. He shook his head.

Dumb ass. Deserve to get shot.

He retrieved her other gun and stuffed them both into his backpack, then carried his backpack and the duffels to the bedroom. Michael glanced at the other duffel, sticking out from the bed, but decided it could wait. After that, he played orderly for an hour, washing her as best he could with wet towels and soap, then moving her to the mattress after he'd set it up with sheets and blankets. He moved the cot out of the way so he could push the mattress next to the table and fluids stand and dressed her in fresh clothing from the collection he'd brought. The shirt was a problem, but he managed to work the fluid bags and tubing though the arms and push the sleeves above the IO needles.

With her stable, Michael took all the soiled clothing, towels, even the cot, and dumped it all in the shower. He flipped the hot water on and aimed the shower head to hit as much of the mess as possible. It all needed to be trashed, but he didn't want to deal with the stench in the interim.

Once it was all rinsed, Michael laid the cot on its side near the outer wall of the bedroom under a window overlooking the narrow alley and used it to hang the clothes and towels to dry. He moved the second mattress into the main room next to the patient and put fresh linens on it. He laid out some basic supplies—snack bars, bottled water, wipes—next to it.

Lying down parallel to her, he studied her face. Her nostrils faintly flared with each shallow, quick breath. It had been close. Another day and she'd have been gone. He set the alarm on his watch to ring in an hour and closed his eyes.

Michael's eyes snapped open, his hand already silencing his alarm. She was awake, looking at him through heavily lidded eyes. He rolled over, grabbed a bottle of water, held it to her lips. She blinked, and her mouth opened a sliver.

On the razor's edge.

He sat up and put a hand under her head, raising it a few degrees, and poured a trickle of water into her mouth. He could feel tremors in her neck as she tried to support herself. She swallowed, her eyes drooped shut. Michael lay her head down and turned his attention to her arms. This time he found some workable veins.

"Ariana."

It was the barest whisper. Michael lay back down on his mattress facing her. She hadn't opened her eyes, her lips had barely moved.

"Your name?" he said. "Ariana?"

"Ariana."

"I'm Thomas. Thomas Paine."

Her eyes flickered open for a moment, a ghost of a smile traced on her lips.

"You want to tell me what's going on?"

The smile was gone if it had ever been there. "Tired."

Her face went slack. She was sleeping. Michael took his time, working carefully to insert an IV in each arm without harming the veins. He set up a blood tranfusion on one and continued the fluids in the other. After removing the IO needles, he bandaged the entry point on each shoulder.

Michael lay back down on his mattress and set his alarm to go off in an hour. He closed his eyes and slipped off to sleep.

CHAPTER SIX

$\mathcal{T}$he night passed. The sun rose, lighting the room though the thin curtains hung on the window opposite the front door. Michael fretted. Ariana hadn't regained consciousness again. With the fluids he'd pumped into her through the night, he was pretty sure her bladder wouldn't last much longer, and he had no interest in playing orderly again. He needed a bed pan, but there hadn't been one in the packages from Joann.

He checked the kitchenette and came up empty. A few water bottles in the small fridge and nothing else. The gym bag in the bedroom proved much more interesting. Ammunition, magazines, an assortment of knives, and a couple weapons harnesses. His mouth pulled into a hard line, and he forced himself to think of her only as the patient, setting aside all thoughts regarding her possible vocation.

At 7:08 AM, he headed out, leaving his pipes and harnesses in the room. The stairwell was empty, and Michael hit the alley without seeing anyone. He followed several twists and turns before stepping into a street that ran roughly at a right angle to the street in front of Ariana's apartment. It was bustling with people and cars. Michael stepped into the flow and found a small market a little over a klick down the road. As he walked, he opened the new phone and was relieved to see it was set up with an account to get apps. He downloaded his translation app and selected Italian.

Stalls held food of all sorts and a few household goods, with proprietors emitting a continuous stream of cajoling Italian. The noise washed over Michael, meaningless. He stepped up to a small stall hung with pots, pans, and kitchen implements, pointed to a wide, shallow pan, and raised his eyebrows in question. The proprietor, an old man sitting on a stool, eyes drilling into Michael, let out a burst of Italian. Michael hit the translate button and held the phone toward the man. His face scrunched up and he gave Michael a hard look.

"I don't speak Italian," Michael said. "Just speak normally."

The man frowned but started speaking again. The app didn't catch it all, but the price came through loud and clear.

"Like hell I'm paying that much for a pan." Michael tapped a number into the phone that was a third as much, hit translate, and showed it to him.

The proprietor sputtered, then unleashed a torrent of Italian which eventually ran dry and ended in a new number that split the difference. Michael paid the man, took the pan, turned, and saw them.

Two large men, well dressed, moving with a graceful confidence that spoke of a capability for violence. They disappeared into a stall selling fresh vegetables, but the one on the left had been looking at him. Their eyes had met for a brief moment, and Michael had seen the man's eyebrows pull together. Had it been consternation?

When instincts cry
it's best to fly
think on the move
try to disprove

Pan in hand, Michael headed out of the market by a different street. He followed a twisting, turning trajectory that carried him in a large arc back toward Ariana. Why had his instincts screamed danger? The whole situation with Ariana stank of trouble. Secret directions to an obscure room. Multiple gunshot wounds. Her own weapons.

He jerked to a stop and closed his eyes. A small man behind him ran into him, but Michael ignored him. He could see it now. When he'd left Ariana's apartment and first stepped out of the maze of alleys behind her building. The two men had been sitting at an outdoor table of a small cafe off to the left as he'd turned to the right.

Michael stepped up to a street peddler selling magazines and pretended to browse the selection. It had to be connected. He'd been marked, and there was no explanation for it apart from Ariana. They were hunting her, and they'd pegged him as a point of contact. Either the organization hunting her was extremely lucky, or very competent, or both.

He pulled out his phone and checked a map. He was two streets over from an alley that could get him back to her apartment. Michael pocketed the phone and walked, his head down, the pan still clutched to his side. One street. Turn. Two streets. He saw the entrance to the alley just ahead and angled toward it.

A well-dressed, large man broke off from the flow of pedestrians and cut across the street toward the alley. Michael kept his head down, calculated the distance. He'd hit the alley just before the man. Should he run? Try to lose them on the way to Ariana's?

It's their home turf.

Running would accomplish nothing, other than to give them, whoever they were, a much better idea of where Ariana was holed up. Michael got to the alley and pulled up a few steps in, waiting for his tail. A man came toward him from the shadows further into the alley. The other man stepped into the mouth of the alley.

Neatly done.

Michael moved to put his back near a wall and waited. The two men converged on him and stopped a pace away, boxing him in. They both wore dark suits, no ties, fancy shoes. The one on the left that had come in behind him stood a little under six feet and wore dark stubble for a hairstyle.

Call him Curly. Other one's Larry.

Larry had an unruly nest of black hair. He was taller, probably only an inch shorter than Michael, and he was thick. They both stared at Michael and said nothing. Were they waiting for the other pair of men, or just trying to unnerve him? Michael didn't intend to wait to find out.

"Gentlemen," Michael said. "How can I help you?"

Their eyes flicked toward each other, then settled back on Michael. Larry slowly nodded, like he'd decided something, while Curly cocked his head to the side and faintly shook it. The effect was superb. Tension crawled up Michael's spine as he waited. These two knew how to shake someone down.

"American?" Curly asked.

It was another blow to keep him off balance. Michael had been sure Larry would speak for them. Curly's voice was thick with an Italian accent.

"Yep, that's me." Michael tightened his grip on the pan's handle, tensed his legs. "How can I help you?"

"You will take us to *Il Falco*," Curly said. Larry smiled and kept nodding.

"The ill fake-o?" Michael shrugged and shook his head. "No idea what you're talking about."

"*Il Falco*." Curly's head shook again, almost imperceptibly. "The Falcon."

"If that's a person, they've got a seriously cool nickname," Michael said, "but I've still got no idea what you're talking about."

"Mister..." Curly's eyebrow inched up in question.

"Paine."

"Mister Paine," Curly said, "You do not know us. You do not know your position. I do not know how she got you here, or why you help her. But it will be very good for you to help us, yes?"

His hand dipped into his coat. Michael tensed, but Curly pulled out a large stack of euros, rolled and bound with rubber bands.

"Take us to her." Curly extended the bills to Michael.

Michael's neck felt hot. His eyes drifted from Curly to Larry and back. Maybe they could take him. Maybe they couldn't. Either way, he intended to find out. Bastards thought he'd roll over for some money?

Something in his eyes must have shown, because Curly's head started shaking again, and he withdrew the money and tucked it back in his coat. Larry shuffled a step closer and smiled.

"You will not help us?" Curly asked.

"Doesn't matter if I will." Michael's neck was on fire. "I can't. No idea what you're talking about. So take your *Il Falco* and shove it up your collective asses."

It happened all at once, stretched out over pregnant moments. Larry's hand dipped back into his coat, and Michael was confident he wasn't reaching for money. Simultaneously, Curly struck. He didn't pull his arm back. No wasted motion. He drove it directly at Michael's solar plexus. His fist met the back side of the pan as Michael snapped it up. He'd known where Curly would target.

It was a powerful blow, but the pan distributed the force. A real professional, to strike that hard from close quarters. Michael heard a crack as the pan was driven into him with force, and Curly reeled backward. Probably a snapped metacarpal. Michael seized Larry's coat by the lapels with his other hand, hindering him from drawing his gun, yanked him forward. He sidestepped and bounced Larry off the wall behind him. Larry's head gave a satisfying thud as it met the brick and rebounded.

Michael flicked a leg behind him and shoved him toward Curly, who was reaching into his own coat. It looked awkward. Curly was holstered for a cross body draw and was trying to retrieve his firearm with his off hand, his dominant hand curled protectively against his chest. Larry slammed into him and tangled them both up for a moment.

Michael leapt forward and push kicked Larry hard in the chest, sending him stumbling backward with Curly until they slammed into the opposite alley wall. He leapt forward and brought the pan down on Larry's head, and the man crumpled to the ground. Curly finally pulled his gun free, but Michael delivered a vicious blow to his hand with the edge of the pan. Bones crunched and the gun tumbled down the alley. Curly slouched, his two ruined hands feebly clutching at each other. He didn't see the pan as Michael brought it down on the top of his head.

Michael patted the men down with the backs of his hands and retrieved their wallets and the large roll of bills Curly had flashed earlier. He was breathing hard, but his body felt fine. No injuries. His mind and emotions, on the other hand, were like dry timber that had just been introduced to a carelessly discarded cigarette. It started slowly, but soon rage and confusion burned uncontrollably. Heat to match his emotions radiated up his neck. He reached for poetry, but his thoughts fragmented.

He walked, coherent thought mostly out of reach, but his subconscious mind guiding him back through the twists and turns to the alley door of Ariana's building. He slammed it open and took the stairs two at a time, emphasizing each step with profanity under his breath. He never saw the young family, a mother and father with a little boy, step through the doorway at the second-floor landing until he was on top of them.

A hand jammed into Michael's chest, and he reacted without thinking, grabbing it, twisting, striking. He pulled the blow at the last instant as his eyes finally saw the family and his ears opened to the woman's scream. The man's arm would wear a colorful bruise for a few days, but Michael had managed to avoid breaking it. The father shepherded his family back through the door into the second-floor hallway, glaring at Michael the whole time, massaging his shoulder.

The door closed, and Michael sagged against the wall. What had he done? Worse, what had he almost done? He drew in several ragged breaths as his neck cooled down. He wasn't wired for civilized life. Chaos was his canvas, violence his paint. In that moment, the black hole of despair and self-loathing that lurked in the deep recesses of his mind flared to the foreground.

for a season, we say

57

yet day after day
the instincts unchanged
the heart still deranged

Ariana. Her name tugged at him, and Michael got moving. He glanced around and spotted the skillet three steps back down the stairs. He'd released it on first contact. Picking it up, he gave it a quick inspection. The handle was warped, and there was a slight dent along one edge, but it was still functional.

Ariana. He glanced up at the ceiling toward her and took a deep breath. Sure, she was in deep with some hard people, but he'd get her safely to Montreal. Even if helping her didn't tame his demons, the money would sure help. He took one more deep breath, and headed up the stairs to the fourth floor.

Michael walked down the hall toward her door, flipping the skillet and catching it by the handle. One rotation. Catch. Two rotations. Catch. Three rotations. Catch. He arrived at her door, pushed it open, and glanced in.

Ariana was gone.

The IVs hung from their tripod on the table, the tubing coiled up on the mattress, twin catheters laid side by side, used medical tape in a ball beside them. Otherwise, the room was as he had left it. Michael stretched his neck to each side and was rewarded with a satisfying click.

He stepped into the room, gently closing the door. He stayed near the wall and worked his way toward the bedroom door, each foot placed slowly and silently. He stole a quick glance into the room and closed his eyes, processing what he'd seen. His shoulders sagged. His backpack was on the floor next to the bed frame to the left, open. The backpack that had held her guns.

"Ariana, it's me, Thomas Paine, your rescue nurse. We good?"

Michael heard a faint response but couldn't discern the words. "I couldn't hear your answer, but I really don't want to get shot, okay? I'm coming into the bedroom."

He stepped through the doorway. Light spilled from the bathroom door left halfway open. He could see her knees to her feet, the pants he'd put on her last night around her ankles.

Ah. So. Guess I won't need the skillet.

He moved to the bed frame and sat so he no longer had a view into the bathroom. "How're you doing?"

"Little dizzy." Her voice was breathy. "Very weak. Found the food you brought and forced myself to eat some."

"Yeah, you'd lost a lot of blood," he said. "It was close."

The toilet flushed in response, and the pants were pushed through the doorway.

"I'm taking a shower," Ariana said.

"Great," Michael said, "except for the part where you're not up to it yet."

"It hurts, yes. Some things are worth it."

"No doubt," he said. "But showers take a pretty wide range of movement, and a lot of energy."

"Thomas," she said. "Thank you for saving my life. I'll be careful. No falls, okay? Now, please shut up and bring me a towel once I'm in. And some fresh clothes."

There was a loud squeak followed by the sound of water drumming on the empty tub. A shirt and panties followed the pants out the door. Lastly, a shoulder harness with the two guns was pushed out.

"Mind them for me," she said.

"Listen, at least sit down in the tub."

J. PHILIP HORNE

He heard a faint grunt in response. Michael got up and retrieved the guns and clothes. He put the weapons in his backpack and retrieved a medium-sized compression bag from one of the duffels for the dirty laundry. As he pushed the air out and tied off the bag, there was a squeak and whoosh of the shower curtain being pulled back, a creak as the tub took her weight, and variation on the original theme as the curtain was pulled closed. Michael set down the bag on the wooden bed frame nearest the bathroom and retrieved a towel from the bedroom closet. The bathroom door was still opened, so he reached in and set it on the toilet seat.

"Ariana?" he said.

"Hmmm?"

Her voice came from down low, so at least she'd had the good sense to follow through on his request.

"You've got to call me if you see any blood in the water, okay? You can't afford to start bleeding again."

"Understood," she said.

"Good. Good. Okay, I'll step out."

"Thomas? Clothes?"

Idiot. Can't remember a list with two things on it.

"Right," Michael said. "Be right back."

Michael grabbed the laundry bag off the bed frame and headed back out to the living room. He rummaged through the duffel for a full set of clothing down to the running shoes and traded it out for the laundry bag. He stacked the clothing neatly and took it to the bathroom where he deposited it on the back of the toilet tank.

"Okay, you're good to go," he said. "How're you doing?"

"Can't do it," she said in a weak voice.

"It? Can't do what?"

"My hair. Can't wash it. Too much stretching. You'll have to do it."

60

Michael frowned. "Just rinse it."

"Washed," Ariana said. "It's a mess."

"I get that," Michael said, "but no one's going to notice."

He heard her sigh. "You cut my clothes off. What's left to hide?"

"Huh?" Michael frowned again. "It's not like that. I just don't like playing orderly."

Arianna pulled the shower curtain open a couple feet, exposing the curve of her back. Her wet hair reached well below her shoulders, the curls pulled straight. He heard a tapping against the side of the tub up near the front.

"I think I'm paying for whatever I need," she said.

"There is that," he said.

Michael reached under the curtain and she stuck the bottle of shampoo into his open hand. Two marriages had taught him this much. Women liked to use a lot of shampoo. He dumped eight times too much into his hand and started washing her hair. He tried to stay medical, to avoid remembering. The feel of her wet, warm hair in his hands, the sound of the water, the curve of her back. It was as he feared. Memories rushed in.

Five days since the divorce. One hundred twenty-seven days since Bethany had served him the papers. One hundred forty-four days since he'd walked in on her and Frank in the shower and almost committed murder. One hundred ninety-eight days since he and Bethany had last showered together, intimately close while so far apart.

"Hey!" Ariana said. Michael's thoughts splintered. "You're hurting my scalp. Less pressure."

Michael shook his head. The memories held nothing but pain.

like spring rains falling
during endless winter, my

heart's out of season

He decided to keep talking.

"Listen, I need you to fill me in on what you're into," he said, working the shampoo into her hair more gently. "I'm gonna get you to Montreal, okay? But normally, my patients have a broken leg, or are sick. Bullet wounds, not so much."

"I'm injured," Ariana said. "Isn't that enough?"

"It would have been," he said, "if I hadn't been followed this morning and jumped in an alley."

He felt her stiffen up at his words. "Who?"

"I'll show you their wallets when you're done. I left them unconscious in the alley where they came after me. They were competent."

She started to turn but flinched away from the motion. "You can handle yourself."

It was a statement, but really a question. "Yeah, I can handle myself."

"I'd hoped it wouldn't be needed."

"Well, it was. But I need to know why. So rinse your hair, then you tell me what's going on. Why'd they jump me, and why are you paying so much? I'm assuming it's all related."

He rinsed his hands in the water and pulled the shower curtain closed. Severe injury had a way of diminishing people, but Ariana was doing just fine in spite of being full of bullet holes. And the sutures seemed to be holding up well. He'd done good work the night before.

"Call me if you see blood," he said. "Actually, ping me every thirty seconds. Need to know you're conscious."

Michael rose and stepped out of the bathroom, pulling the door partially closed. He grabbed a protein bar from his pack and sat down on the bed frame to eat.

"Still alive." Her voice was faint, but Michael was glad she'd taken him seriously.

"Roger that," he said. He took a bite, chewed, swallowed. The bar tried to live up to its branding of being a rich, chocolaty treat, but failed. He took another bite.

"Ping," Ariana said.

"Acknowledged."

Michael stuffed the rest of the bar in his mouth and dropped to the floor. He started with back stretches, then moved outward. Shoulders, neck, arms. Hips, legs, ankles. Ariana continued to check in. He was working his wrists when the water squeaked off.

Getting to his feet, he stepped over beside the bathroom door and listened. Michael heard the shower curtain open, a grunt of exertion that he guessed was her reaching for the towel, then quiet, followed by a creak. He gave her another minute.

"Ariana? How're you doing?"

"Weak." Her voice was barely above a whisper.

He waited for more information, but the only sounds were the occasional creak of the tub.

"Can you dress?"

"Not anymore," she said.

Michael slowly pushed the door open and stepped into the bathroom. She was sitting on the edge of the tub wearing a bra and panties, slumped over with her elbows on her knees and her head hanging down. The towel was wrapped around her hair but already coming unwound. She didn't look up, or move at all. Kneeling down beside her, Michael gently pulled her near arm around his neck, put a hand behind her back and the other under her knees, and lifted her.

She was solid for her size. As he stepped through the bedroom, her head rolled toward him and rested against his chest. The towel made one last effort before falling to the floor. He carried her out to her mattress and lowered her down. She slumped over on her side, asleep. He pulled the blanket over her and stood.

Michael frowned and glanced at his watch. 10:38 AM. The answers would have to wait.

CHAPTER SEVEN

*A*riana slept, and Michael paced. He felt taut and tired. The international travel, change in time zones, and lack of sleep had taken a toll. He walked over to his duffels and found an empty freeze-dried fruit bag and the wrappers to a couple protein bars. Apparently, she'd forced herself to eat quite a bit of food. Michael followed her example.

After eating, he checked on Ariana. She was in deep sleep. Her color looked great considering how close to death she'd been the night before. Food and rest were critical now. She'd gotten the blood she needed and had her wounds tended. She'd eaten. She was sleeping. He'd nursed her away from the precipice. He was sure she'd recover quickly, as long as those men didn't find them.

He grabbed his backpack, put it beside his mattress, and lay down. The sleep would help.

Michael's eyes opened. He'd been asleep on his mattress beside

Ariana's. The curtains on the window no longer glowed with muted daylight. Something was off.

He glanced at his backpack and came alert. Ariana was toward the wall, the backpack on the other side in arm's reach. It was unzipped. He was certain he'd zipped it up before laying down to rest.

The door burst open and men spilled in. Dark suits, guns. Michael caught fragments of images as he exploded into motion. He flung himself toward the door, grabbing his backpack as he launched over it, landed in a shoulder roll. He threw the backpack as he came out of the roll. It caught the lead man in the face just before he pulled the trigger, his shot pulling high.

Michael never paused but followed the backpack forward as more men came into the room. In the back of his mind, a place of unconscious math, the odds felt low. Five men were through the door and spreading out. Were there more? Did it matter? Wasn't five sufficient to end him?

He threw himself sideways and low, slammed into the lead man's legs with his abdomen, kicked out at the man to the right. His heel caught the man in the knee, breaking it inward toward the far leg. Michael simultaneously grabbed the man to the left in the crotch and yanked down.

All three men fell together into tangled mass as Michael rolled back away from them. The final two men came into view as the front three dropped, their guns aimed at him. He was on the floor, unarmed, out of options.

A gun fired behind him with a suppressed roar. Both mens' heads snapped back, bloody holes appearing in their foreheads simultaneously, and they toppled to the ground. Not a gun, Michael realized. Guns. In spite of the three armed men trying to recover on the floor in front of him, Michael stole a glance over his shoulder. Ariana sat on her mattress, arms held forward, a gun in each hand extended toward the men.

Impossible!

"Stay down!" she yelled.

Ariana shifted both guns as Michael froze on the floor, looking back toward the men. The man on the right was clawing the floor, curled into the fetal position. The other two were sitting, swinging their guns around to Michael's left. Toward Ariana.

Her guns fired again simultaneously, their heads snapped back, and they flopped backwards to the floor. Another round was fired, and the last man stopped clawing the floor. The door, now decorated with blood, finished its slow trajectory and clicked shut.

"What the hell?" Michael sat up, taking it in.

Blood pooled under the bodies, reminding Michael of a topographical map. Small tributaries rushed to join together into rivers that fed lakes.

blood pooled a mirror dark
casting back reflections stark

Nothing in his experience gave a frame of reference for what he'd just seen. It went against everything he knew. Adrenaline, motion, speed, accuracy. They simply didn't mix like that. Ariana had, in his mind, achieved a whole new level of dangerous.

"We need to go." Ariana said.

Michael swore under his breath. His adrenaline was pumping so hard he had trouble pushing himself to his feet.

"No, we need to talk," he said, looking over at her as he stood.

"We stay," she said, "and we talk to the *carabinieri*. I don't want to talk to them, but I don't shoot police, understand? We leave and problem solved."

Michaels stepped over to her and squatted. He felt like a coiled spring. "Good call on not shooting police. Now, who are you?" He hooked a thumb toward the bodies behind him. "Who were they? Why were they hunting you?"

Ariana drew herself up, putting her eyes level with his. "I promise we'll talk. But we must go. Now."

"Just give me the two-sentence summary."

Her eyebrows scrunched together, and Michael realized he'd been wrong when he'd first seen her. Ariana's proud nose and strong jaw fit her perfectly, enhanced her underlying beauty. More than that, she seemed to have that rare combination of beauty and cuteness, seen in the way her eyebrows expressed displeasure. He knew it would undermine his resolve. Both his ex-wives had been cute beauties, at least to him. It was his kryptonite. He had to push forward.

"Oh," he said, "be sure to include something about *Il Falco*."

Ariana's eyebrows shifted again. She no longer looked cute. More like dangerous, with something else. Pride? Loss? Michael was keenly aware of the two handguns, now grounded on the mattress, her hands resting on the grips. Two minutes ago they wouldn't have caused fear to dance in his guts. Seeing five men shredded in moments had shifted his perception. He waited, tense, ready.

She scowled and glanced over his shoulder at the men. "They're *Hije*. I'll know with certainty after I see the wallets you collected this morning. They hunt me"—she looked him in the eyes—"for reasons I'll explain when we are safe. They know me as *Il Falco*."

Michael grimaced. "That's it?"

"We are out of time."

One of her hands twitched as she spoke, a hand Michael was carefully watching with his peripheral vision. He stifled a response. He felt like he was sitting in a cage with a lion. Sudden motion might trigger a violent retaliation, but if the lion moved first, he'd need to react instantly to survive.

"And the *Hije*?" He tried to mimic her pronunciation. "What's that?"

"A *fis*. Albanian mafia clan. Imposters, really, but they operate like a *fis*."

Michael frowned, putting the pieces together. It didn't add up to anything yet. He looked her in the eyes, tried to pull out any sense of her identity. Was he enabling a psychopathic murderer? Thus far, he'd only seen her kill in self-defense, but the efficiency had been shocking. And no sign of emotional blowback. She should have been shaking.

Michael's mind flashed back to the moment before it had all happened. Before he'd decided it made sense to beat unconscious a worthless excuse of a junior officer out of West Point. A junior officer whose parents had potent political connections. He'd looked the kid in the eye, seen the smirk, known what had happened, let the rage flood over him.

He forced himself back to the present. In the absence of a compelling reason to deviate, he decided to stick to the plan. Save Ariana. Get her to Montreal.

"Okay," he said, standing. "If you're up to it, where do we go?"

"I'm much better. Not good, but better," she said. "We go through the closet but bring me my harnesses and gym bag first."

"The closet?"

Ariana nodded. "Hurry. The gym bag. Then strip the stuff you brought down to one duffel. And give me the loose jacket. You got a loose jacket? We leave in one minute."

"Yeah, I bought everything on your list," he said.

Michael shook his head but moved quickly. After retrieving her gym bag and weapons harness, he attacked the duffel bags with a fevered energy, tossing the jacket toward her as he worked. He triaged the remaining medical gear, retaining a few essentials to put in with the clothing. The distant two-tone wail of a police siren grew in volume as he worked.

As he strapped on his pipes, he stole a quick glance at Ariana. Straps crisscrossed between her breasts, a gun holstered under each arm, each pointing down with the grip forward. A strap high on her waist carried four spare magazines.

He finished the pipes and pulled on a light jacket. Ariana stood, moving gingerly, and held out her jacket to him. "Help me."

At least three sirens now converged on their location. They were close. Hopefully that closet was more than it seemed. Michael gently maneuvered her arms into the sleeves, turned her around, and zipped up the front. It was lumpy but obscured the guns.

Ariana stepped around him and moved toward the bedroom. "Bring the duffel, your backpack, my bag."

He grabbed the gear and followed her through the door to the bedroom. She'd dropped to her knees and was poking around in the back of the closet near the floor. Michael set down the bags and crouched to see what she was doing. The sirens outside had locked in on two pitches, no longer shifting. The police had arrived.

Something clicked, and the three feet of wall below the bottom closet shelf swung away from Ariana. She crawled in after it and stood, her legs barely visible in the dark space, perhaps two feet behind the back wall of the closet. It looked as though the bottom shelf extended a foot or so back into the hidden space.

"Push the bags in and follow." With that, Ariana's feet disappeared up out of sight.

Michael crawled in after her, pulling the bags behind. Once past the shelf he stood. The space was about the size of the closet they'd passed through, but unlit. In the faint light coming from the closet, Michael could see Ariana standing on the shelf, doing something with the ceiling above her. A small metal ladder was bolted to the wall behind Ariana and led up to the ceiling. Beside him, a pair of two-by-six boards, a bit taller than him and painted black, were leaned against the back wall. One had a metal collar of some sort attached at the top end.

"Get our gear up here with me," she said, continuing to mess with the ceiling. "Then push the door closed."

He pulled the duffel up and set it beside her on the shelf, leaning vertically against the wall. There was no room on the shelf for the other two bags, so he shoved them into the back corner and pushed the secret door closed. It swung shut silently and gave a satisfying click as it sealed off all the light.

Another click from above and dim light was restored. Michael glanced up and saw a narrow opening, two feet square, through the ceiling and the roof a couple feet above that. It was almost full dark, but he couldn't see any stars. The angry blare of sirens continued.

"Help me up," Ariana said. "Can't afford to waste my energy on a ladder."

Michael clambered up onto the shelf, squeezed in with her and the duffel, his head ducked low to avoid the ceiling. He lifted her by the hips as she climbed the ladder and disappeared above.

"Pass up the gear," she said, her voice a whisper above the blaring sirens. "And get the boards."

Michael pushed up the duffel until it tipped out of sight,

grabbed the other two bags and pushed them through, then pulled up the boards, propping them up in the opening. He climbed up the ladder and came out on a rooftop patio inside of what looked like an abandoned aviary. Wood and wire mesh obscured his view of the patio.

Ariana had already opened the little wire mesh door and was sitting just outside the aviary in a patio chair. Michael pulled the pair of boards up after him and pushed them out toward her.

"Grab your gear and move out," she said. "I'll close it."

Michael pulled on his backpack, grabbed the duffel and her bag, and stepped out of the aviary, standing up straight once outside. He glanced around as Ariana headed back in. The light was better than he'd expected. Late dusk more than full night. The entire roof was a once-magnificent patio. Stone planters separated sections of the patio, adorned with the husks of dead plants. Decrepit, rusted furniture was clustered together here and there. A stone parapet outlined the edge of the building. At one end, a roof sloped up from the patio floor and ended in a wall with a door. Stairs back into the building.

He glanced over his shoulder and found Ariana standing just behind him by the aviary. She moved quietly, or maybe the sirens had distracted him.

"Won't they know to check the roof?" he asked.

"Eventually." She nodded toward the rooftop stairway entrance. "The door at the bottom is secured with rusty locks. No one's used it in years. We have a few minutes at least."

Michael nodded. "Where to?"

Ariana pointed to the building next to theirs. It stood the same height across the narrow alley with a flat roof and a small roof patio on the far side.

"Snap the boards together, end-to-end," she said. "We'll use it to cross."

Below, from the front of the building opposite the alley, muffled shouts drifted up. They were moving in. Time was short. Ariana stepped past him, heading for the parapet. Michael fit the end of the second board into the bracket on the first and shoved them together. It was a tight fit, and he finally resorted to banging the boards together using the patio floor. Once in, the collar held about a foot of each board. He looked at the boards more carefully in the dim light and realized they were laminates, like thickly cut plywood.

So these will be radically stiffer than normal boards.

Michael grabbed the duffel and sports bag with his free hand and followed her. The roof extended about a foot past the parapet. The gap to the other building wasn't far, but the roof sloped up from the edge below at a sharp angle and didn't flatten out for several feet, leaving a space of a dozen feet from where they stood and maybe two feet of extra elevation. Michael scanned the alley and saw the silhouettes of men standing in the shadows at both ends. He glanced at her and cocked an eyebrow.

"Put your gloves on," she said. "Pull up your hood. Move the board very slowly. Be one with the night."

Michael grimaced but did what she asked. He slid the unified board across the space until it reached the far roof, then set it down on their roof, wedging it up against the parapet. It formed a narrow ramp, overlapping the far roof with a few feet to spare.

"I'm not so sure about this," Michael said.

Ariana didn't say a word, but pulled her hood down low and jammed her hands into the jacket pockets. She sat down on the parapet, slowly rotated herself around, and calmly stepped out onto the board. Her footfalls were silent, her hips swaying in time to her steps, her balance unwavering. She moved above the empty air without hesitation.

Michael felt a mixture of terror and awe. In spite of her wounds, she had perfect balance and confidence. Somehow, her perfection made his own confidence implode. At four floors up, a fall would be deadly. The board seemed to shrink in on itself, a bare thread stretching across the gulf.

and is it mere height
that nurtures a fright
where no fear should grow
but for the ground below

He picked up a bag in each hand and followed her example, rotating around until his feet were on the board. He looked across the gap. Ariana stood on the far side, a foot firmly planted on both sides of the board to stabilize it, looking him in the eyes. Her hood was back, her face visible in the dim light.

Michael gave himself over to those eyes, deep pools shrouded in shadow. He held her gaze and stood, stepping forward onto the board, his peripheral vision struggling to track the board in the darkness. One foot. Then the other.

He heard the crackle of a police radio down below to his left, followed by muffled shouts. They'd probably found the bodies. Left foot. Right foot. Ariana's eyes seemed to fill his vision. She really was quite beautiful. Her nose was perfection. How had he thought it was too large?

Left foot. Right foot. Repeat. It was strangely intimate, walking forty feet up, enraptured by her gaze. He was three feet away, then two feet. She took one step back as he took two more slow steps and crossed the line of the roof.

"Good," she said, her face looking up into his from a foot away. "I planned this route for myself, but I have"—she hesitated, and quirked her mouth to the side—"uncommon balance."

Michael stepped to the side to get around her and away from the edge. His mouth was dry. "Yeah, well, I'm glad that's behind us. Wouldn't want to have to do that again, you know? So, what's next?"

Her mouth quirked again. "We do that three more times."

CHAPTER EIGHT

The board was just long enough to reach the third building's roof. Ariana once again crossed without apparent exertion, though Michael saw the board flex a bit as she passed over the middle joint. His own crossing was a harrowing experience. It was as though he'd entered a wormhole, traversing not only the street four stories below, but also several years of his life.

The next building was a full story lower. Ariana led him to a far corner and pointed down. A balcony stuck out below, it's floor on level with a roof just across another alley.

"No way you can jump down," he said. "Too much risk you'll reopen your wounds."

She nodded. "Go first. You'll need to lower me."

"Is it an apartment?"

Ariana shook her head. "Art studio. Hopefully empty now."

He'd asked the question almost hoping she wouldn't know the answer, hoping he'd misjudged her precision, the sense that she was an absolute professional. A professional who left dead bodies in her wake.

Michael lay down on the roof, reached down, and dropped the duffel onto the balcony. It landed with a quiet thud. He dropped his backpack and her sports bag onto the duffel, using the clothes within it to provide a soft landing. No one came out.

"Heading down now," Michael said. "You follow."

He slipped over the edge and landed lightly on the balcony. With a couple buildings between him and the source, the sounds of police sirens faded into the background. Turning around, he looked up and found the end of the board inches from his face. He took it from her and set it down, then reached up for her feet. She sat on the edge, her shoes a couple feet out of reach, then scooted forward and dropped down to him.

He caught her shoes as she held the edge of the roof for balance. Once she was stable, he lowered her. Again her balance was uncanny, standing on his hands as she descended, releasing the roof, stepping off onto the balcony once he'd gotten her low enough.

From the balcony, they crossed to the next building. There was no rooftop patio, only roof that sloped upward. Ariana looked a little stiff as she worked her way up. Michael followed with the gear.

"You're wearing down," he said.

She didn't turn. "Weak. And getting weaker."

At the crest, Michael glanced back. They were back on level with the fourth-floor roof of the previous building. Past the crest, the roof extended nearly flat to the edge about fifteen feet further on. Michael was startled to see the gap to the next roof was too wide for their board. Ariana stopped a couple feet from the edge and sat down. Michael set down the gear and took a seat next to her.

The entire journey had filled him with a growing dread.

Ariana was well-armed, had unnatural aim, and maintained utter calm in the midst of killing. She had a bolt-hole equipped with a secret rooftop escape. The fact that her pursuers were self-evidently bad actors didn't make her good. Who was she? Whatever the answer, a dead end didn't fit the pattern.

"What am I missing?" He waved a hand toward the next rooftop. "It's close, but I don't think the board's long enough."

She turned her head toward him. It was full dark now, the passageway between buildings below was another alley and unlit. Her hood was back up, her face hidden in shadows.

"It's hard to see it in the shadows, but there's a recessed balcony directly across from us on the top floor."

Michael didn't like the sound of that. "And?"

She looked away, toward the blotch of darkness that he figured was the balcony. "And I hadn't planned on my injuries."

He shook his head. "You figured you'd jump if you ever came this way, once you'd covered enough ground not to worry about the noise."

The hood moved back and forth a fraction of an inch as she nodded.

"Dammit." He dug into his backpack, pulled out his head-lamp, flipped on the red light.

The dim light revealed a balcony jutting out a foot from the building with a low, wrought iron rail. The balcony extended back several feet under the roof. Thankfully, it was completely barren. No chairs or tables. Michael guessed it was about fifteen feet away and down at least eight feet from the edge of the roof where they sat.

"We just agreed you couldn't handle a short drop to a balcony," he said.

"I know." She looked at him again. "Toss our gear over. Make the jump. Then hold the board so I can cross."

Michael shook his head. "That's crazy. I'd have to lean out and hold it at head height to reach across. Assuming I made the jump."

"Then do it. You're my rescue nurse. Rescue me."

The words ignited a spark in Michael's mind—a clear-cut need that didn't include ethical questions about her vocation or background. He knew he was being manipulated and didn't care. He handed her the headlamp, moved her hand to point at the balcony, and stood. The jump didn't look that bad, as long as he angled it right and got between the rail and the roofline.

Michael heaved the duffel across, aiming with the hopes it would slide to a stop off to the left in the back corner. Instead, the strap somehow caught the dark iron railing and yanked the bag to stop. It landed up against the railing, robbing Michael of the soft target he'd hoped to have for the other two bags.

"Go," Ariana said. "I'll loop the board through the straps and let them slide down to you."

Michael nodded, no obvious alternative presenting itself. He stood and backed away from the edge. Four quick steps forward and he leapt. The dim red light illuminated the balcony as he dropped down to it, clearing the rail and ducking his head to the side to avoid the roof. He reached for the balcony with extended feet and landed, folding his body into a tight shoulder role, stopping inches from the back wall.

He took a moment and breathed, trying to calm his racing heart. Standing, he turned and walked to the railing, testing it to make sure it was sturdy. It seemed solid. Michael saw that Ariana had the board standing vertically, grounded near the very edge of the roof. She was wearing the headlamp, the red light aimed upward at the board, illuminating the edges.

Michael leaned up against the rail, stretched his neck to each side, and reached out with his hands. Ariana glanced at him—her movement revealed by the bobbing red light—and squatted, holding the board near the base on the roof. It tipped forward, picking up speed, arcing out over the space between building. He tracked it, moved over a few inches, reached up for it.

The end of the board slapped into his gloved hands, jarring his shoulders as it jerked his hands down a few inches. He stretched one arm, then the other, holding the end of the board near shoulder height, nearly a foot short of the balcony railing.

"Ready?" Ariana's voice was barely audible.

The red light swept over him, he nodded, the light switched off. In the darkness he felt the board move a bit, heard and then felt as his backpack slid down toward him, a strap looped around the board. He grabbed the strap, holding the board with the other hand, and dropped the backpack to his feet. Ariana's sport bag was already en route and joined his backpack a moment later.

Now I play human bridge. Don't screw this up.

Michael needed to both hold her weight and stabilize the board. He grabbed the board on both sides, his thumbs hooked around the end of the board to keep it from slipping, its weight resting on the heels of his hands. The whole exercise would have been easy if the board had simply reached another foot, but holding it out from his chest was going to be brutal.

His eyes were adjusting to the dim city light. He saw her stand, put a foot forward, felt the increase in pressure on the board. Her hands were held out from her body this time. She moved toward him, the weight increased, the board tried to twist in his hands.

I hold a thread
on which she treads
a sliver, a breath
between life and death

81

Each step she took increased the pressure, made the board seem to come alive in his hands. The whole setup was insane. She was four stories up, descending at a sharp angle, entrusting herself to him. If he let the board twist, or pulled it forward a few inches so the other end fell free of the roof, or did any of a thousand other little things, she would die.

Michael gritted his teeth and focused on her. He willed his arms to become steel, his back a concrete bulkhead. The weight grew and with it the force of each twisting step she took. Her balance wavered, then steadied. She was five steps out. Four steps. Three. The weight was unbearable.

"Get over here now." He forced the words between gritted teeth.

She didn't answer but took another step.

"Can't dismount," Ariana said, swaying gently. "Nothing left."

"Fall toward me," Michael said.

Ariana collapsed more than fell, and Michael wrapped an arm around her waist as she pitched forward over his head, still holding the board with his free hand. He shifted her weight to his shoulder.

"You still with me?" he said. She gave no response. "What the hell am I supposed to do?" Again, silence.

He couldn't just drop her, but if the board fell, it might provide a clue to their pursuers or the police, and he couldn't manage the board with just one hand.

"So screwed," he mumbled to himself.

He heard a noise behind him, shifted around, froze. The door into the building swung open. Light washed out over the balcony. Michael clutched the end of the board with one hand, held Ariana draped over the other shoulder, and squinted into the light. He heard a gasp as a shadowy figure stepped onto the balcony, the features resolving into those of an older man. He held a knife in a relaxed, balanced grip.

The man stepped to the side, revealing a woman standing in the doorway. She looked of an age with the man, maybe late fifties or early sixties, trim and fit. She wore a floral print dress, cinched at the waist, hanging to her knees. She looked Michael in the eye, said something in Italian. The man remained a step to the side, knife at the ready, in a loose stance. Michael's eyes had adjusted to the light enough to make out his pleated khakis and plaid short-sleeve shirt, the top two buttons undone.

Whole world's gone batshit crazy. I'm gonna get knifed by Ward Cleaver. Ward and June freakin' Cleaver.

"I don't speak Italian," Michael said.

The man and woman glanced at each other. In that moment, Michael knew with certainty they'd been married for decades. He could see the silent conversation taking place between their eyes.

June pointed down, twirled her finger in a circle. "Turn her. Face in light."

The words were choked with a thick accent, though it didn't sound like an Italian accent to Michael. Her request presented a problem. Ariana's face was turned to the side, laying against his back. To put her face in the light, he'd have to turn his back on that knife. However, his arm holding the board was on fire, and he knew whatever he was going to do had to happen fast.

"Sure thing," he said, "I'll turn. But put the knife on the ground. Fair enough?"

They exchanged a second glance, and Ward dipped down and rose without the knife. He moved with the buoyancy of a man at least twenty years younger. June flicked her finger in another circle, and Michael turned, exposing his back to them, his neck painfully craning around to keep them in his peripheral vision.

Ward let out a long, slow hiss as the woman gasped.

"Ariana," she said.

The man stepped toward Michael, leaving the knife where it lay at his feet. "I will take her. We help."

Michael tried to process it. Ariana had come this way on purpose, to this very balcony. They knew who she was. Maybe they intended to really help. But what about him? They didn't know him, except as the guy carrying an unconscious Ariana. June must have seen something in Michael's eyes because she snapped a hand out and touched Ward's shoulder, stopping his advance. She stepped up beside him.

"We will help," she said. "We will carry her, yes? Our hands will be busy, yours will be free."

The casual precision with which his unspoken concerns were addressed was more unnerving than the knife had been. But he had no choice. He could only hold the board for a few seconds longer, and he was stuck until he could get Ariana off his shoulder. He gave a quick nod, and they swooped in, rolling Ariana off his shoulder. Ward took her up under the arms, her head resting against his chest, June cradling her legs.

Michael immediately turned and grabbed the board with his now free hand and tugged it toward him. It fell clear of the far roof and swung down toward the side of the building. Holding the end in one hand, he reached down low with the other and pushed hard to slow it's decent. He managed to stop its swing before it smacked the wall below.

A quick glance showed the man and woman carrying Ariana through the door. Michael hauled the board up enough to tip it horizontal on the railing and dragged it forward with him as he stepped through the doorway after them. The room was a study, with wood paneling on the small portions of walls not covered by bookshelves. A red leather couch to his left faced a huge wooden desk to his right, with several wooden chairs distributed around the perimeter, tucked into nooks between bookshelves. A doorway led out of the room on either side.

Ward and June lay Ariana on the couch. Ward leaned over Ariana, blocking her from view, checking on her. He stood and turned, one of Ariana's guns held casually, aimed just to the side of Michael. Ariana's jacket was unzipped a few inches.

Idiot! Of course he felt them while he was carrying her.

"Who are you?" Ward asked.

Michael's mind flashed through the scenario. They had to know her, and she must have trusted them at some level. Ward was taking a strong stance, but avoiding direct, immediate violence. His finger lay along the trigger guard, the muzzle angled off to the side. He'd looked comfortable with a knife, comfortable with the gun. Their concern seemed to be that he was a threat to her. He needed to align himself with her.

"I'm her nurse. Trying to keep her alive."

June stepped up beside her husband, hands folded neatly in front. "The sirens?"

Time to roll the dice.

Michael nodded. "The police probably just found the bodies of the five men who just tried to kill us."

"You?" June asked.

"Did I do the killing?" Michael asked.

June nodded.

"No. Ariana took care of that."

Ward and June glanced at Ariana, looked at each other, and smiled.

Well, that's creepy.

CHAPTER NINE

"Y ou seem honest, but..." June's voice trailed off. An eyebrow lifted a fraction of an inch. "We are not the trusting people. Proof?"

"Sure," Michael said, "but first, can I check her condition?"

"She sleeps," June said. "Proof."

Michael recited her wounds, the sutures, all the details of his work. June nodded, pointed down, moved her finger in a circle. Michael obliged the request and turned back around, facing the desk. It was a beautiful piece. In another life, he suspected it had been a throne. It had a weight to it, a presence. Delicate carvings traced plants up one corner, across the back just under the desktop, and back down the other side.

While Michael inspected the furniture, he heard the woman disrobe Ariana, which apparently took some time given the weapons harness. After that it was quiet for a moment. He heard quiet steps recede, then more quiet.

"You may turn," Ward said.

Michael turned to face them and found only Ward standing between him and Ariana. He happened to be standing so that Michael's view of Ariana's naked torso was almost completely blocked. Michael found himself liking the weird little man. They were in the middle of a potentially violent confrontation and Ward was concerned about Ariana's privacy. June strode back into the room from the doorway past the couch carrying a blanket and pillow. In moments, she had Ariana covered and resting with her head on the pillow.

That done, she stepped up beside her husband and took his free hand in hers. Ward flipped the gun into the air, caught it by the barrel, and extended the handle toward Michael. He stood rooted, unable to process what was happening. He didn't have a category for this sort of thing. Both of them smiled.

"We have decided on trust," Ward said. "I am Ditmir. My wife, Kaltrina. My wife and I are not halfway people. If we trust, we trust. If we are wrong to trust"—he smiled and shrugged—"we would know it now."

Good people. Even likable. But so insane.

Michael shook his head. "Just put it up in the harness and help me figure out how to break down this board so we can close the door."

"Salute!"

Ditmir held up his small glass of grappa. Michael nodded and lifted his glass. He clinked it lightly off Ditmir's. The glasses were slender and flared wider at the mouth, with hardly more than a sip of the yellowish liquid held at the bottom. Though they'd spoken very few words, the man had whipped up a delicious meal of some sort of pasta, white sauce, mushrooms, and thinly-sliced ham. Michael had eaten while Ditmir disappeared for a few minutes. He'd returned to rinse Michael's plate and join him at the table.

"Health seems a good thing to wish for right now," Michael said. He followed Ditmir's lead and downed the warm liquid in one swallow.

Ditmir cocked his head to the side a bit as he lifted the slender bottle sitting between them on the small kitchen table and splashed a bit more into their glasses. "It is not a wish, this thing we do." He lifted his glass again toward Michael and waited for Michael to clink his glass against it before proceeding. He lifted his glass higher, stared at it for moment, then downed the grappa. "It is, ah, a prayer. You see?"

Michael threw back his drink and returned his glass to the table. "And do you pray much?"

"In these times, Thomas Paine, I pray often. But"—he held up a finger, moved it slowly down and tapped the mouth of the bottle—"these prayers are best offered in the company of friends. And if many prayers are needed, it is best to use the wine and leave the grappa on the shelf."

The golden drink was a warm ball in Michael's stomach, leaking outward toward his chest and legs. He poured for the two of them and lifted his glass.

"To good health," he prayed. "For us. For Ariana."

Their glasses clinked and the grappa traced a warm trail down his throat.

"Can we talk?" Michael asked. "While we, ah, continue praying?"

"What is prayer," Ditmir said, "but conversation?"

Michael smiled. He was pretty sure his pastor had said something like that once, though he was also pretty sure his pastor hadn't been referring to a drinking game.

"You know Ariana. How? When did you meet her?"

"We will play a game, you and I," Ditmir said. "I will answer your question, then you will answer my question, yes? Then we will pray." He waved vaguely at the bottle as he spoke. "I would not have God excluded from our conversation."

"Good enough," Michael said. "Proceed."

"I met Ariana when I was but a young man in Albania," Ditmir said. "She was just a little thing in the company of her father. He was not a good man, but he loved her well. She chose me as a, ah, pretend uncle. It is more complex than that. Her father's wife did not even know of her. But I think she knew even then I did not belong in the company of such men. Her affection gave me standing with her father. It was a blessing and a curse. I became the, ah, how do you say, the between person."

"The go-between?" Michael said.

Ditmir smiled. "Yes, I was the go-between for Ariana's father and mother. And for Ariana and her father. And later for her trainers and her."

"Her trainers?" Michael asked.

Ditmir shifted back in his chair and nodded at Michael. "One question. It is your turn to answer."

Ah. Same question to me.

"I met her last night about four buildings that way." Michael pointed off in the general direction of the apartment. "Three days before, she'd called my employer. She wanted transport out of Rome, along with a whole lot of medical care. See, I take work as a rescue nurse when I can. You've probably never heard of that, but it pays better than the construction. What?"

Ditmir had shifted forward, his elbows on the table, eyes intent. "It was Rescue Nurses Worldwide?"

Michael tried to suppress his shock at the question, but his face betrayed him. Ditmir nodded and grinned.

There once was a weird little man

who knew every part of my plan
all my secrets laid bare
it just wasn't fair
it would've made perfect sense if I'd ran

Michael reached for the bottle, strove to control his emotions. It was such a trivial detail, yet Ditmir's casual reference to it had somehow unbalanced him. "I thought we were supposed to pray between rounds of questions."

Ditmir slapped the table, barked a laugh, and sat back. "Please." He waved at Michael. "Continue with your answer. Then pour for us."

Michael set the bottle down and leaned back. "Well, I got the call to come here and render extensive aid. So I did. Found her shot up with hours, maybe minutes, to live. Got her stitched up and topped off."

Ditmir's eyebrow lifted, his head tilted a bit to the side.

"Is that a second question?" Michael said.

"No, no." Ditmir waved off the question. "I do not understand the words. Topped off?"

"A transfusion. She needed blood."

"Ah, I see," Ditmir said. "Our stories are different, yes? But also the same in this one way. Many interesting details"—he waved his hand toward the window above the nearby kitchen sink—"left on the street to fend for themselves. Please, pour."

Michael poured, they drank.

"Walk me forward," Michael said. "You met her in Albania. Now you see me carry her into this—is this an apartment or a house?"

"It is your question?"

Michael shook his head. He'd not waste a question on it, but the building was curious. Ariana was sleeping two floors above on the red couch with Kaltrina hovering nearby. He'd seen nothing of the second floor other than a hallway as they'd descended a tight spiral staircase, and they sat at a small table in a small kitchen on the ground floor.

From the angles and the little bit he'd seen out a window, it looked like the building surrounded a small inner courtyard. He guessed that Ditmir and Kaltrina lived in only half the building, but he wasn't sure.

"I end up on your balcony," Michael said. "You learn she just shot and killed five men, and you looked at each other and smiled. How did we get from little girl in Albania to you looking happy she'd killed five men, just effortlessly?"

Ditmir rocked his head slowly from side to side, scratched his chin, frowned. "The death did not please us. No, but it was proof. Perhaps we are vain, but we were pleased to learn we had guessed the truth these many years. You must understand that Ariana is, well, she has"—he lifted a hand and rubbed two fingers to his thumb—"much money. Bought a lovely estate outside of Rome five years ago when she moved from Albania. She keeps rich company in the city."

His eyes seemed to look past Michael as he spoke. "She was very kind to us when she learned we lived in Rome. It is as though she is our goddaughter. Yet we have long thought that perhaps she was more than that, for about the time she bought the estate, the Albanian boys in the clans, they started to die. *Il Falco* had started to hunt. Since then, little things, innocent things, they add up, and we have wondered. Tonight, you gave us a proof of what we suspected."

Michael felt as though he were watching every tenth minute of a movie and having to piece together the plot. The contours were starting to take shape, but too many questions remained.

"Why do you help her?" Ditmir asked. "You have encountered risks, yes? Yet we witnessed much effort to help her. Why?"

Michael turned it over, checked the angles. Questions regarding his motives felt uncomfortable.

"As you said, she's got money," he said. "And I'm going to have a lot more myself after I get her out of here in one piece. Pretty straight forward."

"I do not believe you," Ditmir said. He held up a hand to forestall Michael's protest. "I believe you will receive much money. But I have my eyes, and I've seen yours. The eyes are the windows to the soul, yes?"

Michael shrugged. Ditmir poured. They drank.

"So why does she do it?" Michael asked. "I'm fine with speculation. Take a guess."

"Guess?" Ditmir said. "I have no need of guesses. If Ariana is *Il Falco*, then she does it for revenge. The *Hije* murdered her father when she was still a girl. Also her half-sister and her father's wife. Her father was not a good man, you see? But he loved her in his own way, and she loved him fiercely. Her own mother had died years before. The falcon has hunted men from all the clans in Rome, but mostly the *Hije*."

"Stop the game for a moment." Michael leaned forward, his elbows on his knees. "Why are you telling me all this?"

Ditmir cocked his head to the side, stared into Michael's eyes. "We will stop the game." He smiled and tapped his temple with a single finger. "I am starting to feel too warm, so it is for the best. But I have one more question for you after this."

"Agreed," Michael said.

Ditmir nodded. "I sense Ariana is doing something big. I wish to move you past the money. I want her to have a true ally. Either fortune or providence brought you to her, and I sense you are what she needs."

Michael grimaced.

Such a crazy, insightful little man.

"Now, my question," Ditmir said. "You are ex-military, yes?"

Michael nodded.

"Why did you leave?"

Michael felt like he'd been punched in the stomach. "That's not something I'm willing to discuss."

"Ah." Ditmir's eyes narrowed a fraction.

Kaltrina stepped into the room. "Ariana is awake and wishes to speak to you, Thomas."

Ariana lay on the couch, propped up by several cushions, her weapons harness draped across her lap. She held a large glass of water in one hand, an energy bar in the other, and took a long sip as Michael entered the room with Kaltrina and Ditmir. Three chairs had been set in a loose arc by the couch.

Kaltrina chose the seat at the far end of the couch, her husband sat next to her, and Michael took the last seat. He nodded at Ariana as he shifted the pipes still strapped to his thighs to a more comfortable position. She nodded back and took a large bite from the bar.

Ditmir slapped his hands on his thighs, leaned forward. "So. Thomas and I have talked for a time. I like him, even if"—his face broke into a tight smile—"he is too big. But now is the time to come together. To put all our things on the table, yes?"

Ariana nodded slowly, took another bite, sipped her water.

"You are not just the rich girl," Kaltrina said, "spending time with the rich boys and girls of Rome."

Ariana swallowed and took another sip of water. "You already know all that."

Kaltrina lifted a hand, a finger raised. "But it is your thing to put on the table, not ours to guess." She spread her hands wide and looked around. "You have fled to our home. You have put us into the middle of your troubles."

Ariana fired off an answer in a language Michael didn't recognize but now guessed was Albanian. Ditmir held up a hand, and she stopped speaking.

"Please." He waved a hand toward Michael. "Let us speak so that all can hear."

Ariana looked at him, and Michael caught his breath. She remained beautiful, yet now his perception of her were pushed by what he'd seen her do into some other realm. On the verge of passing out, still suffering from grievous injuries, she'd all but walked a tightrope. Her sheer will was staggering.

"I came to Rome five years ago," she said, "having spent many years in preparation. Though my family had been taken from me, my father had made provisions that left me significant wealth. I took on the persona of The Falcon. I've been busy since."

"So," Michael said, "this sounds like a comic book."

All three looked at him, Kaltrina's face completely composed and relaxed, Ditmir with one eyebrow lifted, Ariana shaking her head slightly.

"Nevermind," he said. "So how many have there been? Killings?"

They all looked back at Ariana. She frowned, looked up at an angle, tapped two fingers together for a time. Michael felt nervous. There were a lot of taps.

"Prior to the events of the past week," Ariana said, "twenty-nine. All Albanian mafia, some on contract, some not."

Ditmir let out a low whistle.

"And this past week?" Kaltrina asked.

"Eleven, counting the five tonight."

"But what gives you the right?" Ditmir said, leaning forward, his elbows on his knees.

"They gave me the right!" Ariana's face tightened, her eyebrows pulled together, her mouth a thin line. "They murdered my father and his family! He was all I had after my mother's cancer. They spilled blood. Now they meet"—she jabbed her chest with a thumb—"the avenger of blood."

Michael sat still, watching, listening. The pieces were falling into place, and the picture emerging was an ugly mess.

"But Ariana," Kaltrina said, "how does it end? If the murder of your family demanded revenge, does not your murder of these men demand revenge also?"

Ariana shook her head. She bit off the last of the bar, chewed, and swallowed it with a sip of water. "Eye for an eye, the whole world goes blind?"

"It is as you say," Ditmir said.

"No, Ditmir, I don't say that." Ariana looked between Kaltrina and Ditmir. "I say the world is a better place without these men. Every man I have killed has been part of a *fis*."

"But there have been many not from the *Hije*," Kaltrina said.

"Is the *Hije* the only *fis* spreading death?" Ariana said.

"No," Kaltrina said, "but they are the ones who killed your family, yes?"

Ariana shrugged. "I've taken contracts across the clans in Rome to hide my intent, and therefore hide myself."

"But Ariana—"

She cut off Ditmir with slashing motion. "Name a good man I've killed. Name a man who brought life to others."

Ditmir and Kaltrina exchanged a glance.

"But Ariana," Kaltrina said, "if that is your standard, then— I am so sorry, and this is not of your doing—but by your standard your father deserved to die."

Michael was tempted to glance at Kaltrina, but he kept his eyes on Ariana. She had the guns. But she didn't respond. Her face was calm. She sipped her water, then finally spoke.

"They took my family from me. I'll not be dissuaded by your philosophy of ethics."

"Good!" Ditmir said.

"Good?" The word popped out of Michael's mouth.

Kaltrina turned to face Michael. "Yes, good. You do not know the work of the *Hije*. Its evil is so large. Extortion, child sex trafficking, drugs, arms, the rest. We want to know of Ariana's resolve. We would have the *Hije* stopped." She turned back to Ariana. "We will do the things we have discussed."

Ariana nodded, the corners of her mouth twitching up. Ditmir reached over and slapped Michael on the knee.

"It will be good," he said.

Michael looked at him, not knowing what to think or feel. He turned back to Ariana. "To recap. You're an assassin. A very successful one apparently."

At that, Ariana truly smiled. She looked him in the eyes. "Yes."

when the truth is spoken
my innocence broken
now I must decide
I must choose a side

Ariana's smile slackened. "You just did that thing I saw back in the apartment. When I killed the men. And when you first crossed the board."

"What thing?" Michael said.

"You froze, just for a moment, like time had stopped." Her eyes never wavered from his. "You're doing something"—she tapped her temple with a finger—"up here. What?"

Oh, crap. Add "very observant" to her list of finer qualities.

"It's nothing," he said. "Just processing the situation."

"Of course you are thinking." She swept a hand out toward Ditmir and Kaltrina. "We're all always thinking. But you're doing something more. Some sort of ritual. What is it?"

Michael sighed. "My therapist had me use poetry. To process stuff."

"Your therapist?" Ariana said. "Your stuff?"

Ditmir and Kaltrina looked on, their faces masks of polite disinterest.

"I had some issues with anger after, uh, after I left the military. Poetry helped. Got to be a habit."

"A poet-warrior?" She was smiling again.

"This is bullshit," Michael said. "This isn't about me."

Ariana shrugged. "Perhaps."

"So you're an assassin," Michael said. "But according to your code, you'll only off Albanian mobsters."

She nodded. "It is my purpose."

"So, not even Italian mobsters?"

Ariana shook her head. "Not my business."

"And what about collateral damage?" Michael asked. His neck was starting to feel warm. "If a few innocents die along the way, that's okay?"

"There has been no collateral damage," Ariana said.

"How do you know?"

"I'm precise," she said.

Michael could believe that, but the heat on his neck was building. "So you call me in, what? After the whole thing went to hell? Get me to walk right into a trap?"

"You're being paid well." Ariana's face had turned fierce.

"To save your life!" Michael said. "To transport you to Montreal! Not to fight your insane war against this *Hije!*"

"Thomas?"

It took Michael a moment to realize Kaltrina was addressing him. He took a deep breath, tried to steady his voice. "Yes, Kaltrina?"

"I talked to Ariana a little," she said. "Before I came down to get you. She tells me of your capability. I do not know the role you were supposed to have, but I am glad you were with her this day."

Michael knew he was being manipulated, but the words seemed to drain the fight out of him. Had he really believed someone would pay that much for some emergency care? He'd known all along, even if the actual details were way beyond anything he could have dreamed up. No, there was no point in pretending he'd been innocent of the situation. The heat dissipated from his neck, his mind opened back up to the situation.

"What happens next?" he asked. "I call it in and get us on a flight to Montreal?"

"Yes, soon," Ariana said. "But first I have to retrieve a piece of hardware from a building. Then we can leave free and clear. But to do that I have to rest. So we stay here tonight."

CHAPTER TEN

The pub stood on the ground floor of a building nestled between two taller neighbors. The night was held at bay by a single light above the front door. The main room had several small tables surrounded by chairs and a lingering odor of stale beer. A bar sprawled across the back wall and played host to a few old men, one young couple, and a very fat bartender. To the right of the bar, a hall led back past a pair of bathrooms on the left to a lone door. A large man in a dark suit stood sentinel before the door.

The room on the other side of the guarded door felt cramped. Though not large, the space was diminished further by the eleven substantial men, some standing, most sitting, all in dark suits. To the left a door led to the kitchen and through it to the bar. On the wall opposite the door to the hall, a third door led to another room, larger by far, and well appointed. It had no other doors, and no windows.

Four leather wingback chairs were huddled together in the center of the room. They faced each other, perhaps six feet apart, a small wooden table just off to the left of each chair. The room was lit by two lamps at opposite corners of the room, casting sharp shadows across the chairs and the four men who occupied them. They all wore dark suits, though the dim light gave a hint that one wore a shade of dark purple. Albanian was their language of choice, scotch their drink.

"You know this?" Leka Selimaj spoke in a low, husky voice. "With certainty?"

Leka was the diminutive remains of a once robust, larger man. He sat deep in his chair, his face hidden in shadow, hands folded in his lap. His drink remained on the table to his left, untouched.

Valdrin Dushku's slow nod in response to the question was lost in the shadows of his own chair. He was of an age with Leka, yet still powerfully built, and clothed in deep purple. The thick hand that lifted the glass of scotch was missing two-thirds of the ring finger. He held the glass to his nose and inhaled deeply, his eyes briefly closed as he allowed his sense of smell free reign. He brought the glass to his lips and tipped a generous sip into his mouth. The golden liquid slid back across his tongue and he swallowed.

"My man is reliable." Valdrin's voice was gentle and pitched several steps higher than his deep chest indicated. "He was there when the bodies were examined before being moved. The scene indicated two people inhabiting the apartment, but only one shooter. All five men shot once"—Valdrin lifted his glass higher and tapped his forehead with a finger—"here, but not at point blank. No muzzle flash burns to the skin. And their weapons were out. They'd fired only one shot and it was wasted on the ceiling. One of the men had a torn-up knee, so something else had happened, but the fact remains that five men were killed with such ruthless efficiency they didn't get off a real shot."

Leka's frail hand slapped the arm of his chair, then fell back into his lap. "I just lost more men tonight to the Falcon than the past five years. Good men. Two with families. This is unacceptable!"

The other two men remained deep in their chairs, content to let the conversation play out without committing to its outcome.

"I sense that you find our agreement unacceptable, that you would blame me." Valdrin leaned forward as he spoke, his elbows on the end of the armrests, his drink still clutched in his hand. "But what has happened in the past week validates everything I said. It validates this"—he waved his free hand in a tight circle—"agreement the four of us have made. The Falcon, this she-devil, must be stopped at all costs."

"Bah!" Leka waved a hand toward Valdrin, as though he was a fly that could be shooed away. "I have been looking into it since we last met. Prior to this week, yes, we had all lost men to her, but in every case I have been able to unearth contracts. She's to blame, and maybe she seeks out these contracts, but she was fulfilling someone else's wishes."

Valdrin's eyes narrowed. "And?"

"But not your men. Not most of the ones I know about. She's doing it for reasons of her own. Sport? Revenge? I don't know. But either you already knew this and didn't tell us, or you have completely missed that your organization is being hunted. Which is it?"

The other two men leaned forward almost imperceptibly at these words, as Valdrin sagged back in his own chair.

"I have wondered," he said. "The past year, as critical operations were disrupted, as men died, I speculated. What you offer is the first type of proof I've heard, and it is tenuous."

"I think"—Leka paused, pointed a finger at first one of the silent men, then the other—"that the elimination of our men was a distraction. Noise, to hide the signal." The finger now pointed at Valdrin. "The *Hije*, that's the signal. They are the true target."

The finger stayed raised, holding the floor, as Leka paused to take the first sip of his drink. Once the drink was returned to the table, his other hand fell to his lap once more. "You asked if I found our agreement unacceptable. It is not, but the situation is not what we thought. I truly believe that. But now, after tonight, I have five men to bury, and I will have blood for blood. Who is she? Who would have the motive and ability to hunt you?"

Valdrin sat in his chair for a minute, silent. He took a sip of scotch, then another.

"Had my men not happened on her five nights ago, had Nikollë not survived the encounter, we'd not even know it was a woman. That's all we know, and we've known it less than a week. Five years, and that's it! And which of you even believed Nikollë's account of what happened? It was madness, yet after tonight, with five dead"—Valdrin tapped his forehead with a finger—"Nikollë's story sounds like God's own truth." He cocked his head to the side. "Or the devil's."

Leka shook his head. "We also know she has help."

"That's true. A man who tore apart two of my men." Valdrin's eyes narrowed as he spoke. "A very competent man. A man who seemed to know only English. None of it makes sense."

"A woman," Leka said, "who perhaps has motive to see the *Hije* torn down, brick by brick, and a big man who must have rendered aid, maybe even kept her alive, and is highly skilled." He looked at each of the three others in turn. "This is what I say. If both can be killed, good. But if any of us has a shot at the man only, we need him alive. We need what he knows. She's the end of the matter. He's a means."

Four light knocks were followed by a brief pause. The door to the adjoining room swung open and a large man in a dark suit stepped into the room. He closed the door, crossed to Leka, and whispered in his ear. The other men watched, impassive, studying him. The whispered monologue stretched on, though none of the men showed any outward concern.

The man stood, Leka nodded at him, and he left the way he'd entered.

"Perhaps we have something," Leka said. "A man, one not in the room with the investigators, thinks he saw something. It was dark, mind you, but he was positioned at the entrance to the alley behind the building. He thinks he may have seen people passing across the alley from one roof to another."

"Assuming it was them"—Valdrin tossed the remains of his drink into his mouth, swallowed—"and assuming they didn't circle around, you've narrowed their location down to half of Rome."

"I think not. The Falcon was gravely injured. I doubt she went very far. My men took the initiative and looked into the buildings off in that direction for a few blocks. There is one that was interesting. A residence of a married couple from Albania that we've crossed paths with enough times to keep our eye on them. Ditmir and Kaltrina Hajdari."

At the names, Valdrin stiffened, his hands reflexively tightening on the arms of his chair. Leka's eyebrows lifted.

"You know this man, Ditmir?" Leka said. "Or the woman?"

"I know the name." Valdrin lifted his glass, realized it was empty, and placed it back on the table. "He was there at the beginning. When the *Hije* was hardly a clan. It was a messy time." He slapped the arm of his chair. "This is too much for coincidence. They are at that house. They must be."

"If they are involved," Leka said, "we may be able to discover the Falcon's identity. What Albanian entered their life five years ago? Say, new to Rome but with resources. One does not kill so many men without resources. My men are investigating."

Valdrin surged to his feet. "Good. But let's see that it does not matter. Let's go catch a falcon."

CHAPTER ELEVEN

*M*ichael sat on the floor with Ariana perched above him on a bed. He'd emptied the duffel bag and backpack onto the floor, grouping the contents by category. Studying it, he started making choices. Clothing, first aid, food, a giant roll of currency. He'd arranged the clothing for Ariana across the foot of the bed so she could make her own choices, but there was still a lot to sort through.

The second floor of Ditmir and Kaltrina's house was bedrooms, bathrooms, and not much else. They sat in a smallish bedroom that overlooked the inner courtyard. Two twin beds stood to either side of a dark window with a small section of empty floor between them where Michael now worked.

Ariana wore her weapons harness but had the twin handguns on the bed in front of her with an array of other weapons and ammunition from her sports bag. A brace of throwing knives, a discrete handgun that would probably fit in a lady's clutch, a stiletto, two stun guns, and more. She loaded a slender black backpack provided by Kaltrina, weighing the options between weapons and clothing. Michael did the same for his backpack.

"You don't like me," Ariana said, her eyes moving between items on her bed.

Michael glanced up at her. "I don't like what you do."

"Should murderous people go unchallenged?"

"No," Michael said, "but I can't tell if you're talking about the *Hije* or yourself, and that's the problem."

Ariana rolled two pairs of panties, folded them into the cups of two bras, and jammed them into the bottom of the backpack. "That's a nice rhetorical move, but it's a false equivalence. Preying on the weak is not the same thing as stopping the predators."

"I agree." Michael pivoted on the floor to look at her and waited until she made eye contact. "But you pretend assassination doesn't blur what should be clear, bright lines. And it doesn't just blur them. Sometimes it erases them."

She shook her head, her hair bouncing in a way Michael found distracting. "Are you telling me you've never killed before? I've seen you. You went straight toward those men. Not the actions of a man who's never had blood on his hands."

Michael looked down at his hands. "I've killed." He looked back up, her eyes intense, watching him. "I've laid waste to so much life, I sometimes think I must be deranged to live with myself. Maybe what I did was murder, but I don't think it was. Either way, it doesn't make assassination okay."

She looked away, started packing the backpack again. "It's a good idea, to have our essentials ready to go."

So that's the end of that.

"Yeah," Michael said, turning back to the stuff arrayed on the floor. "I'll pack everything left over in the duffel. Hopefully we won't have to run for our lives anytime soon but keep your backpack close."

"You want this?" Ariana held out a handgun. It looked like a close cousin to the two she wore, minus the suppressers.

He shook his head. "No thanks." He patted the pipes strapped to his thighs. "These will do."

"No, they won't," she said. "You don't bring plumbing to a gunfight. Take it."

Michael hesitated, then took it. She tossed him two magazines, already loaded. With quick motions, he broke the gun down, inspected it, and reassembled it. He chambered a round and dropped the hammer with the safety. In his peripheral vision, he could see Ariana watching him.

"What'd you do before the PJs?" she asked.

He set aside the gun and started loading up his backpack. "Marines right out of high school."

Ariana nodded and returned to her own packing. "Why didn't you try for Force Recon? Why the PJs?"

Michael kept his hands busy, his mind calm. Memories clawed at the edge of his awareness. "Got tired of the killing. It weighed on me. The pararescue was a good place for me."

"You were good at it, weren't you?"

He stole a glance, but she was still focused on packing. "Good at what? The PJs?"

"No," Ariana said. "The killing."

This time, when he glanced at her, she was looking directly at him. He shrugged, then nodded. "Yeah, I was good. Very good. Had a knack for it."

"So why'd you quit the PJs if that was the right place for you?"

Michael turned back to his packing. "Not really interested in discussing."

It was quiet for a time, and Michael finished his backpack and turned to the duffel bag. He packed up the items on the floor and turned to the bed.

"I'm done," Ariana said. She was cross-legged on the bed, her back to the wall, the backpack beside her. She patted a small stack of clothes. "I'll take these with me. Going to grab a shower."

"Got it," Michael said.

She stood and crossed the room, the clothes in hand, one gun placed on top of the stack. At the doorway she stopped and turned. "Thank you. You've done great work."

Michael stood up from where he was leaned over the bed, packing up her remaining items. "Sure thing."

There was something about how the door framed her, hair spilling over one shoulder, backlit by the hall light just beyond. A yearning swept over him. He suppressed it.

"When I blacked out, I..." She trailed off, looking down at her hands. "I didn't know if I was ever going to wake up. And when I did, I woke up to you." She looked up at him. "It turned something terrible into something, well, something better."

Michael nodded. "Glad I could help."

"In that first moment, I thought you were an angel."

Michael smiled. "Do you always pull a gun on the angels you meet?"

"Until I've got their credentials." Ariana said. "Okay, I'm getting a shower."

"Leave the door open a bit," he said. "I'm going to wait in the hall once I've finished this duffel. Make sure you don't have any issues in the shower, then grab one myself when you're done."

"Pervert." Her smile disarmed the word.

"Just your friendly neighborhood rescue nurse."

"I'm actually feeling about a thousand times better after Kaltrina's food," Ariana said, "but I'll leave the door cracked open."

Michael's eyes snapped open, Ditmir's face floating near his in the darkness. Michael released his neck. Apparently, his hand had gotten there before he'd really woken up. Ditmir leaned forward to whisper.

"Kaltrina and I, we see activity outside. Men about to approach. Kaltrina will answer and put them off, yes? But be ready."

Michael surged up, grabbed the pipes from under his pillow, and slipped them into his makeshift harnesses. He'd gone to sleep fully dressed other than his shoes and light jacket, both of which he slipped on. Ariana had done likewise, even sleeping in her weapons harness. A glance at his watch revealed it was just after 2:00 AM. A few feet away in the other bed Ariana roused. Ditmir put a hand on Michael's shoulder and tried to push him back into the bed. After a second, he gave up and let his hand drop.

"They will announce themselves," Ditmir said. "We will talk to them. They will leave."

"Who?" Michael said. "How do you know this?"

Ariana sat up on the edge of the bed, leaned forward into their whispered conversation.

"We have regular contact with a couple of the *fise*," Ditmir said. "I believe they are all working together to solve the Falcon."

Michael shook his head. "At 2:00 AM? Nothing good happens at 2:00 AM."

Ditmir laid a hand on Michael's forearm. "I guess that they have talked to their contacts in the police, piecing together what happened. Our house is close by. They want information. You will see."

A chime rang out from somewhere in the house.

"You see?" Ditmir said, no longer whispering. "Kaltrina is good at the talking. She will tell whatever stories are needed."

"We'll see." Ariana slipped on her backpack, pulled her twin guns from under her pillow. "I want eyes on the door."

Ditmir held up both his hands. "No, no, no. You must trust us to do our part."

Michael was ready to go, his backpack strapped tightly in place. "I saw a door just off the entrance."

Ditmir's frowned, gave a terse nod. "A small study."

"Put me there," Michael said. "Kaltrina leads them back to the kitchen if they enter. Ariana, you stay up here." He held up a hand to stop her protest. "Put yourself at the top of the staircase if you want, just keep the high ground."

Kaltrina stuck her head into the room. "I must greet them. Do what you will do but do it now."

Michael looked at Ariana, raised an eyebrow. She nodded, though her eyebrows knitted together, her eyes tight. A poem started to take shape, but he suppressed it. He'd offer no more tells. He turned and followed Kaltrina down the hall to the staircase. They descended, Ditmir trailing Michael by a couple steps.

The small vestibule at the bottom of the stairs was dark, lit only by dim light leaking down the hall from the kitchen. Ditmir headed that way. Kaltrina looked at Michael, pointed at a door to the left of the main entrance. It was unlatched, the hinges silent as he nudged it open and stepped through into a room even darker than the entryway. A faint line revealed the break in curtains covering a window that faced the street out front.

Michael closed the door but for a three-inch gap and drew his pipes. Ariana's admonition to not bring a pipe to a gunfight seemed relevant, but the heavy pipes felt right in his hands. Any action would be close quarters. They'd serve him well.

Through the crack, Michael saw Kaltrina unlock and open the door about a quarter of the way. Greenish-yellow light spilled in from the street, lighting half her face, the other half in shadow. A man's voice, low and harsh, the words in Albanian, hit Kaltrina like a physical force. Her eyes flared open and she staggered back a step, the details of her face disappearing in complete shadow. The door swung further open and light washed over her as a big man stepped past the open door into the vestibule.

He raised a gun to Kaltrina's forehead and pulled the trigger. Michael had started moving the moment he'd seen the fear on her face when the door swung open. He leapt forward, swung the pipe, struck the man across the bridge of the nose just as the gun fired. The man's head snapped back at the same moment Kaltrina's head was flung backwards, blood spraying out of the back of her ruined skull.

Heat exploded in Michael's mind as he saw Kaltrina's body collapsed to the floor on the edges of his peripheral vision. He made no effort to restrain it. The blow had staggered the man, his hand reflexively releasing the gun. Michael dropped the pipe in his right hand and snatched the gun out of the air as it fell. He pivoted, put the gun to the man's chest, fired once. Michael's mind dimly registered the body armor, he raised the gun as the man staggered backwards out of the door, fired again, wrecking his throat.

He fired off two more rounds at the cluster of men in front of the house, flipped the door closed as he turned, sprinted past Kaltrina's body for the kitchen. Gunfire erupted outside, but Michael's mind had worked out that the gun he'd taken was firing hollow points, and the door had felt solid. The door held as he did the math, counting. Probably five men firing shots. His foot slid in pooled blood hidden in the shadows near Kaltrina's sprawled body. He staggered forward and caught the rail of the stairs to steady himself, coming face to face with Ariana.

He checked his swing with the pipe an inch from her temple, snarled, pushed her down the hall, toward the kitchen. Toward Ditmir, who stumbled forward out of the kitchen, emitting a high keen.

"Go!" Ariana said, walking backwards with him, guns extended toward the front door. "Get him back to the kitchen. I'll cover us."

Michael didn't hesitate. He stepped forward and snatched the little man off his feet as Ditmir tried to run by, hoisting him over a shoulder. Michael surged down the hall, waiting for it. The front door banged open, suppressed gunfire erupted behind him. Six shots in quick succession, accompanied by the roar of returned fire from the doorway and cries of pain.

Michael reached the kitchen, lit by a single bulb over the small table. He dumped Ditmir on a chair and stole a glance backwards. Ariana backed into the kitchen, fired four shots in rapid succession—two from each gun—and pushed the door shut with a foot. Michael turned back, whipped his remaining pipe up and out, shattering the bulb. As darkness fell on the room, the windows—one above the sink looking over the street, the other on the opposite side overlooking the inner courtyard— exploded inward simultaneously.

Men followed the glass, feet first, vague shapes in the darkness. Michael moved, his mind turning it over. To burst in with that speed, they'd likely roped in from the roof and swung outward first, the timing coordinated perfectly.

Conclusion? Whole house's compromised by men with real training.

The thought flickered across his mind as he leapt toward the closer man, coming through the courtyard window right next to Ariana. Michael landed on his left foot, his right foot raised high. The intruder landed in a squat, and Michael brought his foot down with a violent ax kick to the top of the man's head. Ariana stepped past the man as he collapsed to the floor and fired two quick shots toward the other intruder.

"Down!" Michael yelled and dropped to the floor.

He landed beside the man he'd just downed. A part deep inside Michael screamed, fought the inevitable, but mostly he just felt rage. He reached out with the gun, planted it on the man's temple, pulled the trigger.

Gunfire rang out, men outside the windows firing into the kitchen. Suddenly Ariana was next to him on the floor, her arm wrapped around his neck, pulling his ear to her mouth.

"Mine's down. Plan?"

Michael pulled his head back so he could see her in the faint light. He wasn't seeing muzzle flashes, so the men were still back from the windows firing blind. It was distracting, the curve of her cheek, the faintest light outlining her upper lip. His mind was stuck in a dark place of instinct and savagery. He released his remaining pipe, reached out, pulled her close, and kissed her.

"That's a dead end," he said, pulling away and jerking his head toward the window above them. "We go out the other window, try to shoot our way out."

She didn't speak. He had the feeling her eyes held an intensity that would have been uncomfortable if he could have seen them. His brain struggled toward normal thought. Maybe the kiss hadn't been a good idea. Or maybe it had been with death so near. The gunfire slowed down. They'd make their approach now.

"Cover both windows." Ditmir's ragged voice came from off to Michael's left. The little man was probably under the table. "Give me a few seconds to move around. And don't shoot me. Bastards will pay."

Ariana reached over and tapped Michael's lips with a pinky, still grasping a gun with the remaining fingers. "I'll cover the sink window."

Then she was gone. He could vaguely see her crouching, both guns held high above her head. The window above the sink was significantly higher than the window Michael had to cover. Ariana performed a swaying squat-walk, arms straight up, firing an occasional shot.

What the hell did that mean?

The lip tap had probably been the most ambiguous signal he'd ever gotten from a woman. He shook his head, reached up to put the barrel of his gun on the windowsill above him and squeezed off a slow cadence of shots, changing the angle on each one. Ditmir scurried low to the ground over to the door, reached up, and fiddled with something on the wall. There was a loud clunk, and Ditmir was moving again.

Michael figured the body beside him had to be armed. He reached over with his free hand, found a shoulder holster, and relieved the dead man of his firearm just as Ditmir reached the side of Michael's window. He grasped something on the wall as Michael fired a couple more rounds, then yanked down. Michael pulled his hand clear just before a cover of some sort slammed down, sealing off the window. Michael reached up and felt an unyielding, metallic plate.

Something bumped Michael's feet. In the remaining light from the far window, Michael could just make out Ditmir crawling on his elbows toward the sink. He heard Ariana reload both guns with freakish speed, then resume firing. Ditmir got to the counter and stood with seemingly no concern for Ariana as she fired round after round through the window. He grabbed something, jerked it down. The room plunged into absolute darkness.

CHAPTER TWELVE

*M*ichael flipped on the headlamp to its red light and adjusted the angle of the beam. His rage was on low burn, his mind largely back under control. Ditmir was digging through a drawer next to the sink. He retrieved a candle and matches, stepped over the body by the sink, and put the candle on the small table. Once lit, the flickering pinpoint of light seemed bright in the confines of the sealed off room. Michael flipped off his headlamp.

The windows were blocked off with what looked like steel plates. Michael stood as Ariana walked over to his window and touched it.

"The door is secure as well?" Ariana said, looking at Ditmir, who'd collapsed into a chair and sat with his elbows on his knees, his face in his hands.

He nodded but said nothing. Gunfire sounded from the hallway, but the door showed no signs of stress.

"You made your kitchen a safe room?" Michael asked as he retrieved his remaining pipe and slipped it into the harness on his right leg.

Ditmir ignored him, and Michael heard muffled sobs behind the hands. His shoulders started to shake. The moment replayed in Michael's mind. The gun coming up. The struggle to swing the door open and get to Kaltrina in time. The pipe striking the man's face just as the gun fired. Questions tumbled through his mind. Should he have swung for the gun instead? Or thrown the pipe to disrupt the shot? He had no answers.

His eyes drifted down to the man sprawled below the window, his head wrecked. He shuddered. Then the door shuddered under a heavy blow. And another one. Ariana knelt in front of Ditmir, took his hands, pulled them away from his face. He looked up, his eyes distant.

"Ditmir," she said, "I'm sorry. I promise you, I will avenge her, but we have to go. You must have planned something when you set up this room, yes? How do we leave?"

The door shuddered again. Whoever was slamming into the door was big.

"Tear them down." Ditmir's eyes had come into focus, locked onto Ariana. "Not just Valdrin. The whole *bajrak*. You understand?"

"And the girls," she said.

Ditmir nodded, dragged a hand across his face. "And the girls."

What the hell? Bajrak? Girls? Secrets within secrets.

Boom!

Michael wasn't sure, but it seemed like the door shuddered more with that blow. At the edges of his hearing, two-tone sirens wailed.

"You ask much," Ariana said.

Boom!

"And I've given much," Ditmir said. He glanced around the room, his eyebrows lifting, as though seeing the two bodies for the first time. "You should go."

"How?" Michael felt like his head was going to explode. "How do we go?"

Ditmir reached under the table and yanked on something. He yanked again and produced a metallic handle. It all clicked for Michael.

"Magnets," he said, and Ditmir nodded. "Trapdoor in the floor?"

Boom!

Ditmir knelt and put the handle on the floor. Michael could see it twist a bit in Ditmir's hand, aligning itself to the magnets in the trapdoor. Ditmir tugged, and a section of the tile floor lifted up. The workmanship was incredible. The door had seemingly appeared from a seamless floor. Michael stepped over, flipped the red light back on, and looked into the hole. It was a shallow space but extended out of sight in two directions.

"This goes to the other side of the building," Ditmir said, pointing along the leftward side. "You will find the door one meter before the end of the tunnel. Push up hard and it will open into a hall. There is a door right there to a small library. Go into the library, out the window. Across a small space between buildings is a window down low, by your feet. It is unlocked. It leads to parking under the building. We have a Maserati parked there. Take it."

Boom!

A groan sounded from the wall, like wood pushed past its limits. Ditmir fished a key out of a pocket and tossed it to Ariana. She plucked it out of the air and slipped it into a pocket.

"Okay," Michael said. "We take the car. And you?"

Ditmir stood and retrieved a bottle of grappa from its shelf with a small glass. He popped out the cork and poured. "I will stay and pray. If these men make it in before the police, I will see what I can do. If they flee, I will sow confusion with the police."

Boom!

Michael retrieved both the guns he'd acquired from the floor where he'd left them. "This one's empty, but I'm betting you'll find more ammo on one of these guys."

Ditmir threw back his drink, took the guns, and poured again. "Go. I'll drop the door back in place once you're in."

The sirens were getting louder. Michael looked at Ariana, she nodded. He put a hand on Ditmir's shoulder.

Boom!

"I'm sorry."

Ditmir looked up at him with watery eyes. "Pay your debt. You understand? We sheltered you, and my wife lies dead."

Michael grimaced but nodded. He had no idea what he was committing to, nor time to think about it. He stepped into the hole and ducked down into the narrow crawl space. It extended back under the floor a few feet behind him, making it easier to lower himself through the small opening. He lay nearly flat to get the backpack into the space, then crawled forward on his elbows into the darkness lit only by his red headlamp.

The claustrophobic tunnel extended ahead to the outer limits of his light. Once Michael had worked his way forward a full body length, he heard Ariana working her way into the tunnel. She tapped his foot, he assumed to let him know she was following him. A moment later, the trapdoor closed, cutting off the trickle of light from behind him.

They moved forward, and soon the other end came into view. Once Michael judged himself within three feet of the end, he arched his back and pushed up. The unseen door above him popped free and swung open. Michael worked his way to a kneeling position and looked around, holding the door to keep it from tipping past vertical and crashing down.

The red light of Michael's headlamp revealed a hallway stretching to his left and right with a door immediately ahead. The space was silent but for the wail of sirens, now louder, more urgent. He offered a quick, silent prayer for Ditmir. An image of Kaltrina's head snapping back flashed behind his eyelids with each blink. Still holding the trapdoor, he stepped out of the tunnel. Ariana crawled into view.

"Think I need help." Her voice was faint.

Michael reached down and grabbed her backpack with his free hand. "Hold your arms tightly to your chest. I'm going to lift you out." He spoke no louder than she had.

He gave her a moment to prepare, then lifted her slowly up to a standing position. Releasing the backpack, he took her hand as she stepped up to the floor, then lowered the trapdoor closed. She pointed at the door next to them, and he nodded. Michael opened the door and led her into the dark room, closing the door behind them.

The lived-in look of the room was confirmed by noise from the hallway. Someone was on the move.

"Sirens would wake the dead," he whispered. "Better hurry."

Michael crossed to the window, unlatched it, pulled it open. The sirens were much louder. Glancing down the narrow space between buildings, he could see the reflected glow of police lights. There were no shots. No yelling. He glanced back at Ariana.

"They fled," she said. "Hopefully Ditmir lives."

He nodded and scooted through the window. She leaned out toward him, and he lifted her through. Face to face, he set her down.

"No kiss?" she said and flipped up the hood of her jacket.

He turned back to the window and closed it.

He turned toward the opposite wall. "Disappointed?"

A short distance further back from the street out front, he saw the window down at ground level.

"I suppose," Ariana said, letting the word hang there as Michael's mind race along the implications, "you'd like to know."

He grimaced, reigned in his thoughts, channeled them into the well-worn grooves of poetry.

with such words spoken
hopes unknown broken
words not even cruel
yet painting me the fool

He reached out with the intent to usher her toward the window and was startled when she took his hand. They walked the short distance to the window and Michael crouched, releasing her hand. The window was unlatched and slid open sideways just as Ditmir said it would. Michael crouched lower and looked inside.

The window was set just under the ceiling of a basement that was lit only by an LED rope light a good twenty feet away outlining the steps going up to the floor above. It was a tight little parking garage holding a dozen cars, maybe more. Michael slipped off his backpack, as the window was barely big enough for his shoulders. He dropped down between two cars and reached up to catch his backpack as Ariana pushed it through the window.

A light flashed across the window, and Ariana hissed something. It hadn't been in English, but Michael could tell the intent. She came through the window with her backpack still on. Michael dropped his bag and caught her, lowering her to the ground then closed the window and latched it as a light danced across the glass. Someone was running toward it.

A car chirped behind him, accompanied by the brief flash of orange lights. Michael turned to see Ariana holding up the key fob that Ditmir had given her. She walked to a car facing outward from the opposite wall. The vehicle was hard to make out in the dim light, but it looked like a beast of a car. Michael flipped up his jacket hood, grabbed his bag, and followed.

She went straight to the driver door and got in, sliding out of her backpack as she dropped into the seat. Michael landed in the passenger seat a second later, his backpack dumped at his feet. He reached over and grabbed her backpack while moving his seat backwards. She punched the start button, the engine hummed to life, a light flickered over them, then returned.

"Buckle me," she said, and punched a button on a remote clipped to the driver sunshade.

He leaned across her, ignoring the light, pulled the seatbelt over and buckled it. Ariana had her phone out, a map pulled up, and studied it as he settled in his own seat and buckled up. The light flickered away, and Ariana stuffed the phone in a jacket pocket.

"You have a plan?" he asked.

She pulled the car out of the space and turned toward the back of the building, Past the stairs off to the left, a ramp led up to the street level, an iron gate just completing its slow swing open toward the ramp.

"I do," Ariana said. She pulled the car forward, up the ramp, stopped at the top where it emptied onto a narrow street. "But no plan will get us out of here, only improvisation."

She pushed something on her door handle and both windows lowered. The sirens were loud and seemed to be getting louder. Ariana pushed a button on the center console, then reached over and pushed a button for a couple seconds on the other side of the steering wheel.

"So you know this car pretty well?" Michael asked.

Ariana nodded. "I own a Maserati. Getting us set up. Sport mode. No traction control. I don't think the Albanians are gone, not after getting so close to me. And the police will be a problem. It may take some aggressive driving."

The air was cool, even cold. She edged the car forward so their view cleared the building. The street was lit here and there by lights on the surrounding buildings. Cars zipped by in both directions.

"How can there be this much traffic?" Michael said. "It's getting on toward 3:00 AM."

"Welcome to Rome." Ariana was studying the map on her phone again.

"What are we waiting for?" he asked.

"Making sure I know the terrain. Knowledge is power, right?"

"And the windows? You want to be able to hear the sirens better?"

"No," Ariana said. "That was a courtesy to Ditmir. I don't want to shoot out his glass."

Michael reached over, gripped her arm. "No police."

She nodded. "No police."

The irony was not lost on Michael that it was at that very moment a police car rounded the corner off to the right and headed toward them, siren wailing, lights flashing. Ariana dropped her phone in a jacket pocket and punched the gas. The car leapt into the street, cutting in front of a car coming from the left. She spun the wheel, worked the brake with the gas, and came out of the turn at a speed Michael would have thought was impossible.

They roared down the narrow street as it wound between

the encroaching buildings. She passed a car in front of them, getting back over moments before an oncoming car passed them. The night sky had the glow of a large city, the street alternating between darkness and pools of light. Ariana did not turn on the headlights.

She swung a left turn onto a larger street, working the steering wheel paddles and both pedals. She came out of the turn just as two police cars pulled into the street a block ahead, angling across the street to cut it off. Several cars in front of them braked hard to stop in front of the barricade.

"What was it?" Ariana asked as she threw the car into a hard slide, then gunned it to yank the car around and rocket forward the way they'd just come. The tailing police car turned off the side street just ahead of them, careened across the road just before they shot by.

"What was what?" Michael tried to keep his voice calm, tried to entrust himself to her competence.

"The poem. Back between the buildings. Saw you blank out for a moment."

"Oh," he said. "Of course you noticed. Sorry, my poems are mine and mine only."

She took a left, another left, then a right. The roar of another car came from behind them. Michael glanced back over his shoulder, saw a car running without headlights cross the street they'd just turned off of in pursuit. The street looked otherwise empty, though it curved, limiting Michael's view.

Ariana did everything at once and the car whipped around and was suddenly going in reverse, facing the oncoming car. She flipped the headlights on bright, drew across her body with her left hand, stuck her arm out the window. She fired twice. Michael saw two holes appear in the windshield just before the car swerved and careened into a building.

She hit the brakes, flipped off the lights, and holstered the gun. As they came to a stop, three police cars turned onto the street several blocks ahead.

"We may get lucky." Ariana hit the gas and the car jumped forward. "It's dark enough they may not see us if they're focused on it. Black car and all."

"It" was the other car, hanging halfway out the front of a building and seemingly having started a small fire. She angled to the left side of the street then threw the wheel to the right, aiming for a small side street that descended sharply from their street half a block short of the wreck. A flicker of motion teased Michael's peripheral vision. He turned and saw a car running full speed toward them, its lights off.

It clipped the tail of their car, sending them into a spin as Ariana slammed on the brakes. They came to a stop after three quarters of a turn, broadside to the side street, facing the car that had just hit them. It slid to a stop even with the wrecked car, then accelerated in reverse. The three police cars were coming on fast.

"Well, that sucks," Ariana said.

She hit the gas, turned the wheel, and did a tight donut until they faced the side street again. The Maserati launched down the street just as the other car backed up even with them. Michael heard gunfire, but the slope of the road took them out of sight immediately.

"You think we're in trouble?" he asked.

"No, I've got this," she said. "I know where we are. I just hate giving back the car damaged."

Michael looked at her. Ariana wore a detached look, like she was seeing the street but watching something else. He kept his eyes on her. It made him less nervous than watching dark street fly by, blind curve after blind curve. She turned onto another tiny street, this one filled with even more twists, but no longer descending.

"Ariana, his wife was murdered tonight. He doesn't give a damn about the car."

"Right. Sorry."

She turned onto street after street. Sirens filled the air, but were now distant. Michael sat back and tried to relax as the city flickered by. Ariana swung out into a much larger street, flipped the lights on, rolled up the windows, and settled in with the other cars on the road.

For the moment, the intensity that came from fighting for his life drained out of him. They were just a youngish couple driving a damaged car through Rome in the middle of the night. For the moment.

CHAPTER THIRTEEN

"*H*ow do you do it?"

"Do what?" Ariana said.

"Shoot so accurately." Michael pantomimed shooting. "The whole two guns thing. Hell, no one can shoot one gun like that. Not that I've ever seen."

She flipped on a blinker and executed a tight turn into a parking garage. She kept her hood pulled close and looked down as she grabbed the ticket. The gate lifted. "I've always seen the world as all these lines and curves. I had a lot of struggles when I was young. Had trouble learning to read. Couldn't do math. Even had trouble learning to speak as a toddler. But I saw lines everywhere."

"Lines?"

She drove the car up a level. "If I was throwing a ball, I'd see this line extending from my hand in an arc. As I got better at throwing, as I learned to repeat the same motion, the ball began to trace the line. And I got terribly accurate."

"Okay," Michael said. "Keep going. But first, what are we doing here?"

"Stealing a car," Ariana said. "This one's banged up. Too recognizable. Hand me my backpack."

He handed her the bag. "I'm sorry I asked."

"You're cute," she said, pulling a long, slender case out of her backpack. "You shoot someone in the head, then worry about stealing a car?"

The cold weight of grief pressed on Michael's chest and made it hard to breathe. He'd known it was lurking behind the immediacy of their escape, that it would fight forward and try to drown him. As always, it did not come alone. A line of ghosts, fragments of memories, surged forward. The dead demanded his acknowledgement.

"I did what I had to do."

She'd reached for the door handle but stopped and turned back to him. Her hand reached out, took his. "I'm sorry. I shouldn't have joked about that."

Her hand tightened for a moment, then she was out the door. The car she'd parked next to was facing outward, its driver's door next to hers. She pulled a long, flat tool with a bent end out of the case. She slid it into the door along the glass, fished around for a minute, lifted it back out.

"Can you bring our packs?" She pushed the Maserati's door closed and opened the door of the other car.

Michael shook his head, as though the ghosts merely clung to his face and could be shed like drops of water. He stepped out, grabbed both backpacks, and headed around to the passenger side of the car. It was an older red Fiat that had seen better days. He clambered into the passenger side, found a bar under the seat, and pushed it all the way back.

Ariana was twisted over toward the center console, doing something under the steering column. Her breathing sounded forced. A moment later, the car started and she sat back up. She looked at him. Her face was pale.

"Seatbelt?" she said.

Michael reached across her, aware of her face close to his, a sensation that shoved the dead back into his subconscious. In their place he felt an itch he knew he shouldn't scratch, that he would choose not to scratch. He grabbed the belt and pulled it out away from her and around, then click it into place.

"You don't look great." He sat back and buckled himself in. "You need some pain killers?"

She looked forward, her face hidden by the hood, and shook her head. "Clarity"—she tapped her head with a finger —"over comfort. Don't know how much more I have in me tonight." She glanced at him. "Enough to get home, though."

She dropped the car into gear and drove for the down ramp.

"Is that the plan? Head to your place?"

She nodded. "Best I can come up with. I'd wanted to stay in the city until I'd retrieved that item we discussed. Certainly didn't want to leave any traces pointing to me, but we need a safe place to rest, and I'm running out of options."

Ariana pulled up to the exit and paid the machine some Euros after scanning her ticket. She kept her head averted, the hood pulled close. Michael followed her example. The arm lifted, and they rolled back out onto the street.

"And what is that item? The one you need to retrieve." Michael asked.

"A rifle."

"A rifle. Like what I could buy off the shelf back home?"

"Not exactly," Ariana said. "An MK-13 with a nice setup."

Michael shook his head. "Yeah, not so much. So where are we headed?"

"The grah's right up ahead," she said. "After that, about twenty minutes to my place. Northwest in La Sorta."

"The grah?"

131

"GRA. The Rome Ring Road. It's a loop around Rome. We'll make good time once we're on it."

Michael nodded. "So you visualize trajectories. Is that it?"

Ariana glanced at him and nodded. "More or less. I'm not sure I actually see lines, but it feels like I do. They're there, but they're not."

"So you point a gun," Michael said, "and it's like you have a laser sight on it?"

"Something like that. The suppresser makes it easier, makes the line more accurate, gives me more to work with. The line sort of fades out over distance, but I'm pretty confident at normal ranges."

"Yeah, I noticed."

Ariana turned the car onto an elevated highway. "The GRA."

They rode in silence for a time. Michael tried to process everything he knew, but his mind kept stumbling back to the kiss. What had he been thinking? He pulled his hood down and used the motion to steal a glance at her. She'd already pulled hers down. Her face looked slack, drained of vitality, yet her beauty still imposed itself, forcing him to reckon with it.

And what, Michael wondered, had she meant with the whole pinky-tap on his lips? Nicely done? Do it again and I'll shoot you? He had no idea, but she'd taken his hand after that. He was sure that had meant something, too, but he was also sure that he shouldn't be thinking about it, that he shouldn't care. Yet he did. It was maddening.

So damn weak. A pretty face, some personality, and I'm the sucker. Again.

He forced his mind back to the safety of analyzing the situation. Ariana was an assassin, and a damn good one, but she viewed herself as in the right. As having just cause. Yet it seemed to him nothing more than some sort of extravagant quest for revenge, stretching out over years, executed with patience and expertise. She'd gotten shot up, probably spec'ing out a job if she'd left behind a sniper rifle. She claimed to have killed eleven men in the previous week. He'd seen five die, so she'd killed six men when everything went down and she'd ended up calling Rescue Nurses Worldwide. And Ditmir had known of RNW, so all the stuff Joann had said about them getting a strange call a few times a year was true. Word was out there in the wild about the shadowy side of RNW.

"Why Montréal?" His voice sounded abrupt, intruding on the quiet transition from city to dark countryside as they left the GRA behind.

"Officially, that's where I am right now," Ariana said. "On extended holiday. I flew back under an alias for the work."

"So you get back to Montréal," he said, "recover, then what? Ditmir said three things. Valdrin. Something like barrack, and the girls. Want to fill me in?"

"*Bajrak*, not barrack. You really want to know my plans?"

"*Bajrak*." Michael tried out the word, grimaced, shook his head. "No, I guess I don't. Not more than needed to get you to Montréal."

A few minutes later she pulled off the dark road and came to a stop with the headlights illuminating a wrought iron gate across the stone paving of the drive. "Be right back."

Ariana moved slowly, opening the door, pushing herself to a standing position. She walked to a keypad mounted on a black metal post on the left side of the gate. The gate began opening, and she made her way back to the car. Once back in the driver's seat, she didn't ask about the seatbelt. They pulled forward through the gate, and Michael glanced back and saw the gate start to swing shut in the red glow of the taillights.

The drive ascended a gentle hill, following a broad curve to the left, up to a stone-paved circle drive in front of what

Michael supposed was Ariana's house, though it looked more like a small resort. In the middle of the circle drive, low shrubs concealed lights that shown upwards onto a low-walled pool. Water arced up from the mouths of four stone fish around the perimeter of the pool to land in a pedestaled basin in the middle. Three dolphins in the basin looked upward, water bubbling out of their mouths, the water running into the basin and spilling down to the pool below.

The house itself was two stories with balconies lining the second floor, lit from below. Several shallow steps led up to large double doors at the main entrance. The windows were all dark. Ariana followed the drive around the fountain and pulled onto a narrow extension that went around to the side of the house. A four-car garage stretched out from the main body of the house, kicked out at a bit of an angle toward them. Ariana drove up to the furthest bay door.

"Code's three seven nine eight," she said.

"You pretty much wiped out?" Michael asked.

"Completely." She turned toward him. "It's like my strength bled out the closer we got to home. I'm done. My body's just quit."

Michael dug into his backpack and pulled out his headlamp. He settled it on his head and flipped on its red light, then got out and pushed the door shut. Michael headed around the front of the car to the keypad on the left side of the garage door. Ariana killed the headlights. By the light of his headlamp, he punched in the code, the door lifted, and he followed the car in as Ariana drove it into the garage. She killed the engine and swung the driver door open. The garage door slowly closed.

Michael glanced around the garage. It was lit by the lone bulb on the garage door opener above the car. The dim light showed a clean space, cabinets lining the front wall, two cars parked in the two spots closest to the main house. The nearer one looked like a four-door Maserati. Beyond it, he couldn't quite make out the type of car, but it was a low to the ground sports car. From its angles, he guessed it was probably a Lamborghini.

Ariana still hadn't moved. Michael stepped over and crouched down to check on her. She was leaning back on the headrest, her head rolled over facing him.

"Really tapped out, huh?" he said.

She smiled for a moment, then it was gone, her face slack.

"Okay, let's do this." Michael slid an arm behind her shoulders, the other arm under her legs, and lifted her out of the car.

She didn't protest, but draped an arm around his neck and leaned her head against his shoulder.

"Do rescue nurses expect tips?" she said, her voice a throaty whisper.

"Absolutely," he said as he walked toward the far end of the garage with her. His headlamp swept across the door to the house. "First tip I need is how to get into the house."

"My keys are, oh, damn it. They're in my backpack."

"Mind if I set you down?" Michael asked.

She shook her head, which he felt as much as saw. He carried her to the door to the house opposite the sports car, knelt, and set her down, her back to the door. Michael stood and glanced at the car. It was definitely a Lamborghini. Bright yellow. Expensive looking.

"You okay?" he said.

"Yeah," Ariana said. "It was that damned tunnel. Crawling took it out of me."

"I believe it." He pivoted so he could see both her and the car. "Is that a Gallardo?"

"2013 LP550-2 with the 6-speed gated shifter."

Michael stood "Was that a yes?"

Ariana laughed, a low chuckle. "Yes, it's a Gallardo."

The name rolled off her tongue as though she was speaking Italian, not English. It made the car seem even sexier, and Michael thought it was doing pretty well on its own.

"Good enough. I'll get the backpacks. Then we'll talk about when I get to drive it, okay? Rescue nurses don't really make enough to buy Lamborghinis."

She half smiled. "I thought I was paying pretty well."

Michael nodded. "Truth. Just not Lamborghini good. I'll get our gear."

He walked to their borrowed car, retrieved the backpacks, and headed back to her. He knelt and unzipped her bag. Ariana sat with her head resting against the door, her eyes closed, her breathing slow. He reached out and put the back of his hand on her forehead, then took her wrist and checked her pulse.

"Will I live?" she asked, her eyes still closed.

He released her wrist. "Nothing that sleep and calories can't fix."

Michael's hand drifted up, touched her cheek. Her eyes remained closed, but she leaned into his hand with gentle pressure.

Damn, but she's beautiful.

Her hair glowed in the red light, loose curls spilling over her shoulders. He let his hand drop and stood. Ariana opened her eyes, looked up at him, and smiled. It felt to Michael like an *I know what you're thinking* smile. She looked down, rummaged in her backpack, pulled out a set of keys on a carabiner.

"Help me up," she said. "Pretty sure I can stand if you'll just stay near in case I'm wrong. Need to disarm the security once we're in."

He bent down, took her carefully under the arms, and

lifted her. She turned toward the door and leaned against the frame with a shoulder.

"Can you bring the bags in?" she asked, working the key into the deadbolt. "And no lights, okay? Let's keep the house looking unoccupied."

Michael zippered her backpack closed and slung one backpack on each shoulder. He reached out and took her under the arm as she pushed the door open. They stepped through into a dark room. It looked like an expensive mudroom to Michael, with wooden coat and shoe racks along the wall to the right along with a slender door, cabinetry to the left. On the far side of the room, an open doorway showed an expansive, dimly lit kitchen. Immediately to the left of the garage door, a security box protruded from the wall. She pressed her thumb to a pad on its face. The pad turned green and she punched in a code on a small keypad. It emitted a descending chime and a green light above the keypad turned on.

She turned toward him and grabbed his arm, steadying herself. "I'd give you a tour, but I think I'll pass out in bed instead. Would you be so kind as to take me to my bedroom?"

Michael smiled and pushed the garage door closed. "I don't usually give the bedroom assists on a first date, but you're paying well."

Stepping in close to her, he lifted her, an arm behind her shoulders, the other under her legs. She nestled her head against his neck.

"And the bedroom is?" he asked.

"There"—her arm lifted, her face still up against his neck, her breath warm on his skin, and a finger pointed toward the doorway to the kitchen—"Right out of the kitchen, across the room. Stairs up, door on the right."

Michael carried her through a kitchen that could have graced the cover of one of the magazines at his dentist's office.

Discreet under-cabinet lights highlighted a huge island, honed marble counters, a massive copper oven hood, a host of other details he took in with a glance. Straight ahead was a doorway to a dark room dominated by a large table and chairs. To the right was a massive, arched entryway toward the front of the house. He headed through it and looked around. It was darker than the kitchen, but some light leaked through the curtains on the far side of the room, revealing hints of a huge living space, a very high ceiling, and furniture in abundance. He made his way forward to a curved staircase leading upward. It curved back along the left side of the room and led to a walkway above the arched entry to the kitchen.

Taking the stairs two at a time, Michael carried Ariana up to the walkway and through an open door a short distance to his right that opened into a mammoth bedroom. A giant bed stood against the far wall, lit by a nightlight in the wall extending away from him to his left. To his right, a couple wingback chairs were arranged on either side of a small sofa around a fireplace.

Michael crossed the room and laid Ariana in the bed. He stood, dropped the backpacks near the foot of the bed, and flipped off his headlamp. She smiled deeply, opened her eyes, and found his.

"Home feels so..." She trailed off but kept the smile.

"Right?" he said.

Ariana nodded. "Can you get a bottle of water for me from the kitchen? In the refrigerator. I'm going to hit the bathroom even if I have to crawl."

She swung her legs off the bed and sat up. Her head hung down, her hands clutching the edge of the bed. Michael reached out and put a hand on her shoulder.

"You sure?"

Ariana looked up at him. "You want to improvise a bed pan for me?"

Michael shook his head. "Not really."

She nodded. "The bathroom it is. Then sleep."

"Alright," he said. "Be right back with your water."

Michael headed back out to the walkway overlooking the room below. Two doors stood opposite the railing, and on the far side the walkway extended into a dark hallway. Michael went to the closer door, opened it, glanced inside. A large window and glass door on the opposite wall let in moonlight, revealing a spacious bedroom, complete with a small sitting area at the foot of a huge bed.

He cut across the room to the window on the left side of the bed and looked outside. Balcony overlooking a pool. Pool house. Spa. Ridiculous lawn. Gazebo. A couple fountains. Michael shook his head. His first impression had been right. Ariana's home was more like a resort than a house.

With a final glance out the window, Michael turned and headed back downstairs to the kitchen. It took him a moment to find the refrigerator. He'd never used one that looked like it was built into the wall and stood taller than him. An entire shelf was dedicated to water. He grabbed a bottle and headed back up to Ariana's room.

The first thing he saw as he stepped into her room was the small pile of clothes beside the bed. She sat on top of the covers, leaning back against a pillow propped up on the headboard, wearing only panties and a bra. She was, Michael decided in a glance, as close to perfect as he'd ever meet. He felt a pull, a desire to throw off every restraint, every scruple.

"Thomas?" she said. "You good?"

Michael's mind rumbled back into motion. She was talking to him. He was Thomas. He shook his head.

"Yeah, I'm good." He crossed to her and handed over the bottle of water. "Here you go. Get some rest."

She opened the bottle and took a sip. "More poetry?"

"What?"

Ariana nodded toward the door. "When you came in. You looked out of it. More poems?"

"Oh, that." He shook his head. "No, there's already enough poetry in this room. Didn't really feel the need to add any."

She cocked her head to the side, frowned, then smiled.

"Not bad." She frowned again. "But almost too subtle. I'm not even sure I'm reading that right. Either way, though, can you check my stitches?"

Michael took a slow breath, tried to calm his mind, become clinical. It was surprisingly easy after all the years of practice, in spite of the pull she exerted on him.

"Let's take a look," he said. "I'm going to need my headlamp. Might want to close your eyes."

The wounds, front and back, looked shockingly good, the stitching in great shape. He flipped the headlamp off and stood back up.

"You're in way better shape than you have any right to be in," he said.

She worked her way under the covers, slid the pillow down, and lay back.

"Isn't that bragging," she said, looking up at him, a smile tugging on one side of her mouth. "It was your work."

His clinical disposition wavered, then broke. Looking down at her, knowing what was under the covers, his mind seemed to catch fire.

there's a fire that burns unseen
that foolish men try to tame
but the fire's edge is keen
and sets their lives aflame

"Okay, I'm going to grab one of the bedrooms." He turned

and picked up his backpack. "Mind if I grab some food from the kitchen?"

She was looking at him, her eyes narrowed. "That was definitely poetry. Are you ever going to share it with me?"

Michael walked to the door and looked back. "No, probably not. Now about the food."

"Grab whatever you want," Ariana said. "Just no lights, okay?"

"Yep. No lights." He pulled his eyes away from her. "See you in the morning."

CHAPTER FOURTEEN

*M*ichael sat up, glanced at his watch, and grinned. He couldn't remember the last time he'd slept until 9:00 AM. The heavy curtains blocked most of the mid-morning sun, but enough leaked through to show the contours of the bedroom he'd chosen the night before. Two twin beds stood side by side, each with a bedside table. A large walk-in closet held two dressers. It was on the ground floor near the back corner of the house opposite the garage. Probably intended for servants.

He grabbed some fresh clothes out of his backpack and headed to the bathroom opposite the closet. The bathroom had no windows, so he closed the door and flipped on the light. The shower was stocked with soap and shampoo. Towels hung on hooks next to it. The sink even had mouthwash.

Michael bathed and dressed quickly, repacked his backpack, and took it with him as he headed out of the bedroom. A hall led past a few other rooms he'd checked the night before. Another guest bathroom. Library. Office. A room with a pool table.

He came out into the main living room opposite the staircase. Ariana was in the kitchen sliding what looked like a medium-sized quiche without a crust out of a skillet onto a large plate. A large window over the sink overlooked the pool in back and flooded the kitchen with light. Two places had been set at the corner of the kitchen island closest to him. Silverware, plates, napkins, water bottles, small cups of what looked like steaming cappuccino. Next to the place setting further from him was spread a black felt cloth. A disassembled low caliber gun with various cleaning supplies lay on the cloth.

"Good morning, Thomas." She set the skillet back on the stove. "Sleep well?"

Michael sat down on a stool at the place setting opposite the window. "I slept incredibly. Better than I have since—well, in a long time."

Since I discovered Bethany and Frank in the shower.

Ariana sliced the weird-looking quiche in half, though one half was distinctly larger than the other. "I didn't have any vegetables cooked, so I kept it simple with some spinach, mushrooms, and mostly cured meats."

Michael smiled. "If it'd make you feel better, I'll act like that's a problem."

She stepped around the island and slid the larger half onto his plate, the smaller onto hers. "No acting required. Enjoy."

"You feeling better?"

Ariana sat down and picked up her fork. She waved it vaguely at his plate. "Eat." She took a bite of her quiche. "We can talk while we dine."

"Fair enough." He took a bite. It was perfect. Light, fluffy eggs, a couple sharp cheeses, mildly bitter spinach, some unidentified but delicious meats, and mushrooms. "This is fantastic. I've never had a quiche without a crust, but it works."

Ariana snorted and slapped a hand to her mouth to keep

the food in. "Quiche? You're in Italy, Thomas. It's a frittata."

Michael shrugged. "Learn something new every day."

They ate in silence for a couple minutes. His cappuccino was perfect. "You timed all this pretty well. Still nice and hot."

She nodded. "The shower you used causes a pipe to knock. Need to get it fixed, but it gave me a pretty good idea of when you'd be coming out."

"So how are you doing?" Michael asked.

"Really well." She took a bite, chewed. "The wounds don't feel great, but my energy level is much better."

Michael made a show of looking around. "You've got a nice place."

"Thanks," Ariana said. "Sorry I can't open the curtains. It really is a nice view."

Michael finished off the last of his frittata, pushed the plate back, and cupped his cappuccino in both hands. The whole context felt unreal, having a beautiful woman make him breakfast at what looked to him like an Italian resort, even if it was her home. A beautiful woman who happened to be an assassin, and a damned good one at that.

Ariana took the last bite of her frittata, looked up, and caught him staring at her. A small smile tugged at the corners of her mouth as she chewed. He held her gaze, thinking. He'd told her he didn't want to know any more than necessary, but the situation was so odd he wasn't sure how to distinguish the incidental from the essential. Getting to Montreal should be straight forward, but nothing had gone according to plan yet.

She lifted her own cappuccino, still looking him in the eyes. Her head tilted slightly, an eyebrow lifted a fraction of an inch. Michael set down his drink and grasped for the right question to get her talking. He needed information.

"So what was the whole pinky tap thing?"

What the hell? Where did that come from?

Her eyebrow raised a bit higher. "Sorry?"

"Back in the kitchen. On the floor."

"Ah." She sat back, her eyes narrowing. "Is that really the right place to start?"

"What do you mean? The whole 'tap my lips while clutching a gun' was pretty damn inscrutable."

"I see," she said. "Yet I believe the first question is, why did you kiss me?"

Michael broke the eye contact. "Oh. Yeah, there is that."

"Yes, that."

He shrugged. "No idea. Well, lots of ideas, but no real explanation."

Ariana smiled, both eyebrows lifting this time. "I'd love to hear those ideas."

Michael grimaced, reestablished eye contact. "We were killing. People were dying. Hell, I thought we'd be dying. I go to a very primal place when it's all going down."

"I see. A primal place. Is that what you call it?"

"In situations like that, don't you become instinctive?" he said. "Even impulsive?"

She ignored the question. "When you kill someone your impulse is to kiss me?" She had a mocking half-smile in full effect.

"I don't know," Michael said. "Look, I'm sorry."

She held her cappuccino in both hands like him. A single finger lifted, wagged side to side at him. "I didn't ask for an apology, just an explanation."

Michael started to laugh, but it died in his throat. He shook his head. "You are cloaked in ambiguity."

"Perhaps." She leaned forward, her elbows on the island. "And does my warrior poet have a poem about his impulses?"

It came to mind unbidden, a fragment of verse. He cleared his throat and spoke.

"In Rome, city of seven hills,
there he met she who lives to kill.
The rushing currents of her life
grabbed hold and swept him into strife.
And though he aimed for Montreal,
she needed more, yes she took it all.
Hands red, for her he carried on.
This bird of prey, this dark falcon."

She sat back, her face blank.

"Sorry," he said.

Ariana's mouth moved, silently voicing a fragment of the poem. He was pretty sure she'd said *she took it all*. He looked down at his empty mug.

What the hell was I thinking?

"Yeah," Michael said, "that was a little more intense than I'd intended."

"And wasn't really about kisses or impulses."

He glanced at her. She looked pasty.

"It's not like that. The poetry channels it. The impulse. The darkness." He shrugged. "I'm not an actual poet, right? It's more about processing things. Tends to be melodramatic. It is what it is. I shouldn't have voiced it."

She slowly raised her cup to her lips, tilted it, then pulled it back and frowned. She stood, took his cup with hers, and walked to the corner of the counter where a stainless cappuccino machine hulked. She looked back at him.

"You want another one?"

"Yeah, sure."

Ariana busied herself for several minutes as the machine gurgled. Michael sat, thinking. He felt his anger lurking in the background, waiting. Ariana beguiled him. Beautiful, stunningly competent, rich, possibly evil, definitely an assassin. He didn't have a category for her. She made his emotions, his desires, act like a drunk who'd just stumbled face-first into a spider web.

Ariana cleared their dishes and slid the black felt over to her place, then returned to the machine as it let out a loud hiss. Michael sat, breathing in a careful cadence, forcing his mind clear of questions. He knew his mission. Get Ariana to Montreal. They'd retrieve the sniper rifle that night, be on a plane the next morning. His money earned, he'd fly back to Rome, drop his alias, and return home. He didn't need to know about the *bajrak*, the girls, the rest of it, but the unknowns gnawed at him.

Two men had died at his hands in support of a mission that might be nothing more than glorified revenge. Were his own motives ever black and white? No, he felt it probably didn't come down to one or the other. She'd likely tried to tangle her revenge up in some larger scheme to make the world a better place. The universal excuse for most every war and many crimes.

Ariana brought the steaming cups of cappuccino over to him, set his down in front of him, and took her seat.

"Thanks." Michael lifted his cup and took a tiny sip of the searingly hot liquid. Bold, mildly bitter, perfect.

"You weren't made for the Marines, in spite of the fact you were good at it. And you found your place as a PJ, but then you dropped that too. Instead, you're a rescue nurse. Is that pretty much it?"

Michael looked at her, ignoring the heat on his neck. "Let's talk about your childhood in Albania instead."

Her smile caught him off guard. "Did you play this game with Ditmir? He loves trading questions over port or grappa. Or, when I was little, tiny sips of wine."

Michael lifted the cappuccino to his lips to buy time. He'd

thought he was pushing back by taking the conversation to Albania, but it hadn't fazed her. He put his cup down.

"Yeah, we traded questions over grappa."

Ariana set her own cup down and her hands immediately busied themselves with the gun now laying in front of her.

"I'll do the same, minus the grappa, if you'd like," she said. "Here's the first question. What's your real name?"

Michael sat back. "I'm not sure I'm comfortable with the question."

"But you only intend to ask me questions that I'll like?"

Her hands continued moving as she spoke, her eyes on Michael, flickering down only occasionally. In seconds the gun was fully disassembled.

"We've been through a lot together," Ariana said. "I hate having to use an alias. It'd be like if I'd made you call me Falcon the whole time. I just need a first name. One you're obviously used to hearing."

"Fair enough," he said. "My name's Michael."

"Thank you, Michael. That feels much better."

"Of course," Michael said, taking another sip. "My turn, I guess. Ditmir mentioned he was the go-between for you and your trainers. We didn't get much further than that. Can you explain?"

"My father discovered my talent when I was very little and developed it aggressively." Her hands continued moving, meticulously cleaning the various parts of the gun. "Not just guns. Knives. Hand-to-hand. All of it. I was a pretty badass little girl. Mass will always count for a lot, and I was smaller than all the boys who wanted to bully me, but—"

"Wait," Michael said. "You were bullied? I thought your father was some scary mafia guy."

She held up a hand, one finger lifted. "That's not how the game is played. We trade questions."

"Right." Michael grimaced. "Should have let you keep talking, I guess."

Ariana shrugged. "We all make mistakes. Are you married or in a relationship?"

Michael ignored the twisting pain in his gut. "My ex-wife divorced me six days ago. For the best given her issues with faithfulness." He took a sip of his cappuccino, suppressed the emotion that he knew would channel into anger. "My second ex-wife, I should say. My high school sweetheart all but divorced me during my first overseas deployment. Formalized it right after I got back."

Describing the horror of his relationships in cold, barren terms felt like a bandaid being torn off. Painful, but it somehow made it easier to keep the rage in check.

"Maybe you're attracted to bitches?"

The momentary shock gave way to the humor of the situation. Michael grinned. "You're the second person in a week to say something like that. But it's a second question. It'll have to wait."

"Touché." Her hands kept moving, her eyes steady on him.

"So, bullies in spite of your father?"

Ariana nodded. "They wouldn't have done it if they'd known who my father was, but he was an invisible part of my life, and my mom didn't exactly have a high place in the community. Then there were my issues"—her hand reached up, a finger tapped her temple—"my mind didn't seem to work like everyone else's. I struggled in school. I was easy prey. But outside of school I learned well, and untrained mass only counts for so much against real skill."

Her hands stilled for a moment, her eyes focused in the distance. "I think that's what he wanted, my dad. He wanted me forged. When I got older, I realized he could have intervened, made the boys leave me alone. No, he had plans for me, and their torment helped prepare me. I really do believe he loved me, but he was a hard man."

Her eyes focused once more on his, her hands began moving again. "Why'd you leave the pararescue?"

Michael studied his cappuccino, took a sip, watched the liquid's slow turbulence as he lowered it back to the counter. "That's not something I really talk about."

"You think I normally talk about bullies and absent fathers?"

He looked her in the eyes and felt a bond of sorts with her. Together, they'd survived a night of madness. They'd both saved each other's lives. Something clicked, and words tumbled out.

"We were sent in to extract these wounded men. Army Rangers. The active fighting had moved on, about a half klick away. Not a big deal, really, but we were in the area, and they needed medical aid fast. We were brought in and started patching up guys to stabilize them for the helicopter ride out."

He took a sip, continued. "Something was off. There was one guy, this cocky SOB who was the only one not injured. No one was talking, but the wounds on one of the dead guys were all off from the scenario they described. So while we patched up the men and shipped them out, I asked questions. Subtle ones, or subtle enough for scared, injured men hiding a secret."

Ariana was assembling the gun with confident movements, her eyes intent on his.

"Anyway, I pieced it together. Of the three dead guys, one of them hadn't been killed by the enemy. It was friendly fire. And the little prick had been the one who shot him. Maybe an accident, or maybe he had motive, but he shot him, and they were covering for him. I confronted him, and I could see it in his eyes. I was right, and he didn't care if I knew. He wasn't going to admit to anything, but he thought he could get away with it."

Michael stopped, closed his eyes, lifted the cup to his nose. The aroma soothed him, helped hold the rage and hurt at bay. There was a final click of the magazine sliding into place, a round being chambered, and Ariana's work went quiet. He opened his eyes and glanced down. The gun was assembled, suppressor attached. She was watching him but made no comment.

"Well, something snapped. I lost my mind. I beat him senseless in the few seconds before my pararescue team could restrain me. I beat him so badly they ultimately had to induce a coma to save his life. And then I found out why he thought he was above it all, why he'd thought he could get away with it. He *was* above it all. His dad had potent political connections, and there was hell to pay."

He took a sip and drew it to a close. "So I'm not a PJ anymore, and let's just say it wasn't an honorable discharge."

"No benefits?" she asked. "No, what, college tuition?"

"Rules, Ariana, rules," Michael said. "My turn. What's this about 'the girls'?"

"You sure, Michael?" She looked him in the eye, sipped her cappuccino. "I give you those details, and you don't strike me as the kind of guy who can just drop me off in Montreal and call it quits."

The word 'yes' was on his lips, but he stopped. For some reason, Sherry's face came to mind. Waitress and aspiring photographer. Lived next door, not a universe apart like *Il Falco*. Normal. Michael needed normal, not more beautiful disasters. It struck him that finishing this job—getting her to Montreal right away—was the path to normal, not staying in Rome. His heart cried out to say 'yes', but where had his heart gotten him? Two divorces and a general discharge that had been a hair's breadth away from being a dishonorable discharge.

"No." Michael looked her in the eyes. "No, you're right. I don't need to go down that hole."

He pulled his phone out of his pocket. "I'll call it in. Get the tickets set up for early tomorrow, right? We grab the gun tonight then get out of here."

"You just have a phone number to call it in?" Ariana asked. "I was expecting something a little more secure."

"No worries then." Michael unlocked the phone, held it up to show her the screen, picking up his cappuccino in the other hand to take another sip. "Secure app. No phone numbers."

He hadn't seen her take the gun in hand. It flicked up, let out a cough. As the phone fragmented and flew out of his hand, he flipped his cappuccino toward her with his other hand, all the while processing what he'd seen. She was firing subsonic .22 LR rounds. Nothing else would be that quiet. And she wasn't trying to kill him, or he'd probably be bleeding out, not very much alive and throwing his cappuccino at her.

As she'd fired, Ariana had shoved off the island with her free hand, tipping over her stool and launching backwards. She reached back for the floor as his cappuccino sailed over her, somehow turned her fall into something akin to a back handspring. She came up on her feet and staggered backwards into the wall, one hand holding the gun trained on Michael, the other clutching her side.

Michael reached forward slowly, retrieved her cappuccino from where it still rested. He took a sip, set the cup down.

"Your move," he said.

"I really wish you'd asked about the girls." Ariana grimaced and leaned back against the wall. She looked spent. "I could see it. You wanted to know. You were so damn close. Doesn't matter now. There's been a change of plans."

CHAPTER FIFTEEN

*M*ichael sipped the cappuccino and waited. Ariana stood leaning against the kitchen wall, now splattered with his cappuccino, shards of his cup scattered on the floor at her feet. Her gun stayed trained on him, unwavering.

"Sorry about the phone," Ariana mouth was pulled into a frown. She let the gun drift down, away from him. "We need to talk. I'd prefer to not do it at gunpoint. I trust you. Can I have your word you won't harm me long enough for me to say what I need to say?"

"You're worried about me harming you?" He waved a hand toward her. "I'm not the one holding the gun."

Ariana's frown deepened. "Don't. We both know you'd crush me in anything short of a gunfight at range. Do I have your word?"

Michael sat still, mastering the adrenaline pumping through his veins. He lifted the cup, took another sip, and allowed himself a sliver of satisfaction that his hand was steady. There'd been a split second, as the gun flashed up and fired, that he'd thought he was going to die. It wasn't the first time he'd been sure death had come calling, but the feeling was utterly incongruous with the setting.

The strangest part was that his neck felt cool. The rage had stayed in its corner. He'd thrown the cappuccino at her, realized she wasn't trying to kill him, and mastered his response. It puzzled him, even gave him hope.

On the flip side, she'd royally screwed up the whole operation. He had no way of directly communicating with Joann to make travel arrangements, an outcome she must have intended. She wanted him here in Rome and had tried to entrap him with vague statements about some girls. In a way it had worked. Now that he didn't have any options, he was truly curious what was actually going on.

"You have my word," Michael said. "Let's talk it through."

Ariana stood for a moment longer, then dropped the gun's safety, flipped it over and caught it by the barrel. She extended it toward him as she stepped back to her place, still clutching her side. It was déjà vu, Ditmir flipping the gun around and handing it to him. Ditmir, in the final hours he'd spent with his wife. Had it really only been the previous evening?

Michael reached out, took the gun, and set it on the counter between them as she righted her stool and sat down.

"Thanks," she said. She let out a slow breath. "That move cost me. I felt so good this morning. I forget how bad the wounds were. Anyway, I need your help."

Michael nodded. "Understood. I'd thought getting you to Montreal was the help."

Ariana drew in a deep breath, opened her mouth to speak, then closed it, her lips pulled in a line. She reached out and took his hand in hers. He waited, his face impassive, his emotions careening madly about. By what power did women exert such control over him, he wondered. What possible madness could explain the insane desire to please her that surged forward at her touch? To do whatever she asked?

She looked at their hands, then raised her eyes to meet his gaze. "I haven't been entirely honest with you."

"So you're saying you've been mostly honest with me, or are you still being dishonest?"

She shrugged, her hand retreated. "I'll tell you what I need. You can decide."

"I'm listening," Michael said.

Ariana nodded, took a deep breath. "The *bajrak* is the group of men at the top of the *Hije*. Its executive committee. The six men who run things. As best I've been able to learn, those six, and only those six, have all the key account info to access the *Hije's* financial resources."

"Ditmir was saying he wanted you to, what? Kill these six men?"

Ariana nodded. "Kill them, and the *Hije* is crippled, maybe permanently, if they lose access to their money. You killed one of them yourself. Luftar. The man who murdered Kaltrina."

Michael's mind flashed to that moment. The gun coming up. Kaltrina's head snapping back as he struck the man in the face. His second shot taking the man in the throat.

"He's not the only one who's already dead," Ariana continued. "This whole thing started when I was scouting a shot I was planning to take. That I'm still hoping to take. Tonight, but I'll get to that. I was checking wind conditions between buildings. Walking the street level route the bullet would take. Getting a feel for it. I stumbled onto two of the *bajrak* who hadn't been in Rome in a while. They'd been out and about in Europe, leading two groups who snatch teen girls."

"The girls," Michael said. His stomach clenched up at the thought.

"Yes, the girls Ditmir mentioned," she said, "but we'll get to that. There I was on the street, and Tefik and Ermal walk out of a cafe next to me. It wasn't totally random. They were probably in the area for the same reason I was, more or less. Anyway, it was stupid, but I couldn't pass up the chance. I put them both down and ran. Got away, barely. You already know the next part. Got shot up in the process. You saved me. Here we are."

Michael processed what he'd heard. There were still gaping holes in what he knew, but several pieces fell into place all at once. "You've got intel on a meeting. Time and place. You're going to take a shot. Kill one of the *Hije* leaders. And it's got to be tied to what, the kidnapped girls? Human trafficking maybe? They're being sold? Is that why those two guys you killed were in town?"

Ariana looked at him for a moment before speaking, lips pursed. "Very good. We believe a transaction will be negotiated late tonight in Rome between Valdrin, the head of the *Hije bajrak*, and buyers from the Middle East. We think it's extremely likely the girls are being held somewhere in Rome in preparation for the sale."

"Tonight," he said. "That doesn't feel like a coincidence given you just destroyed my phone."

"It isn't."

"The 'we' being you and Ditmir?" Michael asked.

"And Kaltrina," Ariana said. "But yes. Me and Ditmir."

"I'd thought they didn't know you were the Falcon."

"They didn't, not really. But we were working together to gather intel on the *Hije*. They knew I have reasons to hate that organization, that I want to take it down. They do too for reasons of their own. I'd told them I'd find a way to get any evidence we gathered to the police anonymously. They'd probably figured out early on that I was passing info to the Falcon, and maybe more recently guessed that I *was* the Falcon."

Michael leaned forward, his elbows on the island counter,

took the last sip of cappuccino and set the cup down. "We haven't really covered that yet, have we? Your motive in all this?"

Ariana looked down at her hands, folded together on the counter. "The *Hije* murdered my father, his wife, my half-sister. I didn't even know I had a sister back then, and really, I'd prefer to not go into it right now." Her gaze pivoted up to him. "There's more to cover about the here and now."

"Right," Michael said. "The meeting tonight."

"That, and more." She sat up, drew in a deep breath. "Much more. I need to get my laptop. Show you some files." Her eyes drifted down to the gun between them, then back to his. "You good if I go get it?"

Michael nodded, tried to keep his face impassive. Ariana stood and headed for the stairs up to her room. He felt an unnatural calm that came from the absolute certainty that if she'd wanted to kill him, that first shot would have taken him in the eye. He retraced the steps of their conversation and couldn't detect anything that would have caused her to reassess yet.

In spite of that knowledge, his back faced the staircase as he stared at the cappuccino-adorned wall, and it made him nervous. Did he really know her well enough to predict her intentions? No, but she'd made it clear enough she needed him. He'd make it another day without being shot in the back.

He heard her coming down the stairs and took the last sip of his cappuccino. Her cappuccino, he corrected himself. Ariana sat back down in her seat, flipped the laptop open, entered the password. She pushed it over in front of him.

"Some PDFs," she said. "Some websites. You don't need to read it in detail but take a look."

The top window was a PDF that looked like it had been made from some European news site. Probably British given it was English. He glanced at the photo next to the text. A bright-eyed girl stared out at him, smiling. That rare combination of a ginger with a decent tan.

YOUNG WOMAN GOES TO ROCK CONCERT, NEVER SEEN AGAIN.

The provocative title summarized the contents of the article pretty well. Sixteen-year-old Amanda Patterson's family had been visiting Germany with another family. The four teens, Amanda's older brother and twin seventeen-year-old brothers from the other family, went to a concert at a club. Amanda went into a bathroom during the concert and hadn't been seen since. It had been three weeks.

Michael flipped to the next article, then the next. The pattern was pretty obvious. Starting two months ago and working forward to a couple weeks prior, girls aged fifteen to eighteen, away from home and on the mainland of Europe, had been snatched. They all had a certain sweetness to their look, an innocence.

He knew he was being manipulated, that she was pulling his strings. But was it really manipulation if she was simply clipping news articles? Making him aware of a hard reality?

Michael pushed the laptop back a few inches. "I've read them. Well, skimmed them."

"We think," Ariana said, "that these are the girls the *Hije* is selling. Here in Rome, at a meeting late tonight."

"What's the link? Why these girls? These could be random kidnappings. There had to be others in that timeframe."

Ariana shook her head. "Ditmir has an insider in the *Hije*. He doesn't get much info, but he was getting the locations of Tefik and Ermal as they traveled around. These girls were all taken in towns where one of them was staying at the time."

"Okay, not foolproof," Michael said, "but reasonable if you knew that's what they were up to."

"That's what they were up to."

Michael considered it, decided to take it at face value for the time being. "So these are the girls. You've more or less made it clear you need my help. And you want me very motivated. So let's get to it. What is it you're hoping I'll help you do? Is it taking this shot tonight?"

Ariana shook her head, then stopped, reconsidering. "Yes, but that's not the hard part. No, what I have in mind for this afternoon will be far harder."

"Which is?"

"I need your help taking down the *Hije* estate—more of a fortress, really—where all their financial books are kept. Up to twenty men onsite at any time. And their security setup defies planning as far as I can figure it. No way to do it but to go in and start killing."

Michael blinked. "Yeah, you need me motivated."

CHAPTER SIXTEEN

*a*riana pointed at the laptop. "You saw all the girls, right?"

"Yeah," Michael said, "I saw them."

"Here's the situation." She stood, stepped carefully around to the far side of the island where there wasn't glass covering the floor, and started pacing. "I take the shot tonight, I kill Valdrin, and it throws off the whole transaction. At that point, what happens to the girls?"

"You tell me."

"They're dumped into the local sex market or they're killed."

"Then don't kill Valdrin," Michael said. "Put everything into locating the girls."

"If he doesn't die, the transaction takes place." She stopped pacing for a moment and looked at him. "The girls disappear forever. The *Hije* gets richer."

"Is this about the girls or furthering your vendetta?" he asked. "I'm getting mixed signals."

Ariana stepped back over to her stool and sat down. "No,

you're not, but it's all tangled together. I'm trying to tell you that you don't have to buy into it to want to help me. And besides, my vendetta has found meaning beyond itself."

"By attacking some fortress. Guarded by twenty men. With no plan."

She grimaced and shrugged. "I exaggerated. Not all the men are guards per se, and I have a plan, but it's more of an approach, a method. And there's no hope unless I have a second. Do you remember when we left Ditmir's kitchen?"

The question felt sideways to Michael, but he nodded.

"This is the debt Ditmir was talking about. He wants you to help me save these girls."

Michael's mind whirled. Faces of young women snatched from their families spun through his thoughts. He hated being used, but it felt childish to ignore a very real need to make a point with Ariana. And if what she was saying was true, she was offering him the chance to be part of a real mission. A clean mission. One already loaded up with a debt to Ditmir.

"Let's back up," he said. "Before we talk tactics, what's the goal of shooting up this place? You mentioned the finances."

"That's right. There's three goals." Ariana held up a hand with one finger extended. "First, kill Kushtrim. Member of the *hajrak*, one of three still alive." She lifted a second finger. "Second, get the financial records which may have a clue as to where the girls are being held. We can get Ditmir to help us scrub them for info." A third finger. "We keep copies, but we pass the originals to the police with an anonymous tip regarding the girls. It's evidence against the *Hije* and gets more eyes looking for clues."

It made sense, so long as he could trust her. Which he couldn't, though she did seem to operate with some sort of twisted moral code.

"Okay, let's go with that for now," Michael said. "Give me a high-level view of your plan, or method as you called it."

The corners of her mouth twitched up toward a smile. "You're considering it?"

He shrugged. "I want to hear you out."

Ariana's smile blossomed. Radiant, magnetic. "I could kiss you."

"Might even help convince me." Michael thought he was joking, but he wasn't sure.

She raised an eyebrow. "Michael, I can be very convincing. This matters to me. It's everything, you understand?"

Michael grimaced and sat back on his stool. "Don't say crap like that. Just, don't."

"Fair enough." Her smile was gone. "I was just playing along with what you said."

Had that been all it was? Michael doubted it. "You're right. Sorry."

Ariana waved a hand, dismissing his words. "Let me give you the overview. It's a large estate on a small hill. I've scouted it endlessly the past four years and developed a couple informants among the cleaning staff, all done very anonymously. There are always at least eight men there, and up to twenty. More if there's something going on at the estate, which is often. A few of them are always patrolling. They walk the building in pairs. And they do it well. Never the same route or timing, and every single square inch that can be seen from the outside gets patrolled at least every thirty minutes if it's not occupied. But it's random, like the routes they walk. Sometimes it's five minutes between pairs, other times it's thirty minutes."

"Huh." Michael squinted in thought. "Maybe a computer program setting up the patrol routes to randomize things but still ensure everything is covered on schedule?"

She shrugged. "Probably. So there might be three pairs

patrolling, maybe more, with no set shifts. And usually a lot more people onsite. Guys arrive and stay for four hours, other times twenty-four hours. Sometimes much longer. "

"And the target? Kushtrim?"

"Almost never leaves, almost never seen from any exterior view. The estate surrounds a large courtyard. He seems to live there like a toad in a damp hole. They bring in girls sometimes. There's a party at least once a week. But the patrols never stop."

Michael processed what she'd said, his eyes coming to rest on her gun. It all clicked. "You want to handle this like, uh, like a video game, with Kushtrim the boss level at the end."

"Go on," she said.

Michael nodded toward the gun between them. "The gun. Sure, you had it out as a contingency to take out my phone, but you were also prepping it for this afternoon, right? Suppressed subsonic .22LR rounds. A round that's shockingly quiet when suppressed, yet still capable of being lethal, at least with your aim. You want to move through the estate taking out pairs of men without alerting all the others. I mean, with that security setup, they'll have to know, but it will be surveillance, not actual ears and eyes until we're on top of them. And I agree, that would be suicide by yourself, even for you."

Ariana's smile was back. "Again with the analysis. Very nice." She leaned toward him, elbows on the counter. "I've seen you in action. Drop all the humility, okay? You were a monster in urban combat, weren't you?"

This time Michael's eyes dropped to his hands. "My fire team was very successful at completing our objectives."

"Because?"

He looked up at her, eyebrows pulled together. "Because what?"

Ariana slapped the counter. "Because you were a monster!

166

Listen, I've got the gear. Whatever you're thinking you might need, I've got it. We go in together, move through the house rapidly, hit them hard one pair at a time before they have a chance to group up and organize. We can do this. Our odds are fantastic against any two of them. We just need it to play out fast several times in a row, before they can organize."

Michael got up, paced into the living area, hands held behind his back. If he could truly help those girls see their families again, he'd do it. He had to. But would it help them, or would he simply be helping Ariana kill someone she hated? And the scope of the mission creep was unreal.

Ariana followed him into the room and sat down on a couch, watching him. He glanced back at the kitchen, confirmed the gun was still on the island. How far could he trust her? Was trust even the right word when he had to verify she wasn't about to shoot him? He turned and faced her.

"I came here to save someone's life. Your life. And get you to Montreal. I've already been forced to kill two men, and helped you kill five others. I didn't sign up for any of this."

"I know," she said.

"You said there'd been a change of plans," Michael said, "but there hasn't, has there? Not really. You were never planning to go to Montreal."

Ariana held his gaze for a long moment. "I was never planning to go to Montreal, no."

"No," he repeated. "I was brought in to patch you up. Keep you going."

Ariana stood up, faced him. "But I also wasn't planning for Kaltrina to die. Or to take a shot at Kushtrim, or involve you in any of it. I'm improvising. I told Ditmir I'd take out the *bajrak*, and I'll die trying if I have to. I assumed that's what it would take when I made the promise. You understand? I figured I'd die today making a run at him. But last night I realized that if we went in together, we'd have a solid chance at pulling it off. Ditmir figured all this out sitting there in his kitchen, but I'm starting to catch up."

She reached out, took his hand. "Michael, I know you're better than me. Or at least that's how your morals would sort it out. But together, we have the capability to stop truly evil men, maybe even save those girls. I've seen you in action. You have a gift. Maybe it's a gift you'd prefer not to have, but it's a gift all the same, and it's needed now. Sometimes, it takes real killing to preserve life."

Jeffrey's words bubbled up, unbidden, and Michael rocked backwards as though struck, releasing her hand. *Sometimes, the way you help someone is by shooting someone else.*

"What?" Ariana stared at him, lips pursed, eyebrows pulled together. "What is it?"

Michael shook his head. "That's twice now you've practically quoted a buddy of mine."

"Good," she said. "Maybe that will help you see I'm talking sense. And listen, I don't know what portion of the payment you're getting, but I'll triple it."

His mouth opened, but she held up a hand to silence him. "I know you're not going to do this for the money. Not the killing. I get it. You probably have no interest in being a mercenary. Great. Do it because it's the right thing to do. I'm still going to pay you."

She was right. He didn't want to do it for the money. On the flip side, another hundred grand was insane. He'd have the chance to figure things out, maybe go back to school. It was game-changing money, and in spite of himself he felt it exert a pull on his will.

"Give me a sec," Michael said. "Need to think it through."

"Understood. I'm going to clean up the cappuccino decorating my wall, then take a short nap. You've got 45 minutes, okay? Time is tight."

Michael nodded and headed back down the hall toward the room in which he'd slept. He turned into the office he'd previously passed. The curtains on the window across the room were thin, filling the room with a diffused light. A large wooden desk and leather chair stood in front of the window, with three leather wingback chairs arrayed facing it.

He stepped around the desk and sat down. The chair was the perfect balance of firm yet accommodating and tilted back with just the right amount of resistance. Michael leaned back further and put his feet up on the desk, crossed at the ankles. Eyes closed, he focused for a moment on his breathing, letting the world fade to the background.

He couldn't do it. Ariana had masterfully churned up his emotions into a tangled mess of kidnapped girls and piles of money, with just a hint of wondering if there might be something between them. Michael grimaced, opened his eyes, stared at the ceiling. There were moments when self-loathing threatened to overwhelm him—recognizing how easily beautiful women manipulated him was one of them. Even his poetry, bad as it was, seemed to have abandoned him. No verse jumped to mind to help him process what he felt.

The stark reality was simple. Ariana was right. He was the right man for the job. He wasn't invulnerable—what she proposed would probably get them both killed—but he had an aptitude for managing chaos and violence. But was the job itself good and right? And was he willing to pay the price? Not the price of death, but rather living with the memories of what he'd done if they succeeded?

Michael sat thinking for several minutes before he finally resorted to something he knew should be a bit more central to his life. He prayed.

Forty-five minutes later, Michael stepped back into the kitchen and glanced around. Ariana wasn't there. Neither were the traces of the cappuccino he'd tossed at her. He looked toward the front of the house and spotted her on the floor in a painful-looking yoga pose, like she was trying to impersonate a sea lion.

"Hey," he said, walking over to stand beside the couch. "I'm in."

Ariana lowered herself to the floor, rolled over onto her back, and sat up. She stuck a hand out and he pulled her to her feet. She looked him in the eyes for a long moment and nodded, her hand still in his.

"Thank you." She reached up, cupped his cheek, her eyes intense. The moment stretched, her hands dropped to her sides, and she turned toward the kitchen. "Let's gear up."

Ariana led him back to the room between the kitchen and garage, to the narrow door beside the coat and shoe racks. She pulled it open and flipped a light on as she descended a steep flight of stairs.

"No windows in the wine cellar," she said as he followed her down.

She flipped on another switch at the bottom, and Michael stepped down into a low-ceilinged, cool room filled with wine bottles. Shelves lined the walls, and two free-standing shelves dominated the middle of the room. It wasn't a large space, but Michael guessed there had to be hundreds of wine bottles on display, maybe as many as a couple thousand. The sections of walls not covered in shelving were paneled in a dark wood that matched the shelves.

Ariana nudged him with an elbow and nodded toward the far side of the room. He followed her to a blank section of wall between two shelves where she squatted and manipulated something in the paneling. A half door, maybe three feet tall, swung away from her into a dark space.

"You're all about the secret doors," Michael said.

Ariana shrugged. "I wouldn't want this to be easy to find."

She scooted through the opening and stood, a bright, clinical light suddenly flooding the space, spilling out into the cellar. Michael hunched down and ducked through after her.

The room matched the width of the wall it shared with the wine cellar but was barely five feet across. Michael took it in with a glance. Bleached wood floors, white walls, stainless shelves lined with black felt. And a massive selection of weapons and other armament.

"Oh," Michael said, slowly pivoting, cataloging what he was seeing.

"Now you know all my secrets," Ariana said.

Michael glanced at her. "I doubt that."

She shrugged. "Okay, not all, but some of the big ones."

He stepped forward and lifted a gun off a shelf about chest high. He ran a hand along along the hand guard and suppressor. Glanced at the trigger group and confirmed it was an S-1-F. A fantastic, short-barreled military rifle for urban combat.

"The very one I had in mind for you," Ariana said, stepping up beside him.

"Suppressed M4A1 CQBR. This'll get it done if we have to light it up. You've got magazines and pouches?"

"It's all here. Magazines, armor, knives. I'll set you up with a SIG P226 as backup. Custom armor-piercing 9mm rounds. The works."

Michael set the gun back on the shelf and turned toward Ariana. "Some of this stuff isn't just expensive, it's practically impossible. How'd you..."

He trailed off. Did he really want to know? Would she

really want to answer? She looked at him, waiting, the corner of her mouth twitching up.

"With this gear," he said, "I've got to think our odds of survival today are at least five times higher than I'd assumed. We've got to be up to five percent, right?"

"You're not factoring in the med kit I've put together," she said. "If we can both keep each other from bleeding out, keep our trigger fingers working, I figure we're at something much closer to thirty percent."

Michael tried to laugh, but it died in his throat. He couldn't tell if she'd been joking.

CHAPTER SEVENTEEN

"*P*oint of no return," Michael said. He shifted in the driver's seat to look her full in the face. "Committed?"

"More than you can know," Ariana said.

She pulled on a black ski mask made from an ultra-lightweight, stretchy material. Michael carried its twin in a pocket. Ariana gave him a long look, reached for her door handle, hesitated. She turned back toward him, yanked the mask above her nose, and kissed him deeply. By the time he'd recovered from the shock, she'd pulled away.

"I get impulsive in the moment," Ariana said. "You understand, right?"

Michael was pretty sure the phrase 'wicked grin' had been coined for the exact smile she flashed at him before pulling her mask down. The door shut behind her and she disappeared into the brush and low trees surrounding the small stream bed that wound along beside the road.

His heart raced, his mind buzzed, the car idled. Michael regained control as he counted a slow one hundred, then dropped the car—her sedan was another Maserati—into gear and rolled forward. Go time. Deep breath, quick glance at his gear behind the passenger seat, and he accelerated forward as he unbuckled the seatbelt. A tight bend to the right and the gated entry came into view.

Just as she'd described, the stream was channeled through a large culvert under the short drive up to the gate, a small guard booth off to the left. Michael turned in and stopped a bit short, trying to block the view of the stream bed on the far side of the drive from the booth. A guard approached him from a door on the side of the booth. Another man stepped out behind the first but didn't approach the car.

"Here we go," Michael said, and rolled down his window.

The man was dressed similarly to all the *Hije* men Michael had seen thus far. Dark suit. Expensive looking. A slight bulge in his coat under his left arm. He came forward, his hands extended out and down, as clear a *stay put* as one could communicate without words.

"Hello!" Michael said. "Do you speak English?"

He stuck a hand out the window and waved. The sudden move had the desired effect of bringing both pairs of eyes into sharp focus on him.

"English?" he repeated as the closer man approached the car. "I seem to be lost. Do you know which way to go to get to the city? To Rome? Are you understanding me?"

The man stopped a few feet away, shook his head, and pointed back toward the road. "You go now. Go back."

Michael threw his hands up in exaggerated frustration inside the car. "Yes. I want to go. I just need to know where to go. How do I get to Rome?"

The man took a step closer, shook his head, jabbed a finger toward the road. "You go away now."

"Look," Michael said, "my phone battery died. I just need

some directions to get me on the way to Rome. I've got a map here. Can you help."

He turned away from the man, shuffled through some blank papers on the middle arm rest. Michael heard the man step forward, sensed his closeness as he leaned toward the car.

Michael turned back and jabbed a finger at a blank sheet of paper. "Look here. See?"

The man's eyebrows came together in bewilderment as he leaned in next to the open window, trying to make sense of the blank sheet of paper. Michael snaked a hand out, grabbed his shirt, and yanked him forward. The man's brow met the roofline of the car just above the open window and rebounded. Michael bounced his head off the car once more for good measure, then let him topple to the ground.

The second man by the booth hit the ground face first at almost the same moment. Ariana stood behind him, gun in hand. Michael swung the door open and walked around to the passenger side. She looked remarkably clean given she'd just traversed the culvert.

Ariana pulled a small can out of a pocket, reached up, and shot a tight stream of black paint at the security camera mounted to the eave of the booth, then disappeared inside it while he got in and started gearing up. The gate jerked into motion, opening away from the car, and Ariana stepped back out and walked over to the car.

Her gun made its coughing sound, Michael winced, and she dropped into the driver's seat.

"Did you have to?" he said. "He was out cold."

"I did," Ariana said. "And I will for every single one of them, you understand?"

Michael shook his head, but kept belting on his body armor, ammo pouches, and weapons. It was challenging work in the confines of the car.

"I didn't hear the first shot," he said.

Ariana pulled the car forward through the gate and up a winding drive lined by trees on both sides.

"I timed it with your guy's head hitting the car." She shrugged. "Guess the noise didn't really matter, but I like to stay sharp."

With his armor on, ammo in place, sidearm holstered, knife sheathed, and M4 strapped on, Michael retrieved the mask from its pocket and pulled it on.

"And the code worked?" He grinned, though the mask hid it. "I mean, I guess I know it did since the gate opened."

"I've been paying those maids every week for two years for the codes just in case I had a shot at it. Sloppy, really. They shouldn't have given non-*Hije* any part of their security."

The road twisted to the left, and the house came into view through the twin row of trees. It looked more like a fortress. Straight, vertical walls with narrow windows, three stories tall.

"It's like this all the way around?" Michael asked.

"Exactly like this," Ariana said. "Three stories, a giant square around a large central courtyard that shows up pretty clearly on satellite map views. Here we go."

She pulled the car around a curve that swept along the front of the house and off to the left side where there was a small parking lot. Seven cars were already parked there. Ariana didn't bother with a space but parked right up next to a large door into the house. He handed her the small backpack and she slipped it on over her armor.

"We move fast and quiet. Maybe they saw all that, or maybe they're just wondering why the gate camera is down. Let's hope they have questions, not answers, and try to keep the element of surprise. Avoid firing that thing"—she nodded toward his M4—"but if you do, unleash hell, you understand?"

Michael had made his peace. He closed his eyes, saw the

faces of Amanda and the other girls. He'd do what was required, pay whatever was required. A quick nod, and they surged out of the car.

Ariana had a copy of the maid's keys, and the door opened into a short entryway. Michael's heart tried to race, but he controlled his breathing, kept his pulse in check. The world opened up to him, a heat searing the back of his neck. The entryway ended at a hallway cutting off to the left and right. He stole quick glances, saw two men walking away from them off to the left. Michael moved toward them, cutting to the far side of the hall to leave room for Ariana, his gun at the ready.

He heard Ariana's gun cough, the man to the left stumbled forward, a wound opening on his neck at the base of his skull. Her accuracy still shocked him, in spite of what he'd already seen. It shouldn't be possible.

The other man whipped around, a gun in hand, stumbled sideways and collapsed. Blood leaked out of his ear. She'd shot him in the ear! Michael shook his head in disbelief.

Guess that's one way to make sure the skull doesn't deflect the subsonic rounds.

He was relieved to see the hall didn't go the full length of the side of the house. It turned to the right just past the bodies, also to the right about twenty feet back past the entry they'd used. Long halls would have played hell on any element of surprise they still had.

They hurried forward to the first door just short of the two bodies. He glanced at her, she nodded, he swung it open. Clear. Past the bodies. Next door. And the next. Around the turn, onward. They skipped the stairwell behind the fourth door. Another bend.

The fifth door was a bedroom. A man and a woman embracing, mostly undressed, just inside the room. Ariana took the shot, the man released the woman, grabbing the side of his neck as blood poured out of a ruptured artery. Michael leapt forward, struck the woman just behind the ear toward the neck. Her eyes rolled up, the scream dying on her lips, unvoiced. He caught her and lowered her to the ground.

Michael looked up just in time to snatch the small, black case Ariana had tossed toward him. She'd already turned toward the door after retrieving it from her backpack. She stood watch as Michael opened it, made a guess at the woman's weight, filled a syringe, and injected her.

"Sleep tight," he said.

He crossed to Ariana, returned the case to her slim backpack alongside the med kit, then they were moving. They approached another turn, heard the noise just before the men rounded the corner a few feet away. Michael's neck burned, his mind cleared. No thought, only instinct. He conjured his knife, leapt forward, took the man on the left in the neck as he strode into view. The knife stuck in a bone, he released it, lashed a foot out and caught the middle guy in the stomach, doubling him over. The middle guy. There were three men, not two.

Ariana fired, the third man stumbled backwards clutching his forehead, but he stayed on his feet. The middle guy, doubled over, threw himself at Michael's legs. He was a big guy, but Michael was already moving. He leapt, twisted, got a hand on the hilt of his knife, wrenching it from the first guy's neck as he tumbled toward the ground. The knifed man clutched his neck and collapsed backwards. Michael landed hard and rolled toward the man Ariana had shot. He whipped his arm around with the rotation and released the knife.

It should have been a terrible throw, but somehow the blade caught the man Ariana had shot under the chin, driving the blade upwards into his skull. Before his body hit the floor, Ariana had fired twice more, and the other two men were dead.

Michael rolled to his feet, retrieved the knife, and cleaned the blade on the man's designer suit coat before sheathing it. Ariana moved over to him, her eyes everywhere, and put a hand on his shoulder as he stayed in a crouch, taming the cadence of his breathing.

"Michael, you good?"

Michael breathed, tried to clear his mind, gain control of his thoughts. He reached up, gave her hand a squeeze, then stood. "Let's keep moving. Eight down."

She nodded, stepped to the next door, waited for him to open it. Empty.

"Amazing throw," she said, so low he almost missed the words as they continued down the hall.

He nodded. "The ear?" he said, his voice pitched to match hers. "Did you really mean to do that?"

She shrugged. "Maybe? I'm aiming for softer parts with these rounds, but it all happened pretty fast."

The hall branched and opened up into interconnected rooms. A gym with a narrow indoor lap pool, numerous bathrooms, a couple more staircases leading up, and finally a mammoth kitchen. Michael stood looking back down the hall while Ariana crouched and leaned carefully forward to scan the kitchen.

"One man, one woman." Her voice was barely audible. "Both cooks, I'd guess. Wait. One more woman coming out of a pantry."

Michael stood at ease, the M4 a comfortable weight in his hands, his eyes focused at the middle distance, his peripheral vision alert to any movement. He hoped she kept up her end of the bargain, that only the men of the *Hije* would die. Surely she wouldn't consider the kitchen staff targets. It would be hard to incapacitate all three without doing permanent harm or allowing them to raise an alert, but they had to try.

Men burst into view from the stairway on the left side of

the hall, twenty feet away, all pretense of secrecy demolished. The alert had gone out, they knew they were being attacked. The men—four of them—launched into the hall, laying down fire. Michael's mind emptied, his senses opened. He dropped to a crouch and squeezed off four shots before a bullet punched him in his armored left shoulder. A baseball bat might have been gentler. It spun him, opened him up directly toward the men, and another shot caught him in the middle of the chest. Had a ribbed cracked? The question evaporated as another bullet traced a line of fire across his left thigh.

His wounded leg tried to buckle as he was thrown backwards, off balance from the first two hits. Michael scanned the hall as he slammed into Ariana, back to back, and pushed hard off his right leg to push them both past the corner into the kitchen.

Michael rolled off her onto his stomach, getting the M4 in position, flipping it to full auto. His chest was convulsing, his shoulder ached fiercely. When he spoke, his words were breathy and forced. "Cover the hall! Two down, two up."

He sensed her movement beside him, but his focus was wholly forward, looking for an angle. There, between numerous stainless-steel table legs and cabinets, he could make out the lower third of a large doorway on the far side of the kitchen. His leg burned, his ribs were on fire, but he held steady. He knew what was coming.

Men poured in through the doorway. Four? Six? It was hard to tell from his obscured view of their legs. Michael unleashed the remaining twenty-six rounds in his magazine, an eruption of sound and fury that lasted under three seconds. He rolled to his back, released the empty magazine, and retrieved another one from an ammo pouch. In his peripheral vision he saw Ariana as he reloaded his gun, saw her dive forward and slide out into the hall, firing her 9mm. Saw blood spray from her left arm as she was hit.

Michael flipped the gun to semi-automatic, stayed low, and scrambled into the hall. Images flashed before him. Ariana barrel rolling to the far side of the hall, blood marking her passage. Three bodies lying in the hall. A man up and diving back toward the staircase out of sight. Michael fired before he registered the details. His shot clipped the retreating man in the shoulder, spun him around before he made it around the corner. Ariana's shot took him in the throat. He collapsed.

A bullet hit Michael between the shoulders and punched him forward into a shoulder roll. Pain flared down his spine from the blow, but the armor did its job. He came out of his roll well down the hall, safe for the moment from the gunmen in the kitchen. Ariana rolled back toward him, a hiss escaping as her body compressed her injured arm.

Michael stood and gave Ariana a hand up, their backs to the wall, out of the line of fire from the men in the kitchen. "Stairs. Up. Go!"

Ariana nodded and stepped past him, her 9mm at the ready. She slipped around the corner. No gunfire. The stairs were clear. Michael stepped to the kitchen corner and stole a quick look. The noise of gunfire echoed into the hall as he pulled his head back, and plaster sprayed off the corner where the shots they'd taken at him struck. He stood with his back to the wall and processed what he'd seen. Three men, spread out, coming across the kitchen. Motion near the far door, down low. Maybe an injured man. A couple of the cooks in view, on the floor, covering their heads.

Michael flipped the selector to F, pictured where the men were. He picked the one furthest from the cooks, stuck the gun around the corner, and sprayed that area of the kitchen. The moment his magazine emptied he was moving toward the stairs. He dropped the spent magazine, reloaded, and flipped the selector to semi-automatic. When he stepped over the last body, the one with the ruined throat closest to the stairs, his injured leg tried to give out. He careened into the wall, caught his balance, and pushed forward around the corner.

Ariana was at the top of the stairs, which ended in a hallway that led off to the left. Ariana glanced around the corner down low, then stood and stepped out of sight. Michael struggled up the steps and followed her into the hall.

Ariana waited, kneeling near the wall, her gun pointed down the short hall, her free hand digging through her backpack. She pulled out the hemostatic gauze packets and a couple wraps. Michael stopped next to her to keep watch as she set her gun down and went to work on his leg. She was not gentle, but very fast.

Once the wound was packed and wrapped, he took a last glance around the corner down the stairs, then did the same for her left arm. The bullet had hit halfway between the elbow and shoulder and scored her outer arm. She gasped as he jammed the gauze in the wound, but her gun stayed steady in her other hand, pointed down the hall.

"So far so good."

Her words sounded distant. He nodded. "Stay up tempo. Go! Find Kushtrim."

The next two minutes were a blur. Michael figured out his injured leg's limits, and they cleared rooms. He knew at any moment the men from the kitchen would catch them from behind. He stole frequent glances back over his shoulder. They rounded a corner into another short, empty hall. Ariana took the lead as Michael waited with his gun trained down the hall they'd just traversed.

A pause, then all hell broke loose.

CHAPTER EIGHTEEN

he door beside Ariana burst open and a man surged through, ramming her into the far wall. Simultaneously two men rounded the far corner back toward the stairs. Michael whipped around, stepping forward to get out of sight of the men behind him, fired three rounds at the man who'd hit Ariana. The man's arms spread wide and he fell. Ariana somehow landed on her feet, but her gun clattered to the floor. She dove toward Michael. Gunfire hit the wall where she'd been, and a man came through the doorway, then another.

They were close, and Michael lashed his right foot up and out, caught the lead man in the chest, knocked him back into the trailing man. His injured left leg gave out, and he crumpled to the floor next to Ariana where she'd landed. He twisted around as he fell and started firing into the open doorway where the men struggled to regain their balance. He felt a tug at his waist, ignored it, kept firing. Eight rounds. Twelve. Both men jerked around, stumbled backwards, and collapsed.

He pivoted on the ground toward the hall corner, realized

he was too late. The two men from the kitchen rounded the corner, guns extended. And died as Ariana shot them each in the face with Michael's handgun that she'd pulled from his holster. Two shots. Two men.

"Damn, we're good," Ariana said as she rose, her gun still pointed over the men from the stairs.

The words no longer sounded distant. They were achingly close. Michael clambered to his feet.

"Not sure good's the right word." He glanced at the bodies sprawled around them. A pain beyond his damaged ribs and torn leg flared in his chest, cutting through the heat of his rage.

"You think too much," Ariana said.

She backed up, her gun still covering behind them, until they were level. She reached up, put a hand on his face. He looked her in the eyes and was surprised to see something akin to compassion.

"These men needed to die. They died. Isn't that enough?"

Michael nodded, pulled away from her hand.

the dead don't speak
they don't have the words
yet what they say
from the silence of the grave
haunts me

If the price was more ghosts, he'd pay it. He stared down the hall and called to mind each face, each girl needing rescue. It was enough. It had to be enough. Ariana bent to retrieve her handgun from the floor and winced.

"Hurt?" Michael asked.

Ariana stood and returned Michael's gun to his holster. "My hip hit the wall pretty hard. Not working well, but I don't think it's really injured."

"Can you manage?"

She nodded, turned, and continued down the hall, favoring her right leg. Michael followed with his own limp, his thigh burning. They checked three rooms and came to a stairwell with stairs going up to the third floor and back down to the first floor. Ariana glanced at him, nodded toward the stairs up.

"Might as well," Michael said. "If they've already exited the building, we can't catch them."

Ariana shook her head. "They haven't left. They've got to assume there's more than two of us. They're sitting tight up there. I'm sure of it."

Michael shrugged. "Either way, up."

They worked their way up the steps. Michael took two at a time with his right leg, trusted his left leg only to hold his weight. Ariana grimaced and walked up a step at a time, her gun dead steady, aimed at the opening on the third floor.

"How many left?" Michael took two steps, paused, repeated. "Best guess."

"One?" Ariana said. "Four at the most."

Michael nodded and swapped out a fresh magazine as they neared the top of the stairs. His ribs felt like he was being punched with each breath, his thigh a burning ache. The pain was beyond distracting. Ariana didn't look much better. The bandage on her upper arm was soaked with blood and the stairs initially proved challenging for her hip, though her gait improved as she went.

They reached the top of the stairs. From his place two steps below Ariana, Michael could see the stairs emptied into a hall that stretched off to both the left and the right.

"I'll check left." His voice was low, quiet compared to the hiss of his breathing. "You check right."

She nodded and waited for Michael to shuffle across to the other side of the stairs and ascend the last two steps. They looked at each other, Michael nodded, and he turned and stole a brief glance out into the hall. It was empty and turned a right corner a short distance away. He pulled back and leaned with his back to the wall, facing Ariana.

"Short hall, then turns a corner to the right," he said. "You?"

Ariana smiled. "This is it. There's a door on the far side of the hall about twenty feet down the hall. That side overlooks the courtyard. Door was open, a man was keeping watch, head sticking out of the room."

"He see you?"

Ariana nodded.

Michael brought his gun up, aimed toward the hall just to the side of Ariana. "We good with that?"

"Not sure," Ariana said. "He didn't react. Just looked at me."

Michael's eyebrows pulled together. "What the hell does that mean?"

Arian shrugged. "No idea. You ready?"

"No." Michael stretched his neck, tried to fight off the rage, stay rational. "They've got something planned. Let's go."

The mask hid her face, but Michael sensed a smirk.

"A man of action," Ariana said. "I knew I liked you."

She didn't wait, but whipped around and spun out into the hall, her gun aimed down the hall. Michael was a step behind her. He saw the doorway, double doors, both opened inward and out of sight into the room just ahead. The only surprise was the lack of surprises. No one waiting. No gunfire.

They crossed the hall and stood a few feet away from the open doorway, pressed against the wall. Michael pressed his mouth to the outline of Ariana's ear in the thin mask.

"I'm going to cross the opening. See what I see."

Ariana looked at him for a long moment and nodded. He tensed, prepared to leap across the opening in a shoulder role, biasing toward his good leg.

"*Il Falco!*". The voice was reedy, thin, old.

The words that followed were in another language, maybe Albanian. Michael ignored them and leapt. He rolled off his shoulder and back to his feet on the far side of the doorway. The words streaming from the room had cut off the moment he'd flashed into sight. He tried to breath, tried to calm the raging fire in his ribs.

Michael turned and signaled to Ariana. A man in each of the far corners of the room, armed. A man in the middle of the room. He couldn't figure out how to sign the most important part.

To hell with it.

"Old man at a desk." His voice was breathy. He still couldn't seem to drive enough oxygen through his lungs with the pain in his ribs. "Dead man's switch. Really obvious bomb vest. Wants us to see it."

Ariana's shoulders slumped. She reached her good arm up, still clutching the gun, and pulled her mask off. Her mouth was pulled in a thin line.

"I'm sorry, Michael."

"Sorry?" Michael said. "About what? That's Kushtrim in there, right?"

"It is English we speak?" The voice of the old man was defiant, forceful. "I will, ah, speak it also then."

"Why are you sorry?" Michael said, ignoring Kushtrim.

"He must die," Ariana said. "No matter the cost."

"But the bomb. He dies, we die."

It all clicked, and Michael moved. Ariana calmly stepped into the doorway and fired a single shot as Michael leapt toward her. He heard echoes of at least two shots as he slammed into her, felt the punch to the back of his bad leg as they careened out of the doorway. Heard the blinding roar of the bomb, then lost track of reality.

CHAPTER NINETEEN

*T*he world spun. Michael coughed, gasped for air. He opened his eyes to a murky haze. He tried to push up off the floor, but noticed the floor seemed soft. No sound, just severe pain in his left ear.

Michael pushed up again, and the floor fought back. He looked down and discovered he was draped across Ariana. He rolled to the side off of her, still trying to catch his breath. Ariana sat up beside him.

"You okay?"

Ariana's voice sounded like they were talking via a string between two paper cups. Distant, hollow. He saw her clearly for a moment, then his eyes drifted towards one another and he couldn't seem to focus on either of the two Ariana's struggling to her feet.

"Up, Michael. We need to move."

He tried to sit up, but up seemed ambiguous. Hands gripped him under his right arm and tugged him. He closed his eyes and trusted Ariana was pulling him in the right direction. He got his feet under himself and pushed toward her.

Pain blossomed in his legs and back. He gasped and almost collapsed, but Ariana's grip stayed firm, guiding him upward. Michael grunted and stood. He opened his eyes, found the world was obeying the basic rules of physics again.

"Not sure I can walk." His voice was stretched thin from the pain.

Ariana nodded, stepped in close, and pulled his arm over her shoulders. "Lean in."

Michael leaned, and they shambled back down the hall to the stairs. He stole a glance back at the ruined doorway and debris-strewn hall.

Shouldn't be alive.

Ariana read his mind. "He wasn't bluffing, but it wasn't a large bomb. Just enough to clear that room and all the financial records he kept."

They reached the stairs, and Michael clung to the railing with his free hand as Ariana helped him down one step at a time.

"So we failed?" The question was bitter in Michael's mouth.

He felt more than saw her shrug. "Kushtrim's dead. We don't have the records, but their finances are total chaos now. That's something."

They reached the second floor, turned, and continued down to the first floor.

"But the girls," Michael said. "How do we find them?"

"First we get out of here. Then we patch you up. I'll contact Ditmir, let him work on it. We get Valdrin tonight. With Kustrim dead, I bet it shakes them up, provokes a misstep. We'll find them, okay?"

He had no standing to argue, an odd collision of literal and metaphorical challenges. "How'd you make it out so well?"

"You hit me full on," she said. "Threw me clear just as the bomb detonated, shielded me with your body."

Michael nodded. "Guess I'm a hero."

"Pretty much."

They reached the first floor, opened a door into an empty hall, and slowly made their way toward the exit.

"How are you doing?" Ariana asked. "Pain manageable?"

"Not really," Michael said. "Let's just get to the car. You making it?"

He felt her shrug. "Very weak. Feel like I'm going to pass out."

They continued on. The pain intruded at every step, comprehensive and terrible. His back felt as though he'd been attacked with razor blades. Though his right ear was starting to recover, his left ear ached and felt muted, dead. Pain ravaged the back of his left leg and his ribs burned.

He struggled step by step, leaning heavily on Ariana. She limped but bore up under his weight. No one intruded on their slow retreat. They turned a corner, covered the short hallway, and pushed through the door into bright sunlight. A few steps later, and he leaned against the car as Ariana opened the passenger door for him and moved the seat back as far as it would go. Sirens drifted into the limits of his diminished hearing.

Michael gasped as he dropped into the seat. "Think there's shrapnel stuck in my left ass, uh, glute."

Ariana closed the door and swung open the driver door a moment later. She dropped her small backpack in his lap as she got in. "You're going to have to manage." She closed the door and started the car, slipping on her seatbelt. "Sirens are closing in. We need to be gone."

Michael pulled his seatbelt on and leaned back, trying to lift some of his weight off his butt. His legs resisted the effort, and each gasp set his ribs on fire. Ariana dropped the car into gear, accelerated through a tight U-turn, and headed for the entrance to the estate at speed. In spite of the trauma they'd endured, she handled the car like an extension of her body.

Ariana glanced over at him. "Get a bandage and some pressure on that left hamstring. You're bleeding."

Michael unzipped her backpack and retrieved a hemostatic gauze packet and wrap. He couldn't properly pack the wound, but the gauze and tight wrap were better than nothing. As he worked, Ariana rocketed through the still open front gate, swung left, and raced away from the estate.

The ride became a hazy blur of pain and sharp turns. For a time, the sirens got louder, but several turns later they started drifting into the background. Michael focused on the pain, embraced it, breathed it out. He searched for poetry, a distraction, but found none.

"You with me, Michael?"

Ariana's voice sounded distant with his muted left ear closer to her. He rolled his head toward her and nodded. "Pain's bad. Everywhere. Not hearing much with my left ear."

"Red case in the backpack." Her eyes stayed on the road as she spoke. "Morphine auto-injectors. Dose yourself. Use the largest injector. I'll have us back to my place in thirty minutes, but I've got to take the scenic route. Hopefully I'll stay conscious."

Michael nodded and opened the backpack. He dug to the bottom and found the red case. He snapped open the top and pulled out the largest of six injectors.

"Glad you have these."

Ariana nodded. "Right in the thigh."

"Oh, I know." Michael flipped off the cap and jammed the applicator into his left thigh. "Ten minutes. I got this. How you doing?"

"Badly," she said. "Actually, pretty well considering, right? Arm is more of a flesh wound. Nothing broken in my hip. Just some bruising and stiffness. Main problem is fatigue. I probably need more time to recover from my original injuries."

"You think?" Michael's smirk faded. "Why'd you do it?"

"Do what?"

"Take the shot. Try to kill us."

"I wasn't trying to kill us," Ariana said. "Not exactly. But standing around talking wouldn't have worked in our favor. Cops were on the way in. And *Hije* reinforcements. Kushtrim wanted time. That's what the bomb was for. Create a stalemate, get us talking."

"So you ended the stalemate by, what?" Michael said. "Killing everyone?"

Ariana glanced at him, then reached over and pulled his mask off. "Do we look dead?"

He shrugged. "Close to, and no way you took that shot without being ready to die."

"True." Ariana drove in silence for a few moments. "I was ready to die, but I didn't expect to."

"What did you expect?"

She took a fast turn, pulled onto an empty, straight road through the countryside.

"You," she said.

Michael grunted. "Me?"

Ariana glanced at him and nodded. "I expected you to save us. To save me. It's what you do, right?" She smiled, eyes still on the road. "My rescue nurse."

Michael shook his head, sat back, and tried to endure the pain. He closed his eyes and breathed as Ariana drove them on a roundabout trip back to her estate. He felt simultaneously heroic and unnerved. Yes, he'd saved her, but there'd been no hesitation when she took the shot knowing he could easily die trying to protect her. They'd lived, but it almost felt like she'd manipulated him. And risked using him up.

The thoughts felt incongruous with the warm glow gradually spreading through his body, granting relief from the pain. He shook loose the concern and settled on the twin ideas that Ariana had simply done what was necessary, and he'd been heroic. Within a few more minutes the pain was more of an echo, the dark thoughts quieted. He drifted, lost track of time.

"We're here."

Ariana's words jerked him back to reality. The car wasn't moving. Michael opened his eyes and looked around. They were in the dim light of her garage. He tried to take stock of his injuries, but there was a gauzy pleasantness wedged between him and the wounds.

His door opened, which was odd, since he hadn't opened it. He looked over at Ariana to ask her what was going on, but she was gone. Confused, Michael turned to his door and found Ariana standing there. His mind crawled toward a conclusion.

I'm seriously doped up.

"How much morphine was in that injector?" he asked.

"A lot. You're a big guy." She reached in and took him under his near arm, sagged against him for a moment, then straightened. "Let's get you in and clean you up before it starts wearing off."

Michael nodded and struggled to swing his feet out the door. For some reason his butt felt like it was on fire. He got his legs planted on the garage floor and—with Ariana's help—rose unsteadily to his feet. A glance revealed his car seat covered in smears of blood. Ariana stepped in next to him and ducked under his arm to support him. He looked down at her face as she tilted it up toward him.

"You're cute." He frowned. "No, beautiful."

She smiled and shook her head.

THE RESCUE NURSE

"Both." Michael nodded. "That's it. Both. And hot. That's different, right?"

"And you're sweet when you're high."

She stood there with his arm draped across her shoulders, the dim light hiding some details but showing her rather perfect form. Michael wanted time to stop to give him the chance to drink it in. No more killing. No more *Hije* or kidnapped girls or people to kill. Just Ariana and this lighting and this moment.

"I believe, madame, you mean to say I am most honest when high." Michael smiled down at her. "For you would still be hot even if I stopped being sweet."

Her smile grew, and she shook her head. "Let's go."

Michael staggered along beside her, his left leg rebelling with every step. She led him into the house and to the kitchen island. She ducked out from under his arm and got him leaned up against the island's countertop.

"Can you stay here for a sec?"

Michael tested his lean. It felt steady. The world was moving around a bit, but he was pretty sure he could stay put. He nodded. Ariana disappeared from view. Michael could feel long seconds drift by. He blinked, and she was back, a folded blanket in her arms, a headlamp strapped in place on her forehead.

"Hey," he said.

She flipped the blanket out on the island at full length, but folded narrow so it was several layers thick.

"Up you go," Ariana said. "It'll be easier to work on you if I'm not crouched over. Lay on your stomach first. I think your backside is worse than your thigh."

Michael clambered up slowly and lay down. It was surprisingly comfortable. The blanket was thick and isolated him from the granite countertop. He flipped his head around to the other side so he could see Ariana and get his good ear

195

facing up, but she was gone. Words bounced around in his head.

> "I came to Rome seeking fortune,
> never expecting to find a falcon.
> Only motivated to start anew,
> yet I followed where she flew.
> And now I wonder..."

His voice trailed off as Ariana stepped into view. Michael realized he'd been speaking out loud.

Ariana set down a variety of supplies beside him. Injectors, bandages, antiseptics, a large basin of steaming water, wash clothes and a towel. "What do you wonder?"

Michael tried to shake his head, but it didn't really work laying with the side of his head pressed into the blanket. "Not sure. Lots?"

"This trip is you starting over?"

Michael tried to shrug, but that didn't work well either. "That's what I'd thought."

"And now?" Ariana stepped out of sight toward his feet as she spoke.

Michael wasn't sure what to say. His mind felt sluggish, his thoughts chaos. He felt a tug on his pants by his ankles, and Ariana stepped back into view as she worked her way up up the pants to the waistband, cutting them away from his legs along with the bandages. His underwear went next, then his shirt.

Michael frowned, but was mildly excited. "Feeling a little exposed."

"Deal with it," Ariana moved his left leg around, and Michael stifled a groan as pain clawed its way through the fog. "Looks like a bullet is lodged in your hamstring. You must have taken a shot from one of Kustrim's guys right before the bomb detonated. I'm going to have to dig it out and stitch it up. Your butt's a mess. Looks like you got torn up by shrapnel. More stitches there." She paused, and Michael felt her hand lightly trace his back. "Your back's got some cuts, but isn't that bad."

Michael rested his head in his arms and closed his eyes. "I'm hoping some of those injectors are local painkiller."

"They are, but you're still going to feel it when I retrieve that slug."

The next hour was not pleasant, though the morphine kept him wrapped in a fuzzy sense of reality. Ariana kicked off her work by making a cappuccino for herself. Retrieving the slug from his hamstring was the worst. Arianna had a sense of what to do but lacked competence. She struggled to find the slug and retrieve it. The ordeal left Michael in a cold sweat.

Afterwards, she washed his entire backside and bandaged the myriad of small injuries he'd taken from the explosion. When he was finally stitched up and bandaged, Ariana had him roll over on his back, allowing him the dignity of using a dishtowel to gain a little privacy.

Compared to his backside, the injury to his thigh was relatively straightforward and took only nine stitches after she'd thoroughly cleaned out the wound. The worst of it was having weight on his injured butt and back. And feeling utterly exposed in front of Ariana as she leaned over his legs. It was as though the dishtowel kept shrinking the longer she worked, and Michael found himself struggling to not fixate on her proximity.

At last Ariana stood up. "I doubt it's up to your standards, but it's the best I can do." She shifted to stand opposite his chest, leaned over, and lightly touched the bruises on his chest and shoulder where the vest had stopped bullets. "What about your ribs and ear?"

Michael sat up—keeping his weight off the injured side as

much as possible—and flipped an edge of the blanket over his legs and mid-drift. "Nothing you can do about either. Eardrum is probably perforated. I'd guess I've got a cracked rib, but my lungs are doing okay. I'm going to go wash up some more in my bathroom and put some clothes on. Be right back to stitch up your arm."

"Take your time," she said. "I'll leave my arm bandaged, but I'm going to grab a shower before you work on it. And contact Ditmir."

Michael slowly scooted off the island and stood, wrapping the blanket around him. "I'll be ready to stitch you up when you're done."

Ariana turned and slowly walked towards the stairs, bracing herself on each piece of furniture she passed. Michael watched her until she crept out of sight, moving up the stairs. He began his own slow journey to the guest room. His backside felt taut, and he had to force himself to breath normally instead of taking shallow breaths to protect his ribs. The gentle fog of morphine felt tenuous, and pain stood ready behind it.

But outweighing the pain and fog was a growing elation. He was alive. They'd torn up a fortress, survived a bomb, and were still walking. Each move, each shot, had made sense, a harmony of carnage. They'd effortlessly coordinated every insane step through that madhouse.

Is that possible? Without empathy? Understanding? A relationship of some sort?

Michael shook his head as he stepped into his room and headed to the bathroom. Questions, but what was the point? He had to think about Ariana as a colleague, a fellow warrior, a companion in a shared mission. Not as a woman who kindled excitement in his blood, who beguiled him with her beauty.

He stepped into the bathroom, closed the door, and flipped on the light. Standing in front of the bathroom mirror, he let the blanket fall to the floor. So little to see. A dark blotch on his chest, another on his shoulder, stitches in his thigh. Most of the damage was on the backside, but those same injuries prohibited him from twisting around to get a view of them in the mirror. He settled for using a washcloth to wash more thoroughly under his arms and elsewhere.

Getting dressed was difficult, and Michael was pretty sure it would have been impossible if not for the morphine still encouraging his brain to ignore the pain. He slowly donned another black outfit and made his way back to the kitchen. Ariana was still upstairs, but her med kit backpack sat on the island countertop, along with the supplies she'd used to clean him up.

Michael dug the red case out of the backpack, sat gingerly on a bar stool, and removed the smallest of the remaining injectors. He hesitated a moment to assess how he felt. There was no way the morphine was already working its way out of his bloodstream, but the ordeal of being patched up had left him frayed. He sat down half on a stool, keeping the main injuries clear of the seat. He jammed the injector into his thigh, waited a moment, pulled it free. He set the injector on the countertop and lay his head in his hands. Time crawled by, the warmth returned.

"Take another hit?"

Michael looked up. Ariana stood with a hand braced on the back of a chair. She, too, was in another all black outfit, though Michael didn't think he'd turn heads in his getup like she would.

"I know you're hurting. And exhausted." Michael nodded, warming up to the topic. "But damn you look good."

"Morphine got your tongue again?" She stepped up to him, her face a bit higher than his from where he sat on the stool.

Michael shook his head.

"No?" Ariana smiled. "That was just you dropping the compliments?"

He reached a hand up and tapped his temple. "Morphine's got my brain. Tongue follows."

Ariana smiled and shook her head. Then she pulled her shirt up and off in a quick motion. Michael struggled to understand, struggled to do anything but stare at the smooth curve of her breasts hidden behind a lace bra.

"I, uh, what?" The words dribbled out of his mouth.

Ariana smiled with sharp edges and stepped over to the medical supplies. "Hard to stitch me up if you can't see the wound, don't you think?"

"Oh!" The word burst out. Michael pushed up and stood. "Yeah, no, of course. Let me look at the arm."

He did careful work to minimize the scarring, though the bullet hadn't cut as deeply as he'd expected, leaving the muscle largely intact. His abstract medical mindset eluded him, but he soldiered on, feeling simultaneously drawn to her and inhibited. His scruples didn't extend to flings, yet he'd never met an Ariana before. And had his marriages proved to be much more than extended flings?

Michael tied off the final stitch and stepped back. "Good to go."

Ariana glanced at her arm and turned toward him. "I contacted Ditmir. Before I got in the shower."

"And?"

Michael retrieved her shirt off the island counter and handed it to her, hoping she'd take the hint. He was tired of being distracted, of feeling taut. She slipped it on without comment.

"And he's working it and will pass along anything. We go tonight, which means I need sleep."

"Of course you do," Michael said. "How long can we rest?"

Ariana glance at her watch. "Four hours. We eat and prep. Then I kill Valdrin. And we hope..."

Her voice trailed off, her eyes on the floor.

"We hope we can figure out a way to find the girls before it's too late," Michael finished for her.

Ariana's eyes flickered up to his. "We'll find a way."

CHAPTER TWENTY

$\mathcal{M}$ ichael stood at the kitchen island and finished his caprese salad. He'd tossed and turned for about thirty seconds before falling into a drug-induced sleep, waking four hours later to his watch alarm. The house had descended into shadows, the sun sinking below the horizon.

Ariana had provided him another small dose of morphine along with the salad. He stood in the darkening kitchen and ate, gradually relaxing as the morphine tamed the searing pain in his backside.

"How you feeling?" Michael glanced up at Ariana as he spoke, her eyes hidden in shadow.

Ariana shrugged. "A lot better than you." She took another bite. "Can you be ready to go in twenty minutes? I need to finish packing our gear in the car, but I want to hit the road at full dark."

"We taking the Maserati?" Michael wasn't convinced he wanted to sit in his own dried blood.

She nodded. "I'll put a towel on the seat and swap out the license plate. It'll be fine."

"Of course you have spare license plates stashed around."

"Pretty important detail." Ariana shrugged. "Most of my life comes down to executing well in the details."

Michael smiled. "Wasn't meant to be a criticism. More of a compliment. Twenty minutes." He nodded. "I'll be ready."

Ariana headed to the garage. Michael savored his remaining salad. He'd always loved the simplicity of the sliced tomato, mozzarella, and basil dish. After polishing off six small stacks, he walked carefully to his room to hit the bathroom one last time.

With the door closed and light on, he leaned in toward the mirror, a hand resting on each side of the sink. "The hell are you doing?"

Who was he to help an assassin kill a man? Another man, after all the rest. But not an innocent man. Any doubts about the innocence of the *Hije* had evaporated when Kaltrina's head had snapped back. That moment flashed by in Michael's mind with each blink of his eyes and galvanized him. Ariana would take the shot, and he would be there supporting her the whole way. After the insanity he'd already experienced, what was one more death? One more shot taken by a woman who had a capacity for killing that seemed to border on the sacred, or perhaps demonic.

The man Michael faced in the mirror looked tense, unsettled, a stark contrast to the morphine-induced warmth he felt. Was he really going to help assassinate Valdrin? And were such concerns even relevant given the trail of bodies he and Ariana had left in their wake earlier that day? What right did he have to claim any moral qualms after so much killing?

His head sagged down and he closed his eyes. Instead of bodies and bloody mayhem, instead of Kaltrina's head being laid open in the blink of an eye, he saw the shape of Ariana beneath the covers. She was intoxicating, but Michael felt certain that only heartache would follow were he to pursue her. He pulled his head back up and opened his eyes. He was shocked to see a tear tracing a line down his cheek.

The clarity of the mission, the sense of doing right in violent, confusing theaters of war, had always emboldened him to do what was necessary with no thought to the consequences. Follow orders. Complete the mission. Until he'd almost drowned under the weight of it all. Maybe that weight had never left. Maybe he was still drowning.

Michael stood staring at himself, wondering who he was truly seeing until a glance at his watch told him it was time to go. He flipped off the light, pulled open the door, and headed back to the kitchen through the darkened house. He didn't need a mirror to tell him who he was. He was what he did, mixed together with the reasons lurking in his heart for those actions. And today, he was a man who was going to see Valdrin dead with a bullet to the head.

The distance between that settled goal and his original mission was vast, almost unintelligible, yet each step between the two had made sense in the moment. Michael paused in the dark shadows of the hall a few steps short of the kitchen. He drew in a breath, slowly released it, letting his thoughts flow out, emptying his mind. The girls were the mission now, and Valdrin. No room for doubt. He strode into the kitchen.

Ariana sat on the island in a meditative-looking yoga pose, her features hidden in shadow. She swung her legs out and slipped off the counter. "Ready?"

"I'm ready."

She handed him the SIG and two extra magazines. "Shouldn't need this, but..." Her voice trailed off and she shrugged.

Michael took the gear, looked it over, and tucked it into an interior pocket on this jacket. They walked side by side to the garage door and slipped through once Ariana had armed her security system. With Ariana hovering next to him, Michael carefully levered himself down into the passenger seat of the Maserati. As promised, Ariana had covered the seat with a dark towel. Once he was settled, Ariana headed around the front of the car and dropped into the driver seat.

"Rest for a bit," she said as she backed out of the garage. "It's going to take a while to get into the city."

Michael lowered his seat back. "I think I will."

The car was quiet, the surroundings a mixture of the darkness of night and bright lights, and Michael drifted. Scenes flashed by in his mind's eye. Prom with Ann. Being swept away by young love. Joining the Marines, and joining Ann in marriage. His first time in the madness of war. Returning to a different sort of war with a distant wife.

"Hey."

A hand gripped his arm. He rolled his head toward the voice. Ariana glanced at him, her brow furrowed.

"You were flipping your head back and forth and mumbling something. Seemed bad."

She pulled her hand back to the steering wheel, her eyes once again forward.

"Oh." Michael blinked, looked around. They were definitely in the city. "Sorry. Must be the morphine."

Ariana nodded. "We're close. You going to be okay?"

Michael wasn't sure how he felt. The morphine remained a blurred glass, allowing him only glimpses of his emotions. "Yeah, I'm fine. We got this."

He closed his eyes and waited, swaying slightly with each turn, feeling the hum of the engine rise and fall in pitch. Such a simple job. Accompany Ariana. Wait while she took a shot. Exit the scene. The next part was more daunting—try to figure out where the girls were stashed before it was too late.

Michael felt the car take a couple tight turns and come to a stop. He opened his eyes. They were in a dimly lit, cramped parking garage.

Ariana got out and flipped her seat forward. She reached behind it and pulled out a substantial duffel bag. "Time to move."

Michael nodded and opened his door. He pushed himself up and out, checked his gun, and turned to find Ariana beside him. She dropped the duffel at his feet. Another garage, dim lighting, her beauty, a smile toying with the corners of her mouth. Michael shut his door and leaned back against the car. She stepped over the duffel toward him, still looking up at his face.

He hooked an arm around her waist and pulled her in. In some remote part of his mind, he was babbling on and on about all the trouble he'd bring down on his own head. That she wasn't simply capable of breaking his heart, that she could probably break his arm or any other of his body parts given his current state.

It was all a muted buzz behind the velvet curtain of the morphine. Less than noise, easy to ignore. Michael leaned forward and kissed her. He sensed no surprise, no hesitation on her part. Her embrace was firm, her mouth warm and responsive.

Ariana's hands slid up to his shoulders in a caress that ended with a firm push, separating them. Her eyes were down, and Michael wasn't sure what he was seeing on her face. Sorrow? Guilt? Her eyes drifted up to his, and she shook her head.

"We have a job to do," Ariana said. "Let's just do it."

Michael let his gaze fall to his feet. His heart was racing. "Yeah, sorry."

"No, no apology needed. Not from you."

Michael looked up and caught that same ambiguous look on her face. Something was eating at her.

can a kiss speak across the distance
between two souls so very different
what led to her resistance
was shame or sorrow apparent

She bent and hoisted up the duffel bag. "If I help you get it on your back, you think you can manage this?"

Michael didn't think he could manage anything touching his back, but he nodded and slowly turned. She helped him settle it gently in place, the weight in line with the bulkiness of the bag.

He turned back toward her. "What's in this?"

"Mainly rope. Also my rifle." Ariana turned away from him and strode toward a door on the wall directly opposite her car. "We've got about a block to go. Hood up and go slowly. I know you're hurting."

Michael flipped up the hood on his light jacket and followed her through the door onto the streets of Rome. He kept his eyes on her legs and matched his slow steps to hers as she found a way along the crowded street. The duffel chaffed on his back, tugging at bandages on still-fresh wounds. Something else was tugging on his mind. A memory. Something about the rifle.

"Ariana?"

She glanced back at him for a moment but kept walking.

"Didn't you tell me," he said to her back, "when we were with Ditmir and Kaltrina, that we had to retrieve the, uh, item from the roof? The item we're carrying in this duffel? That it was already there and that's why we weren't leaving for Montreal right away?"

She stopped and turned to face him. "You now know the entire Montreal thing was lie. Did you think everything else was the truth?"

Michael shrugged. "Hadn't really thought it through."

"It's in the duffel. Not on the roof. Let's keep moving."

Michael went back to watching Ariana's legs and matching her stride. Two hundred thirty-seven steps and three turns later, the legs stopped, and Michael pulled up short before running into her. She fished a small badge out of a pocket and scanned it on a small reader beside a door in the tall building in front of them. He heard a faint click and she pulled open the door. Michael followed her into a dark entryway, down a short hall, and through a door into a stairwell.

"We're going up seven flights to the rooftop entrance," Ariana said. 'We'll take our time. No need to drain what energy we have."

The stairwell was lit by a solitary light above the door they'd just entered, and dim light drifting down from a higher floor. He grabbed the railing and ascended the stairs behind her, trying to puzzle out the question eating at him. Why had he kissed her?

"How'd you set this up?" he asked, trying to find something to think about other than the taste of her mouth.

"I have a spot in that parking garage leased under another identity, and an associated office in this building that I picked up just before I got shot up in case I ended up needing access to the roof. It seemed likely given the location, so it made sense to set it up."

"And the ropes?" he asked, wishing their weight wasn't bearing down on his back.

Ariana shrugged as she turned on a landing and started up the next flight. "These stairs are the only way off the roof. I like to have more than one exit for a job like this."

"And they just gave you access to the roof?" Michael turned the next corner, continued climbing. "Like that comes with the office?"

Ariana glanced back at him and smirked, her head shaking. "No, I let myself onto the roof. There's actually a security camera with a view of the rooftop door. I dressed up. HVAC service uniform. It was tricky picking the lock while pretending to fiddle with an actual key"

"And tonight?" he asked. "We just keep the hoods up for the camera?"

"Tonight we blind the camera. They'll know something happened tomorrow morning, but they won't have us on video."

They trudged up the stairs, taking a short break at each landing, preserving what strength their damaged bodies retained. Ariana was doing markedly better than him but paced herself to ensure he kept up. Michael followed her, trusting her to lead, not counting the floors or steps. At last she indicated a stop, a few steps short of the next landing.

"Next flight is a long, straight shot up to the roof."

Ariana signaled to him and he lowered the duffel to the floor. She crouched beside it and tugged open a zipper, revealing the ropes she'd mentioned, their body armor, and a sizable gun case. She reached in and pulled out the two masks they'd worn earlier that day along with several other items. "Just in case."

They pulled on the masks, and Ariana handed him a pair of gloves. He pulled them on as she donned her own pair. Finally, she handed him a small mirror and flashlight. She tapped the flashlight. "It lights up a tight cluster of infrared lasers, with one visible laser to help you aim it."

She pointed up toward what Michael imagined was the corner at the top of the stairwell by the door to the roof. "Hit the camera up there and hold it steady." She pulled another of the laser lights out of the duffel. This one was mounted on a small tripod. "I need about ten seconds to get this set up. Got it?"

Michael nodded and stepped up to the last step before the landing. Like all the landings, a lone light shone just above the landing's door. He leaned against the wall on his left to steady himself and reached the mirror up so he could see up the next flight of steps. It took him a second to find the camera perched in the corner at the top of the next flight of stairs in the tiny reflection. It took him another ten seconds or so to get a steady beam on it with the laser flashlight held in his other hand.

"This is not straight-forward," he said, bracing himself more firmly to steady his hands.

Ariana shrugged and stepped onto the landing, crossing to the far side. "Just don't move." A few seconds later, she had her little tripod-mounted light on and aimed at the camera. "All good. You can relax."

Michael sagged against the wall, surprised how tense he felt. Ariana retrieved the mirror and light from him, packed them in the duffel, and headed up the final flight of stairs carrying the bag. He followed her, hugging the wall opposite the camera to make sure he didn't block the light she'd set up.

The stairs led directly to a door with no landing. Ariana stopped two steps below, retrieved a couple tools from a pocket, and picked the lock in less than ten seconds. The door swung away from them and they stepped out onto the roof. The air was calm, cool.

A nice counterpoint to my life.

CHAPTER TWENTY-ONE

*M*ichael ran a thumb underneath the harness that encircled his waist and thighs in a vain attempt to relieve the sensation of being pinched in seven different places at once. He'd never liked climbing gear. The shoes were torture, the harnesses possibly worse. Now, with wounds decorating his backside and likely a cracked rib or two, he had transcended discomfort and attained a much more literal torture.

He reached up and shifted the body armor that was once again strapped in place. He'd argued with Ariana. Told her there was no way he could function with all that gear in place and his wounds tormenting him. She'd gone toe to toe with him and had come out on top. It didn't help that he'd known she'd been right.

"Here we go."

Ariana's voice was faint, but the words bounced around loudly in Michael's head before landing heavily in his stomach. She was stretched out prone on top of a large, metallic box about chest-high to Michael that housed HVAC gear. She cradled a sniper rifle, her backpack off to the side opposite him.

Motionless, she sighted down the scope toward a building about half a klick away. It stood a couple stories taller than the intervening buildings, on a level with theirs. The side facing them was dominated by a large balcony backed by a wall of glass on the top floor. Though he couldn't make out the details, she'd had him take a quick look through the scope when she'd first gotten set up at the then empty board room.

Michael breathed in for the count of four, held it, let it out slowly. "You see him? Valdrin?"

"I see him. And his men. And here come the buyers."

"How do you know for sure? That it's him?" Michael tried to contain the rising anxiety from his voice.

"Haven't told you, have I?" He could almost hear the smirk in her low voice. "Valdrin has this thing, this personal style, a weird vanity. He always wears the purple of royalty, and there's only one purple suit in that room. It's dark, but it's purple."

Michael's eyes flicked along the length of Ariana, down to the ropes tied off on the HVAC's steel girders that held the large box a couple feet above the rooftop. The ropes ran to the low parapet encircling the roof, where they lay neatly coiled, ready to be pushed off and put to use for a quick—if terrifying—exit. She'd laid them out so they were hidden from the door up to the rooftop by the blocky HVAC. The empty duffel bag and gun case were tucked up under the HVAC.

He took another slow breathing cycle, then another, and struggled to understand why the panic was surging forward and trying to overwhelm him. The rooftop, the mission to kill Valdrin, they had nothing on what they'd accomplished earlier in the day. It couldn't be fear. His mind cycled backwards, sifting memories, looking for a counterpart to the tightness in his lungs. No, it went beyond fear.

What am I doing? How did I think this was a good idea?

Michael looked up at the night sky but found no answers in

the few low-hanging clouds and partial moon. It had all made sense in the morphine high back at her house. He looked down and frowned. Was it as simple as that? He'd been injured before, but never at the outset. Was his body confusing his mind and heart? Was he interpreting simple pain and bodily exhaustion as panic?

More morphine. That should help.

It sounded stupid to him, yet Michael suspected it was true. Block the pain, block the misinterpreted signals. His eyes zeroed in on the backpack.

"You taking the shot now?" Michael pitched his voice low to match hers.

Ariana disengaged from the gun, pulled her phone out, and propped herself up on her elbows to look at it. "No. They're all moving around. Soon as they're seated."

Her thumbs moved in a blur on the dimly lit screen.

"You're texting? Now?"

Ariana flicked a glance at him, then continued typing. After a moment she returned the phone to her pocket and rolled onto her side to give him her full attention.

"You look like hell." She reached behind herself and grabbed her backpack, lifting it over the gun and setting it on the edge of the HVAC nearest Michael. "Get some morphine and settle in. They're going to go through the motions for a little. Could be some time before I can take the shot."

"But, you were texting?"

Michael pulled the backpack over and started rooting around for the morphine injectors while he waited for her answer. The masks they'd removed once they'd gotten to the roof were on top, the case just beneath.

"Ditmir," she said. "He's got a lead on the girls. We'll see, but for now we've got to take out Valdrin. That will poke the hornet's nest and hopefully lead to a mistake."

Michael pulled out the case and flipped it open. He picked an injector and jammed it into his thigh. Had her voice just cracked with emotion? He couldn't make sense of it but wasn't sure he cared. The pain was starting to burn raw and hot, and it messed with his perceptions. He pulled out the injector and returned the spent cartridge to the case, the case to the backpack.

Just hang in there for a few minutes.

He folded his arms on the top of the HVAC and put his head down. Within a few minutes, the warm glow began spreading through his body, walling him off from the fire of his injuries.

"Michael?"

He thought about lifting his head to look at her but decided he was way too comfortable. "Yeah?" His voice was muffled by his arms.

Her hand tousled his hair and sent fire along his spine, a heat entirely different than the pain. A heat that cut through the morphine. "Listen, we're just about there. I've got to get in the zone, be ready to take the shot when it's presented. I need you to guard the door. You understand?"

Guard the door. Sure.

"Why?" Within the privacy of his arms, he frowned, confused by his own question.

Her hand retreated. "Because I need to know I can take the shot no matter what happens. You understand? Whatever happens, you make sure I'm able to take him down. Fire through the door if you have to."

Michael slowly lifted his head. She still lay on her side facing him over the rifle. "What's gonna happen?"

Ariana smiled. Her eyes glimmered like diamonds in the dim moonlight. "Nothing. But I like to cover all the contingencies, okay? Stand by the door and don't let anyone through. Understand?"

Michael wasn't sure he was capable of understanding much of anything in the warm embrace of the morphine. He stood erect and nodded, then turned toward the door.

"Michael?"

He turned back, wondering at the pain in her voice.

"I'm sorry," Ariana said.

Michael struggled to understand the moment, the weight of it, but there was no nuance behind the bright blanket of morphine. "Sorry for what?"

It felt like a stupid question in his ears, like he should have been able to grasp the significance but was missing some key to understanding her intentions.

She looked away and took up her position at the rifle once again. "For all of it. Every last fucking thing."

This time, Michael was sure he'd seen tears in her eyes.

What the hell is going on? Why's she getting emotional?

Somewhere deep behind the morphine, alarms were going off in Michael's mind, but he felt only an anxious curiosity in response. He walked the few steps to the door leading down into the building and drew his handgun to give it a quick once over. Chamber loaded. Safety off. He took a position behind the direction the door would swing out if opened.

I stand above the city
surrounded by night
a bringer of death
straying from the light
she lays beside her gun
tears light up her eyes
I struggle to see the truth
when everything's a lie

217

The poem was horrible, but it served its purpose and centered Michael's chaotic thoughts, helping his mind find rest. There'd been moments of clarity in among the insanity of the day. He'd seen a need, counted the cost, and made a choice. He would guard the door. Nothing would stop her from taking the shot.

"Hodor." The word was barely a whisper, and the accompanying chuckle died before it started.

He stood and waited. The minutes stumbled by and Michael's mind kept spinning back to that last look at Ariana's face. Tears brimming in her eyes, resolution etched in her jaw. They'd accomplished so much. Why the tears? Why the apology? What did it all mean?

Was it possible she was falling for him? He almost laughed at the thought, but there'd been moments of tenderness. Always ambiguity, but there'd been moments. Was she finally worried about losing something that mattered to her? He couldn't piece it together.

He wanted to believe she was feeling the same confused attraction that threatened his equilibrium, but it didn't feel right. Not entirely, at least. He suspected some sort of affection had snuck up on her. They'd been through hell together. Been through hell and lived to tell the tale. It only made sense. Was she now wondering what it would be like if there was something more? Something beyond comrade in arms?

Michael grimaced and shook his head. If Ariana was wrestling with thoughts like that, she was barely keeping up with him. His mind kept wanting to wander off on fantasies of a future where he held her in his arms, just a man and a woman and a moment and no more running and killing.

The door shuddered under a heavy boom. In spite of the morphine, the confusion, the suddenness, the weightiness of his thoughts, Michael acted instantly. He pivoted to square up with the door just beyond the arc of its swing were it to open and fired all his rounds through it, spacing his shots out in a broad circle. Through the thickness of the door now sprinkled with holes, he heard the loud cry of what had to be cussing, though it wasn't in English. He bumped the switch, the emptied magazine fell to the rooftop, and the whip-crack of Ariana's rifle shattered the momentary quiet. She'd taken the shot.

As he slammed the new magazine into place, the door burst open under another blow. Light from the stairwell silhouetted two men in dark suits pushing forward through the doorway onto the roof, one slightly in the lead. Behind them, at least two more men were coming up the final couple steps. The angry cries continued from further down the stairs.

Five men. Maybe more.

Michael drove forward, his left arm raised to check the lead man high on his chest with his forearm. He held the gun low in his right hand and fired as he rammed into the man. It should have been simple. Kill the first guy, push them all back down the stairs under fire.

The man grunted with each shot, but instead of falling backwards, he surged forward into Michael under the collective weight of the men pushing into him from behind. As they slammed together, the man brought his head down in a vicious blow aimed at Michael's face.

Shit. Wearing armor under that suit.

Michael flinched back, shifting his weight to his heels, avoiding the blow by a fraction of an inch. The man continued forward, their chests collided, and Michael was flung backwards. He fell to the rooftop and rolled away, expecting death to rain down on them from Ariana. She'd taken the shot. Now to make their escape. She'd have a handgun or two out and mow them down.

Except there was nothing. No shots. No men recoiling in the stupor of death.

He glanced over his shoulder. From his vantage point lying on the rooftop, he could see underneath the HVAC. She was crouched low on the parapet, clipped in to one of the ropes. She looked at him, bit her lip, hesitated, then disappeared over the parapet. The rope pulled taut and moved in a slow rhythm back and forth a few inches.

Michael's mind floundered, unable to understand.

Then the men were on him, using their weight to subdue him, blows raining down.

How? They came through that door like they knew. Like they knew we were here before she fired that gun.

A well-aimed blow struck Michael just behind the right ear.

Darkness.

CHAPTER TWENTY-TWO

*M*ichael had only a hazy memory of the one time he'd come out from under anesthesia. It had been an inguinal hernia repair in early high school. A fluke problem that the doctor had said belonged to older men, not high school students. The surgery had gone well, his recovery flawless, and life had gone on.

Except for the recovery room. It hadn't felt very flawless. Oh, the nurses had been encouraging and patient. The surgeon said Michael had handled the anesthesia well. But none of them had lived the terror, the sense of drowning, of not understanding anything while feeling so much, as he'd risen out of the deep sleep on the recovery room bed. There'd been no surge toward clarity, just a slow slog through confusion, pain, and feeling dislocated from his body.

His crawl back toward consciousness about five minutes after the blow knocked him out felt similar. Pain shimmered through his skull, echoing from back to front and side to side. Nothing seemed to work. His arms were impotent, his eyes blind, dampened pain dominated his body. And there were no kind nurses this time, no encouraging babble of words that had little meaning yet provided emotional strength.

Alive. I'm alive.

The thought cut through the fog, gave him guidance. He needed to assess, to gain some advantage. He tried to keep his breathing relaxed and his body limp. He didn't know if he'd already thrashed around and signaled his return to consciousness or still had some element of surprise.

The pain in his head was terrible and gaining focus behind his right ear, yet even that pain did not bury the fire in his wounded ribs and backside. On the flip side, he was still doped up with morphine and it gradually asserted itself, offering warm comfort that muted the pain. As the sensation of pain diminished and his mind gained clarity, Michael began to decipher his circumstances. He was stretched out on his side, slumped toward his stomach. The air he was breathing was stuffy and close. His wrists burned and his arms felt twisted behind him in an unnatural position, though he could no longer feel the bulk of his body armor. The surface he lay on vibrated and swayed.

Arms restrained at the wrists. Hood over my head. Thrown into the back of a van. On the move.

Michael struggled to remember the details. He knew he was screwed, but what exactly had happened? He'd been on the roof with Ariana. She'd taken the shot. How had he ended up restrained in a cargo van? He zeroed in on the shot. How'd he know she'd taken it? He remembered the sound of the rifle firing. His spent magazine hitting the rooftop.

Why'd I fire all my rounds?

The magazine had hit the rooftop, the door had burst open. There'd been a momentary struggle, more shots fired. He'd been thrown backwards to the rooftop. With sudden insight, he saw again under the HVAC to the parapet. Saw Ariana disappear over it, the rope taut and moving slightly side to side in time with her rapid descent. Saw her abandon him to the *Hije*.

She betrayed me. Fucking left me to them.

It stung. He'd been on the very edge of a fairy tale in which she saw something in him desirable that went beyond his knack for violence. Something to match his own turbulent but growing feelings. A bitterness welled up to match his body's pain, a twisted sense of relief that at least the betrayal had happened prior to the wasted years and endless heartache of his two marriages.

The van took a hard turn and Michael willed his body to remain limp in spite of the stabbing pains in his legs and back. He breathed the stuffy air in the careless cadence of the unconscious, wondering if the small deception even mattered. Conscious or unconscious, what did his captors care? He was harmless, totally at their mercy. Yet he remained limp as the vehicle took more turns.

Could it have been the money? Was this her way of clearing the table, withholding payment because there was no one to pay? Or maybe she wanted to regain her secrets by taking him off the board. Neither option made much sense. Money seemed to be irrelevant to her, or at the least she had more than she seemed to need. And if she'd wanted him dead, he'd be dead. He'd seen her across the rooftop, under the HVAC. She'd been hidden from the *Hije* men coming through the doorway. He knew her capabilities. One shot to the head, then disappear over the parapet. Michael dead. Problem solved.

But she hadn't shot him. Which meant she'd left him to the *Hije* on purpose, or something else had happened beyond what he'd seen. And then the real question hit him. How'd those men show up right then? And not to scout, but in full force? Like they knew something was going down on that rooftop at that moment. Had her texting been a signal of some sort? And what had they known? Would Valdrin really have just sat there and waited for some of his goons to get on top of a building half a klick away if he thought a shooter was about to light him up? Michael had heard her take the shot, and he had no doubt Valdrin was dead. None of it made sense.

The van took a tight turn, descended a sharp slope, leveled off, and jerked to a halt. Hands grabbed Michael under each arm and jerked him upwards. He gasped and involuntarily jerked his head back as pain lanced through his ribs for a brief moment. He heard the van's rear doors opened—with another metallic noise further out that he couldn't quite place, maybe a rolling cargo door closing—and the men dragged him forward. A dim light showed him the inside contours of the loose hood pulled over his head. His feet flopped off the back of van to the floor beneath, causing his wounded hamstring to become the fiery center of his universe for a few seconds as he tried not to vomit into the hood.

The morphine won again, the pain subsided, and Michael returned to coherence as he was dragged along by the two men still clutching him. They knew he was conscious now, so he tried to get his legs underneath him to gain the dignity of walking between his captors. He couldn't seem to pull it off. They were moving at a fast walk, and between the morphine and the hood he was too disoriented to exert that level of control over his body.

So he strove to get as comfortable as possible given he was wounded and being dragged along by two men who did not care for his welfare, and started tracking the twists and turns they took. After three lefts and two rights, they stopped for a bit, stepped forward, swung around, and stopped again.

Elevator. Wonder how high we'll go.

The elevator descended briefly, then they were moving

again. A left turn out of the elevator, long hall, left again, and a short distance forward toward a searingly bright light, bright even through the coarse weave of the black hood over his head. Michael was dumped into a wooden chair, his arms held out to fit over the low back. The flash of pain as his wounds were slammed into the wooden seat was bad, but no worse than what he'd already experienced. He managed, controlled his breathing, tried to keep some dignity.

Quick hands secured his ankles to the chair with what Michael assumed were zip ties, and the rope binding his wrists was tied down to the back of the chair. Their work done, he heard the footsteps of the men retreat back the way they'd come. He knew what was coming next, and knew that they knew that he knew. He almost giggled as his mind wound backwards through cycles of him knowing that they knew he knew. The silliness of his thoughts was his first real warning that he was terrified. No heat on his neck or other tell that he was pissed off and ready to go, just giddy fear bubbling up.

She abandoned me.

He kept circling back to the sight of her disappearing over the parapet, leaving him behind. They'd fought side by side and come out on top, yet she'd left him to whatever hell he was about to experience. It had to have been on purpose. Her farewell, her goading him to guard the door. It all made sense if she knew what was coming. But how, and why? What was her motive? He couldn't figure it out. But the bedrock truth remained. While he'd been stuck in some fantasy wondering if they had a future, she'd planned to hand him over to a bunch of animals.

Be strong, Michael. Be strong. And don't suffer anything to protect that bitch.

The words sounded brave, but a thread of doubt tickled his mind. It didn't make sense. Why would she give him over to them? She had to know they'd give him a slow death, that he'd have every reason to give up every last detail he knew about her. Anything would make more sense than what she'd done. What was her motive? Had she lost her mind?

> *tied to a chair facing the light*
> *no place to run no one to fight*
> *what dignity is left to me*
> *death the only way to be free*

Loud music kicked on behind him, masking all other sounds. He guessed it was some sort of Swedish death metal. Michael loved metal but had always found the incessant double kick drums and screaming vocals torturous. He wanted to laugh. They probably didn't realize he was already being tormented.

Quick hands grabbed the hood from the top and ripped it up and away. He's eyes were seared by the twin lights facing him a short distance away. Eyes watering, he averted his gaze. He didn't see the large man step quickly in from the side and deliver a fierce blow to his solar plexus, robbing him of the ability to breathe, causing spasms of pain through his abdomen and damaged ribs.

As he tried to master his body and wait for his breath to return, he wondered about the opening salvo. It seemed a stupid way to begin if they wanted him to talk, and ineffective if they simply wanted to maximize his suffering. He tried to look up, his eyes a slit to combat the glaring light. The second blow caught him high on the left cheekbone, snapping his head around.

Maybe they'll screw up and knock me out.

Michael sucked in a ragged breath, let his head roll forward onto his chest. The morphine was still there, fighting back the pain, pushing it away. He had no intention of giving away that small advantage to his captors, but he wasn't sure how to fake it. He'd taken blows before, but always with a chance to fight back. A helpless beating was new territory.

Two blows in quick succession hammered into his ribs, and a pain blossomed that far surpassed the limits of the morphine. Michael was certain he now had another cracked rib and wondered if his lungs were still intact. His breathing was ragged from the blow, but he still seemed to be able to draw in air and expel it. The thought of slowly dying from asphyxiation with collapsed lungs was terrifying to him. He'd always expected to die from some unseen gunshot or IED, or maybe even old age. Not some symptom of being steadily beaten to death.

By now his pupils had constricted and he could make out the large man standing just to one side, a dark silhouette in the flood of light. Michael wasn't sure if it would make it better or worse to see the blows coming, but determined he'd face it head on. He lifted his head and waited, but the man stepped out of sight behind him, taking that tiny element of control away from him.

The music cut off. He heard quiet voices somewhere behind him. They were pitched too low to understand, but what little he could make out wasn't English.

"What is your name?"

The voice was jarringly loud, heavily accented. Michael decided to peg him as a Gary. For whatever reason, the name Gary had always seemed to him about the least intimidating name in the universe.

"Thomas Paine." His voice sounded terrible. Thin and warbly.

"You have no ID," Gary said.

Michael hadn't heard a question in the statement but

decided to plow forward. "Nope, not on me. It was in the back-pack up on the roof where you grabbed me. Guessing my partner took it or you'd already have it."

"Thomas Paine?"

That time the question was obvious. They didn't believe him. So they weren't complete idiots.

"Yes," Michael said. "Thomas Paine. You'll find my ID if you find that backpack."

The large man stepped back into sight and delivered a hard blow across the face, somehow connecting with the exact spot he'd previously hit on the cheekbone. Michael was impressed. And hurting badly now in spite of the morphine. He decided to name him Bullseye. Bullseye stepped back out of sight.

"Who is your partner?" Gary asked.

"I think you guys call her the Falcon," Michael said. "I knew her as Ariana."

More whispering, but no blows. They were interested.

"Where are you from?"

Michael spit the accumulated blood out of his mouth. "Texas. United States."

"How did you begin working with Ariana?" Gary said. "And when?"

"I'm a rescue nurse," he said. "My employer got a call—"

"A rescue nurse?" Gary's voice sounded genuinely curious.

Michael nodded. "Yeah, a rescue nurse. We retrieve people who have been injured overseas and render aid while getting them back home for care. I mean, there's more to it than that with the medical insurance and all, but—"

"Your employer was called?" Gary seemed to like to interrupt.

"About a week ago," Michael said. He was starting to enjoy the conversation, the complete liberty to say whatever he wanted given Ariana had betrayed him. And the lack of blows while they were talking. "A woman needed transport from Rome to Montreal. I was sent to help her."

A momentary pause, and Bullseye stepped back into sight, his fist already in motion. Something seemed to give in Michael's face as his cheek was punched for the third time. His vision blurred, but he wasn't sure if it was from the intense pain or some sort of damage.

"You have killed many men," Gary said. "I do not believe that is what you said rescue nurses do."

Okay, he may have an accent, but he knows English well enough to be sardonic.

"Right, okay," Michael said. Speaking hurt, but he pressed forward. "On the call, she specifically asked for someone with military experience. My employer picked me. Because of that."

"What is your military experience?" Gary asked.

"Marines. USMC."

"I see," Gary said. "Combat experience?"

Michael nodded, then immediately regretted it as nausea swept through him. "Lots. Lots of combat experience."

"And then?" Gary said. "After your employer picked you?"

"Came to Rome. Found Ariana. Patched her up, then got dragged along with her through this hell I'm in."

"Why," Gary asked, "did you stay with her? Once you knew what she was doing?"

Michael took a breath, considered how to answer. He decided to stick with the truth unless offered a compelling alternative. "I'm not totally sure, but I think maybe I found the whole thing exciting. Have you met her? She's, ah, beguiling."

"What do you mean?" Gary's voice sounded a hair closer, as though he were being drawn in as they spoke. "I know the word. I want to know how she was beguiling."

Michael shrugged. "Beautiful. Sexy. Stunningly competent. Rich. Pretty much a man-trap. I just got sort of sucked along in her vortex. "

"Was it worth it?"

Again, Gary sounded genuinely curious. Michael finally felt the first flicker of heat on his neck.

"Sure, until tonight," he said. "From here on out? Guess that's up to you."

"It is," Gary said. Michael could picture him slowly nodding his head. "Why did she leave you on the roof?"

Michael's head slumped forward onto his chest.

"I've been asking myself that same question," he said, "and I have no fucking idea. Just nothing, okay?"

"Where do we find the Falcon now?"

Michael slowly lifted his head. "I think I could find her house if you drove me around. Somewhere northwest of the city."

"We shall see."

The loud music surged back to life. Bullseye stepped in front of him and stretched his hands, limbering his fingers. Michael's eyes had adjusted well enough to make out the leather gloves protecting his hands.

Shit. This is gonna suck.

The blows landed with a precision that would have impressed Michael if he'd been able to witness the artistry from afar. Painful, sometimes damaging, but careful to avoid knocking him out or killing him outright. Michael knew blows to the head and torso hurt, he hadn't actually realized just how much pain could be generated with well placed punches to the thighs and arms. His world collapsed into agony and chaos, and though he remained conscious, he slipped sideways into incoherence.

CHAPTER TWENTY-THREE

*S*omething had changed. Something significant. Michael's body was no longer his, stolen by the pain, the morphine a distant dream. But the music was gone, and he didn't feel any new blows. He tried looking around. His right eye wouldn't open, the other had trouble focusing. The light was still blinding, but there seemed to be a dark shape stretched out in front of him. He guessed it was Bullseye, lying on his back, his head seemingly growing larger by the second.

Michael tried to shake his head to clear his vision. It was a mistake. He managed to vomit mostly off to the left side, his breathing cut off by a searing pain in his lower chest as his stomach contracted. His stomach empty, he drew in a ragged breath, his head hanging forward.

I'm dying.

He wasn't sure though. There'd been very little blood in the vomit, and he was breathing again. All good signs. It felt like the right moment for a poem, something to help him process the nearness of death, the uncertainty of the moment, but he didn't seem to be able to get that part of his brain engaged.

Something tugged at his wrists. He tried to pull away from whatever they were doing to him and was shocked to feel his arms swing free. He screamed, fire consuming his arms with the motion, a pain that transcended the other horrors his body felt. He bit off the raw sound and stared at his bloody wrists with his one good eye. Apparently, he'd been thrashing around while bound and torn his skin apart.

Some sort of trick? Cutting me free?

His eye gained clarity and he looked back at Bullseye, stretched out like he'd tipped over backwards. A pool of blood encircled his head, growing slowly larger. One of Bullseye's eyes was a gaping hole, leaking blood. It tickled Michael's mind, the part that could rationally analyze situations and come to conclusions. That bloody wreck of an eye meant something important.

Someone leaned on his right leg and tugged at his ankle. Michael wanted to attack them, level them with a blow, or cut off their windpipe in a hold. But his arms hung limply at his sides, and he wasn't sure he could deploy them to work violence quite yet. Instead, he gingerly rotated his head around to see what was happening.

It was Ariana. She was standing up from a crouch, a knife in hand, then squatting again to cut his left ankle free of the chair.

You abandoned me.

Michael felt ashamed by how much pain he felt at the thought, a different sort of pain twisting up his guts. He wanted to yell at her, but his jaw didn't seem to work, and only a low moan leaked out of his throat. His left ankle free, she stood and slipped the knife into a sheath at her waist. She had two guns holstered on her shoulder harness, and what looked like the M4 he'd used earlier in the day strapped across her back over her slim backpack. Ammo magazines decorated the belt underneath her armor. Ariana's eyes rose to meet his one good eye, then flickered down the length of him before returning to his eye. She didn't flinch, but only held his gaze for the space of a slow breath before looking away.

Her hand reached toward his face, but stopped an inch away, then retreated. "Can you walk? I've got to keep moving."

Michael wasn't sure he could remain conscious, let alone stand. On the flip side, he was tired of those stupid lights aimed at his face, tired of the chair to which he'd been bound, tired of being helpless. He leaned forward and rose to his feet. He felt unsteady, but the pain was no worse standing versus sitting. With careful steps, he turned around by slow degrees.

The room was large and mostly empty. The wall behind where he'd sat had a single door that stood ajar and a large pair of speakers with some other audio gear just off to the left. Michael took a step toward the door, then another. It felt like he was twenty feet above the floor, precariously balancing on stilts. However, with each shuffling step, his mind gained clarity, his body felt a bit closer to earth. Step by step he inched toward the door. Ariana followed, hovering close by but not touching him. As they neared the door, she drew first one gun and then another.

Five feet from the door, he stopped and pivoted toward her. Ariana faced the door, a gun trained on the slender opening leading to the hall. Michael cracked open his apparently broken jaw a fraction of an inch and spoke a single word.

"Why?"

Ariana kept her eyes fixed on the door. "We had to find the girls."

Her stance, her tone, all of it pointed to the importance of her words. She was trying to convey something significant. Michael couldn't see it, but felt a sense of growing horror. He knew the girls were the goal. That had been the point of trying to get the financial books. What was she really saying?

Ariana glanced at him, then returned her gaze to the doorway. Her face seemed to sag. "There was no way we were going to find them in time. I'm sorry. Truly. We had to."

Michael knew he should understand the meaning behind her words, but though his mind was awake, it seemed unable to grapple with her statements. One thing jumped out, though. She seemed to think she knew where the girls were.

"Girls," he said in a stronger voice, his jaw still immobile. "Where?"

She looked at him again, and this time held his eyes, or at least his one eye that wasn't swollen shut. Tears sparkled in her eyes.

She shrugged. "Pretty sure I'm going to find them here. That was the point." She looked back at the door. "You've done enough, okay? Sit tight."

Here?

That couldn't be a coincidence. His mind finally lurched into motion and grasped the obvious conclusion. His neck prickled with heat.

I was bait. To lead her to the girls.

His hand shot out to grasp her upper arm. Just as fast, she had the other gun's muzzle nestled up under his chin. Their eyes met, and now Michael could see the tears flowing freely. He wanted to feel compassion, to empathize with the decision she'd been forced to make, but his neck was aching with heat. At the same time, he realized she was compromised emotionally and had a gun ready to end him.

He made a show of opening his hand and releasing her arm. "How? Track me?"

Ariana pulled the gun away from his chin and returned her focus to the door. "Two trackers. One in each of your trainers."

Michael couldn't help himself. He looked down, but there was nothing to see but his black sneakers. He was at least glad to discover he no longer felt as nauseous when moving his head.

"Shoes?" He tried to sound calm in spite of the fury chipping away at his control. "When? How?"

"It's simple, really," Ariana said. "Pulled a plug of foam out of each sole near the edge, inserted the tracker, glued the outer edge of what I'd cut out back in place."

"But when?"

"Back at Ditmir's and Kaltrina's place." She stole a glance at him. "When you were in the shower."

Michael's mind reeled. Before Kaltrina died. Before her promise to Ditmir. Before they'd shot up the *Hije* fortress and killed Kushtrim. Before the financial records had been destroyed by the bomb. Before any of it, she'd set him up to be bait. He stumbled sideways, caught himself against the wall next to the door.

"Whole time?" He kept his eye on the floor. "Through... everything? Just bait? A Trojan horse?"

"No." She sounded uncertain. "Not really. It was, well, Ditmir wanted a contingency, I didn't know what to do, but he insisted, and it made sense at the time. We didn't know how to find the girls, and we were running out of time. Listen, I'm sorry, but I've got to keep moving."

Michael stood up straight, released the wall. His jaw hurt like hell but seemed to be loosening up. "Wait. The text? On the rooftop?"

"Just a note to Ditmir." She was no longer looking at the door. Her eyes were unfocused. "To tell him it was time."

"Ariana, hurts like hell to talk. Stop making me ask questions."

Her eyes came into focus and she nodded. "He sent messages through a contact to warn the *Hije* that an investigative journalist was shooting photos of their meeting from a rooftop about half a kilometer away. Our rooftop. This journalist, he's known to the *Hije*, and not loved. It was made to sound plausible and urgent. The sort of excuse to take real action against him. Permanent action."

Michael slowly nodded. It all made sense and stoked his growing anger. A danger to Valdrin that demanded immediate action but not a reason to call off the meeting. It was the perfect ruse. The men had burst through the door into a scene far different than they'd expected but had reacted supremely well. But their appearance had been Ariana's signal to take her shot.

"Did you kill him?"

Ariana nodded.

The simple elegance of the plan should have impressed him, but Michael could feel only a simmering rage. One detail, though, felt off.

"Why would they take me to the same place as the girls?" He forced the words out through his swollen jaw in a snarl. "And what's next? While I sit tight?"

She wasn't fazed by his intensity. "I'm going to play a game called last man standing, and the woman's going to win. I can tell you the rest later, but I have to move."

The fire in his neck burned hotter than the pain in his broken body. She'd betrayed him. Allowed him to suffer at the hands of the *Hije* as a means to an end. She'd used him, seen to it that he was used up. And now she planned to walk away and finish the mission without him. It all made sense. Was possibly brilliant. He didn't care. Rage consumed him, displacing the pain and confusion.

"Fuck that."

Her head jerked around to look at him. He ignored her and grabbed the M4, tugged the strap over her head with spastic effort as his arms tried to rebel, made sure the selector was on semi. "How many rounds left?"

Ariana moved her eyes back to the door, but Michael didn't think it was really needed. She was avoiding his gaze again. He hoped she felt guilty as all hell. He slipped the gun's strap over his own head, got it adjusted.

She used me as bait!

"All thirty," she said. "I've got two more magazines for it."

He'd already spotted them on her belt. He snagged one of them and jammed it into his pants pocket. "Let's go."

Ariana hesitated and looked at him again. Her eyes were raw with anguish. Michael growled low in his chest, reached past her, pulled the door open. Gun at the ready, he stepped into the hall. It was more of a shuffling forward than a decisive step, but it did the job and got him through the door. He checked off to the right back toward the elevator, trusting that she'd cover the other end of the hall. A body lay crumpled on the floor in a pool of blood about ten feet away, another at about twenty-five feet. The hall was otherwise empty.

Betraying bitch. But competent.

"Clear," she said just behind him.

Michael nodded. "Clear. Your work?"

Ariana stepped up beside him. "Yes. Very light security at street level and here. They're disorganized, caught off guard. Best guess is the girls are next floor down at the bottom. I left Ditmir in the main electrical room. He should have cut off power to that whole floor by now."

"So they'll know we're coming."

Ariana nodded as she moved forward around the bodies. Michael followed with a shortened, shuffling gait.

"So why here?" he asked. He tried to speak with a calm voice. "The girls?"

"Lefter's the only—"

Michael cut in. "Who's Lefter?"

"*Hije bajrak.* Last one." Ariana stopped in front of a door to the side of the elevator. "You sure about this? Can you manage stairs?"

"We're going down?"

Ariana nodded.

"I can manage," Michael said. "Lefter. What of him?"

Ariana pushed the door open and flowed into the stairwell, her two guns at the ready. Michael followed more slowly. His anger had settled into a crystalline structure, a maze of hard planes and sharp edges. Once the door closed behind him, Ariana reached up and shattered the small fluorescent light mounted above the door with the extended reach of the gun's suppressor. Light still filtered in from above and below.

"He had nowhere else to go." Ariana started down the steps, her voice barely above a whisper. "Fortress compromised. The *bajrak* dead other than him. But this facility was already secured. Almost certainly by him. He was probably here when I killed Valdrin. He would have had his men bring you to him."

She betrayed me.

Everything she'd said made sense. If saving the girls really was the goal, giving him up had been terribly effective. But betrayal wasn't just a tool to use to further the mission. They'd hidden the plan from him and lied to get him to go along with it.

Ariana hit the landing and turned to descend the last half-flight of stairs to the bottom of the stairwell. Michael stumbled along behind her, one hand clutching the handrail, the other on his gun, trying not to groan with each step. He knew he wasn't ready for whatever happened next. His body was too limited, too distracting. Yet the one thing that had remained true in spite of the betrayal and lies was the very thing that had motivated him to cast aside the original scope and go all in—the kidnapped girls. If Ariana's gamble with his life paid off, they were somewhere beyond that door.

She stopped at the bottom of the stairs and waited for him to descend the final few steps. Her face looked hard, the tears wiped away. He lumbered down to her, biting his lower lip to silence the gasps that struggled to find voice. Ariana once again reached up and shattered the fluorescent light, leaving only a whisper of light from two floors above. She leaned in close.

"I'm sorry it came to this. Truly." She looked him in the eye, held his gaze. "I hate what you've been through. I'm going to make every single one of them pay for that and so much more. But you need to know I'd do it all again. You understand? That's who I am. I'll use anyone up if that's what it takes to destroy the *Hije*."

Michael's crystalline anger shook but held steady. "Great pep talk."

"That's not the point." She looked down at the guns clutched in her hands, then to the door. "In another life, maybe there's something between us. I wasn't expecting that, and maybe you feel differently, but that's how I see it."

The crystal shattered, his knees went weak.

Does she live to screw around with my emotions?

"But I'm guessing not this time around. Not after... what had to be done." Ariana tilted her head up and looked him in the eye again. "I'm going through that door to lay waste to everything. Understand? You go with me, it's not about either of us staying alive. It's about all of them dying."

Somehow in the whole getting-betrayed-and-tortured sequence, Michael had forgotten how beautiful she was. He could see only her silhouette and hints of details. The curve of her jaw. The outline of an ear holding back her hair. Another perfect moment in a very imperfect situation. He felt like his head was in a new space. All the clarity of the fury of the fight mixed with a longing for beauty and love. His head swam with the potency of the moment. His free hand rose, he brushed her cheek with the outside of his fingers.

"Too much drama for me." His voice cracked under the strain of pain and emotion. "I'll see you on the other side."

CHAPTER TWENTY-FOUR

*M*ichael had expected to charge through the door shooting after making his heroic pronounce-ment. It had sounded great to his ears, or at least his one ear that wasn't ruptured, a perfect lead-in to a guns blazing fight to the death. Instead, Ariana holstered both her guns and swung her backpack around to the front. She retrieved two small canisters, her mask, and a set of night vision goggles. She quickly resettled the backpack, pulled the mask over her head, and strapped on the goggles.

"Flashbangs?" he asked.

She nodded. "I don't have any gear for you. You sure about this? We're going to be, well, you're going to be fighting blind."

Michael shrugged. "I'll manage. You ready? I'll get the door."

Ariana nodded again, clutched both flashbangs in a hand and pulled the pins. "Narrow opening, okay?"

"Not my first rodeo," he said. "Here we go."

He grabbed the door handle and yanked it toward himself a foot or so, hoping the metal door was as solid as it looked.

Gunfire erupted from somewhere beyond, and the metal door pinged loudly as it was hammered by bullets. Ariana tossed both flashbangs through the dark opening and pulled out her guns. Michael closed the door all but a fraction of an inch and looked away. The gunfire stopped, and for a split second all was quiet.

The flashbangs detonated with devastating noise and Michael yanked the door fully open. Ariana was through the doorway before he'd let go of the handle. The hall was nearly pitch black and choked with smoke. Gunfire erupted off to the left, loud and close by, there was a scream to the right, and two shots rang out from that direction. He heard three quick shots from Ariana's suppressed guns, again to the left.

Gun at the ready, he stepped into the hall and angled to the right with his shoulder up against the near wall. The smoke stung his eyes, but he knew that would last only seconds longer. He felt naked without any body armor. Men on either side, apparently firing at will and probably hitting each other. As if on cue, shots rang out behind him.

Michael saw the barest hint of a shape writhing on the ground to the left, shot it twice center mass. A burst of shots from behind. Different guns at different distances, interspersed with Ariana's suppressed fire. A muzzle flash fifteen feet ahead on the opposite side of the hall, then another. Something tugged at Michael's left side below his ribs, traced a line of fire across his skin. He ignored it and put three shots on the flashes he'd seen, heard a thump as something heavy hit the ground. More gunfire from behind, and Michael discovered he was face down on the floor.

What the hell just happened?

His left shoulder was numb. He tried to push up off the floor, but his left arm didn't seem to work anymore. He rolled up onto his right shoulder and got his gun out from underneath him, then pushed against the wall into a sitting position. A tiny square of faint light appeared twenty-five feet down the hall a few feet off the floor.

Shitty time to get a phone call. Idiots and their thin wool pants.

Michael got his gun up on his knees and sighted toward the light using his right arm. He squeezed off four shots in quick succession. The light was gone. All was quiet at both ends of the hall.

Twenty-one rounds to go.

He tried once again to move his left arm and was able to lift it a bit at the cost of an exquisite, stabbing pain in his shoulder. He reached over with his right hand and probed the shoulder. He found the blood-soaked entry wound high on the back-side of his shoulder.

Assholes shot at her and got me.

Michael tucked his left arm protectively against his body and, using the wall, tried to lever himself up to his feet. His left foot slipped out from under him and he sat back down hard. He reached over with his right arm and felt the floor, trying to figure out why he couldn't get traction. He felt a liquid, slick and smeared on the floor. More gun shots rang out from the direction Ariana had gone, though they sounded further off, maybe around a corner or two. He brought his hand to his nose and sniffed.

Blood. My blood. Shoulder must be bleeding badly.

Michael scooted down the hall away from the blood and pushed up to his feet. Knowing he was bleeding badly from the shoulder made him feel lightheaded, creating a puzzle he couldn't solve. Was it the actual loss of blood or the thought of bleeding that much which was making him feel faint? Either way, he doubted he had much time left before his body would quit on him.

One last scan of his end of the hall—still cloaked in total darkness—and Michael cut over to the other side of the hallway and headed back toward Ariana. Running was out of the question, so he settled for a shuffling trot that mainly leveraged his right leg. He passed the stairway door, visible by the slight grayness of the fluorescent bulb two floors above.

A dozen feet further on, he found the first body by tripping over it. With his gun clutched in his right hand, he instinctively tried to reach out with his left hand as he sprawled forward, which accomplished very little other than another explosion of pain in his left shoulder as he tried to jerk it forward. The arm remained weak and basically useless. Thankfully, he found a second body by flopping onto it, breaking his fall.

Idiot! You knew there'd be bodies.

Michael rolled off the inert form, found a wall, and leaned against it. The fall had jarred his body, emboldening his every wound to cry out with pain. He couldn't seem to catch his breath and labored to control the cadence of his breathing. He was slipping, and he knew it. How could he have run—or, his version of a run—blindly down a hall that he knew was littered with bodies? His mind wandered.

Maybe there's something between us.

The words were etched in his mind, the context lost.

Maybe there's something between us.

Ariana's singular focus had caused her to use him, to betray him, yet he found such clarity—such all-encompassing purpose —appealing. Enticing even. And she hadn't just used him. She'd put everything on the line, and from what he'd seen, she had far more to lose than he'd ever have. Michael felt like he might finally understand her, and in understanding he found it harder to rage against what she'd done to him. Lacking anger, his longing surged to the fore.

"You, my friend, are a fucking idiot."

The words were barely a whisper—almost a prayer that someone would save him from himself. What had Jeffrey said over lunch? Something about how he always committed fully, tying himself to women who were bitches. Michael didn't think Ariana qualified, not even for a second. Yet he suspected Jeffrey might find her even worse.

You need to move. You're drifting.

He levered himself up the wall to a standing position once more and began shuffling forward again, his right foot leading as he felt along for more bodies. He knew he was near the end. His body was no longer trying to overwhelm him with pain, though it was still severe and constant. Instead, he felt distant, one step removed from it all.

Michael forced himself to keep moving. It almost proved too much. The darkness gave him no reference points, and he struggled to keep track of which way was up. Each step was a trial, a small victory. He moved around the body on which he'd landed, somehow curved over and ran into the wall he'd just been leaning against. At least, he thought it was that wall. He took the next step, then another.

Would it end this way? Broken, bleeding, wandering blindly in the pitch blackness of a hallway already full of death? He nudged into a body, worked his way slowly around it, leaving the security of the wall behind. It would've made more sense to stay near the wall and step over the body, but he knew that would never work. Michael realized the M4 was hanging at his side by its strap, no longer held at the ready. It seemed significant, but he brushed aside the thought and took another step.

His outstretched right hand felt a wall directly ahead. Was it a new wall? The same one? Michael wasn't sure, but turned to the left, followed it a few feet, found a corner. He stood there for a long moment, then slowly lowered his head into the comforting cradle where the two walls met.

"Michael? Holy shit you're a mess."

Ariana's voice didn't surprise him, which seemed odd. He didn't move. It was too pleasant, his head wedged in the corner, the struggle to remain upright made so easy. He felt something on his now numb left shoulder.

"You've been shot. Lost a lot of blood."

It felt like the right moment for sarcasm, but he let it pass, decided on poetry instead.

"Yeah, I got shot." It was a solid start, though he wasn't sure Ariana would be able to hear his muttered words.

"I think you're hot." Solid conclusion to the first couplet. "Got no more time, and... can't think of a rhyme."

"Oh, Michael." She gently turned him around, her hands lending him balance. "I need one more thing, okay? We've got to get moving. We're almost out of time."

He leaned forward, found her shoulder, and nestled his face into the crook of her neck. "Don't have one more thing to give."

"You do. You have to."

Was she crying? He was pretty sure she was crying. Michael focused, tried to figure out what was happening. Yes, she was definitely crying. He could hear it ever so faintly. He tried to reach up and wipe her cheeks with his good arm but realized he couldn't move it. Realized she was clutching his hand, holding his arm wrapped over her shoulders. Realized they were moving, Ariana half dragging him down a hallway he couldn't see. When had that happened?

Maybe there's something between us.

He giggled. How did he think he was going to wipe her tears? She had that mask on, right? It would've absorbed tears one by one as they fell. No, there were definitely no tears to wipe. Yet her crying seemed to gain volume, increase in intensity, multiply into multiple voices. It made no sense. And his eyes were playing tricks on him. The darkness took on an eerie green glow up ahead. It grew in size and detail as they approached, gaining definition. A doorway, dim green light spilling out.

I'm losing my mind.

The noises weren't Ariana crying. They came from the doorway. Sobs, sniffles, an occasional wail. The sounds of fear. The sounds of many girls in distress. Michael struggled back towards reality. Something about the girls. The mission. They all tied together. He couldn't remember.

"This is it, Michael." Ariana was facing him, her masked head near his, her night vision goggles gone. When had they stopped walking? "I need you to do exactly what I say. Understand?"

Michael stared at her, his broken jaw hanging open. He most definitely did not understand. Was she asking him to understand that he needed to understand? It made no sense. His mind spiraled.

Ariana slapped him. Not hard, and high on the cheek to avoid his jaw. His eye sharpened into focus, his mind asserted itself in response to the shock of her hand.

"You'll see a lot in that room." She was leaned in close again, whispering. "Ignore all of it. Ignore the girls, the glow sticks, the chain link cages, all of it."

Cages? What? How does her breath smell so good?

"You've got one job. One chance for us to keep them all alive."

He strained against the fatigue and numbness. Tried to hear her words and understand.

"You've got to get in there fast, about ten feet in, and plant yourself on the floor. Kneeling on all fours. I need you to be stable, your back and hips rigid."

He gave up. She was talking nonsense. Save the girls by kneeling on the floor?

"Do you understand?" He caught the desperation in her voice. "Ten feet in, you kneel and brace yourself. Nothing else matters."

Ten feet. Kneeling. Braced.

The instructions confused him. Kneeling on the ground to save the girls? And even if it would save them, could he even do it? He looked at Ariana, revealed in the faint green glow from the nearby doorway, his one good eye traveling back and forth between her eyes. She seemed deadly earnest. Maybe he couldn't do it. Maybe he could. He decided he'd give it a shot. One last effort, then he could let go.

A loud male voice shouted from the green room in another language. Ariana's head jerked around toward the door for moment, then she began stripping off her gear.

"Now?" Michael's voice was hoarse, distant.

Ariana held up a hand to stall him as she disencumbered herself. Gun harness, ammo belt, body armor. She removed everything but her clothes and mask, and pulled his M4 off and set it by the rest of her gear on the floor. Taking one of her guns in hand, Ariana pulled her mask up over nose. Michael didn't see the hand slip around his neck but felt her pull him forward to kiss him gently on the lips, careful to not bump his jaw.

Maybe there's something between us.

She pulled the mask back into place. "Now."

Michael lurched forward, stumbled, pushed off the wall with his good arm, and turned through the doorway. He kept his eyes on the floor, desperately trying to stay upright, hunched over and shambling forward. In his peripheral vision, he saw glow sticks scattered across the floor of an expansive room. A crowd of people—girls from the sound of the startled noised when he'd entered the room—clustered just up ahead. A strong male voice, the same one he'd heard from the hall, shouted something at him from the midst of the girls.

He collapsed to the floor, jarring his good arm and sending a shock through his ragged body as he caught himself. Both knees planted, his right arm centered up under his chest supporting his weight, he tried to deploy his left arm to help but failed. The world spun as a wave of dizziness swept over him. He ignored his body's signals as it screamed he was tipping over and focused entirely on pushing against the floor with his good hand and knees.

Ariana sprinted through the doorway and covered the distance to him in three strides. She leapt, planted a foot on his lower back, and pushed off hard. It should have hurt, but Michael had moved past the pain. Instead, he slowly toppled over to the sound of a gunshot and stared at the ceiling above as all hell broke loose.

Maybe there's something between us.

It was a happy thought, so he latched onto it and repeated it to himself as he saw shapes fly by and swirl around him. There were voices, lots of them, and all sorts of screams and crying and commotion. Time slid by, unmarked by Michael, until a group of people encircled him. Hands grabbed him by arms, legs, and head, and lifted him. The ceiling started to move at that point, but the green light seemed to follow.

Maybe there's something between us.

Eventually, even the green light slid into darkness.

CHAPTER TWENTY-FIVE

*T*he staccato beeps wormed their way into Michael's dreams, manifesting first as cars honking at him as he frantically tried to figure out which lane he was supposed to take in a maze of highways, later as his watch alarm telling him it was time to wake. Eventually, he obeyed the shrill demand and struggled up to consciousness.

His good eye cracked open. A momentary confusion followed by comprehension. He was in a hospital room, surrounded by medical gear. An IV fed a tube into the back of his left hand. His body was once again wrapped in the warm embrace of morphine. Michael tilted his head to the right and felt a tug in his nose. He tried to bring his right hand up, felt an impediment, worked it free of the covers. He found a thin tube across his face clipped to his nose. Oxygen. His lungs must have been struggling.

"Ah! Awake at last."

The voice came from the left. He couldn't place it in spite of its familiarity. Michael gingerly pivoted his head to the left and discovered a compact man standing beside his hospital bed leaning on the guardrail. The man wore a white dress shirt tucked into blue jeans. Memory stirred and Michael reached for the name.

"Can you understand me?" the man asked.

Michael's jaw didn't seem to want to move, so he settled with nodding. The little man nodded back.

"Good. Good. You missed a day. Out all yesterday. You must know your story, yes? The police, they will question you soon."

He must have seen Michael's eyebrows pull together a fraction of an inch, because he immediately waved his hand, shooing away Michael's concerns.

"No trouble. You are the victim, yes? You have been at the hotel. You remember? I took you there a week ago. You, the real you, not Thomas Paine. You are tourist, ah, visiting Rome to meet beautiful woman you met online, yes? Dark-haired beauty named Ludovica. You are at the hotel, and you are mugged and treated"—he waved his hands indicating the length of Michael's body—"in horrible way. So bad, you do not remember it all. Many injuries over several days. So many you do not know all of them. You understand?"

Michael took several breaths and processed what he'd just heard.

A girl I met online. Dark-haired beauty. Ludovica.

"Understand." The word was forced out through his nearly immobile jaw. "Wallet? Phone?"

Leonardo. His name is Leonardo.

Leonardo smiled. "Yes, yes. They were"—he made air quotes with his fingers—"found by an anonymous person who turned them into the police. I think they return them when they talk to you."

"Not Thomas anymore?"

Leonardo smiled, nodded. "Right!" He shook his head.

"You are not Thomas. Michael, yes?" He smiled again. "But I am still Leonardo." The pronouncement was followed with a wink.

Michael's functioning eyelid felt heavy, but he forced himself to stay engaged. There were so many unanswered questions, starting with the most important one. How was he still alive?

"How?" He tried to put emphasis on the word, make Leonardo recognize its significance.

Leonardo smiled again. "I go now. Time for nurse to check on you." He turned to leave, stopped, twisted around to face Michael. "Ah! One thing. In three days, a rescue nurse from your employer comes to take you home. Good luck, Mr. Grimm."

With that, the little man was gone. Michael took a slow look around his room, frustrated he'd gotten no real answers. The room looked completely normal for a private hospital room, if a bit spacious. Two nurses came in a few minutes later, chatting in Italian, of which Michael understood nothing. Their routine, however, was familiar and comforting. Afterwards he slept.

Michael woke. The pain was still managed. He took in some sustenance through a straw. He was interviewed by two Italian police officers who spoke broken English regarding the horrible mugging and apparent kidnapping that had left him injured and nearly dead. His jaw allowed him to remain vague in his answers and still satisfy them. They returned his passport and phone. He slept again.

He woke to find Ariana standing beside his bed, the dark-haired beauty he'd traveled to Rome to meet. She was holding his right hand, staring off to the side at one of the machines monitoring his vitals.

Maybe there's something between us.

J. PHILIP HORNE

He wanted to reject her, reject the insanity of his fixation on her hint of a possibility. He wanted to still be a PJ. He wanted to marry a woman and live faithfully as husband and wife. His wants dictated so little of his reality. Instead, he seemed destined to be swept along by events and women who did not ultimately care for him.

He gave her hand a squeeze. Ariana shifted her gaze to him and smiled.

"Did we win?"

It wasn't the question he'd meant to ask, though he couldn't quite articulate what he really wanted to hear from her.

Ariana's smile broadened. "Completely. The *Hije* is effectively no more. The girls are being cared for and returned to their families."

"How?" He drew in a slow breath, tried to clarify. "Don't understand. How it ended." He brought his hand to his head and tapped his temple. "Wasn't lucid."

Ariana nodded. "Do you remember the hallway. When I found you?"

Michael couldn't picture it. Only darkness. But he remembered the pain and confusion and feeling of slipping away. And the bodies. He nodded.

"Okay, good. Basically, they were caught completely off guard when the power was cut. They'd been scrambling since Valdrin died, I think. Anyway, with the night vision, I cut through them pretty quickly once those flashbangs detonated."

"Remember crouching." It felt vague, like it had happened to someone else. Stumbling through the dark with Ariana to a green room. "Remember green. And lots of people."

"That's right." She gave his hand a small squeeze. "Lefter had glow sticks scattered on the floor. I'm guessing that had been all the light they used in the room where the girls were penned up. They were drugged, but only mildly. To keep them docile. It was rough conditions, but their basic needs were met. Anyway, he had them all in a cluster around him. Human shields. I didn't have a shot."

"Why?" Michael asked.

"Not sure how he saw it ending, but he was buying time. He had men inbound. Anyway, I figured I had to end it. Right then. I just needed an angle."

"Me crouching?"

Ariana nodded. "You were my angle. Wasn't sure I could do it. I've never tried anything like that. Turns out I can."

Michael struggled to understand. "Your angle?"

"I needed to get high enough to shoot down over the girls and take out Lefter." She shrugged. "So I vaulted off your back. Had one shot right at the peak when he was caught off guard, before he could duck. Took him right in the forehead." She shrugged again and looked away.

Michael's mind locked up trying to guess his odds of taking a shot like that. More likely to win the lottery. Twice in a row. Without buying a ticket.

"And then?"

Ariana looked back at him. "Then I got the girls out on the street as fast as possible. Got a few of the more solid ones to help me haul you out. They made a scene, help started coming, so when the *Hije* reinforcements started arriving, there was nothing for them to do but slip away. With the *bajrak* dead, hopefully it will be permanent. And Michael, the first of the girls were reunited with their families today."

It was too much to process. The morphine not only dulled the pain, it also tore down walls erected to keep his emotions in check. A tear leaked out of his eye.

"How?" Michael disengaged his hand from hers and pointed vaguely around the room, then used it to wipe his eye. "All this?"

"I drove you to another part of the city. Called emergency services. Then showed up here yesterday evening as the hysterical woman you'd come to Italy to meet. Set up the backstory and paid to upgrade your room. In the meantime, I managed to get through to Joann and get Leonardo to pass your passport and phone to the police through a contact." She smiled. "He's a strange little man, isn't he?"

Michael processed what she'd said, reviewed what had happened during his week in Rome, and worked to keep his emotions under control. She waited, watching his face, her hand slipping back into his.

"Always one step behind." He paused, figuring out the fewest words to communicate his intent. "You. Them. Situation. Everything."

"I know. But not because you're slow. I was maneuvering you from one situation to another." She looked down in her lap. "I've had some time to think things through. I'm proud of what we accomplished at the end. I'm not proud of how I treated you."

"Used me." He tugged on her hand, willed her to make eye contact. She obliged.

"I used you. I'm sorry."

Michael nodded. "Forgive you."

Tears spilled down her cheeks, and Ariana began weeping quietly, clinging to his hand. After a few minutes, Michael realized—one step behind as always—that she was mourning far more than her treatment of him. He held her hand, content to offer that small comfort in the midst of her remorse.

When she at last reached the end of her tears, she stepped away for a few minutes to wash her face, then returned. She stood once again beside his bed and took his hand.

"Joann's arranged for a rescue nurse to come get you in a

few days," Ariana said. "The staff here thought travel would be realistic for you by then. I made sure it was first class."

"So," Michael said, "sending me away?"

"I was thinking of it more along the lines of setting you free. I'll have a car to take you to the airport. Your duffel will be in it. Get you home to convalesce. Oh!"—her eyes widened and she smiled—"do you have your bank app on your phone?"

He nodded.

"Check your balance."

Michael released her hand once more and pointed toward a table near the window. Ariana looked, saw the phone, and retrieved it for him. He pulled up the app and logged in. The balance was about a hundred times larger than it had been. Six figures. He'd never seen anything like it.

He looked up at her. She waited, her eyebrows raised in anticipation. Michael set the phone down, took up her hand, gave it a squeeze. Ariana smiled.

"Jaw hurts," he said. "Can't talk. You'll have to. Tell me about yourself. No cover stories. Just truth. What you feel comfortable telling."

Ariana looked at him for a long moment, then nodded. She pulled up a chair beside his bed, took his hand in hers, and talked about herself until the hall visiting hours came to an end a couple hours later.

The flight home was uneventful. He'd transitioned well to oral pain killers and his body was on the mend. By the time he boarded the plane, he could see out of both eyes and walk unaided. Ariana had visited him for a few hours each day in the hospital, and by the second day he'd been an active participant in their conversations. Michael had become content to tune out the future—and forget aspects of the past— and enjoy the company of a beautiful woman.

Once home, he discovered Joann had worked with funding from Ariana to set him up at an inpatient recovery center with on-staff doctors and physical therapists. After an initial moment of irritation at not being consulted regarding the details of his own life, he fully embraced the opportunity to actively pursue a fast and full recovery.

Six weeks later, he drove home to his apartment complex, about ten pounds lighter, a good bit weaker, still needing to heal, but fully functional. He pulled into a parking spot and dropped the car into park. Stepping out, he retrieved his duffel from the back of the car and headed to his stairwell. As he reached the top of the third flight of stairs, he looked up and saw Sherry talking to another young woman.

Shit. What was her name? Liza!

The two women were a study in contrasts. Sherry's pale skin and long, straw-colored hair to Liza's dark skin and near-black, close-cut hair. Michael stepped up onto the short hallway and fished his keys out of his pocket.

"Michael?" Sherry's voice had a breathiness to it, a contained shock. "You're back?"

He looked up from his keys to find both women staring at him. Michael set down his duffel and dropped his keys on top of it.

"I'm back." He shrugged. "The trip took a bit longer than expected."

Sherry walked toward him, Liza a step behind. "You look different. Are you okay?" She stopped a few feet away. "Sorry. Was that too direct? It's just I've been wondering what happened to you."

Michael discovered he had none of the usual awkwardness

when talking to attractive young women. It was a refreshing change.

"All good." He reached out a hand toward Liza. "I'm Michael." He nodded toward his apartment door. "Your neighbor if they didn't change the lock while I was gone."

Liza shook his hand and smiled. She had a nice smile. Relaxed. Self-confident. "Liza. Sherry'd mentioned she'd met you. Then you sort of..."

She trailed off and Michael stepped into the gap. "Yeah, my trip to Italy went a little sideways."

Sherry was staring intently at his face. "It *was* you, wasn't it?"

Michael's eyebrows came together. "Was me what?"

"Little over a week after you left, I was wondering what had happened, so I checked in on news reports out of Rome." Sherry shifted, folded an arm behind her back. "There was a story about some anonymous tourist who'd been kidnapped and tortured, and it freaked me out when I saw the picture. Probably some paparazzi shooting with a telephoto, because it wasn't the best pic. But it sure looked like you, if your face was all mashed up."

"Oh."

"Yeah," Sherry said, staring at his face again. "Sure looks like you went through something rough."

Michael hadn't known any pictures had leaked. He'd worked hard to stay invisible while in the hospital. He wasn't sure how to respond. The silence stretched out for a few seconds.

Liza nudged Sherry with her elbow. "And the second one?"

Sherry glanced at her and Liza raised her eyebrows meaningfully.

"Okay, so then there was this other story," Sherry said, looking back at Michael. "About this insane mafia thing. Bunch of girls kidnapped and up for sale. There were all these dead thugs. Like, lots of them. And all the girls claimed that two people—this masked woman and this large, insanely beat up guy—rescued them."

Michael wasn't sure what to say, so he kept his mouth shut to see how it would play out.

Sherry shrugged, looked down at her feet. "I don't know. Just seemed interesting. The timing of the two things, the timing of your trip, you going missing." She looked back up at him. "And don't lie to me about that first report and claim the tortured guy wasn't you. I'm sure it was. I'm a photographer, remember? I've got an eye for detail. And you look like you've been through something. Something bad."

"Fair enough." Michael said.

He was stalling for time, processing the situation. He had no interest in lying and was impressed with Sherry's intuition. He hated the thought of making her feel stupid by denying what she'd pieced together. She was way out in front of the Italian police, though she had the advantage of having met him prior to all his injuries. What was the downside of them knowing some of the details if they'd already figured out the big picture?

Michael concluded there was no downside. He smiled.

"Listen," he said, looking from Sherry to Liza and back. "My bank account is in a very different place than it was a month ago. And I haven't over-indulged in a very long time. Why don't I host a small dinner party for our hallway? You two pick the restaurant, I'll treat, and I'll tell you a story that you won't believe. You in?"

The two women glanced at one another and their eyes lit up.

"I knew it was you," Sherry said and flashed her electric smile. "I'm in."

"This is crazy!" Liza said. "Sherry's been ranting about this whole thing for three weeks. I wouldn't miss it for anything."

Michael nodded. "Be warned, though. It's harrowing. I mean, there's mafia killers, kidnapped girls, betrayal, murder, torture. All of it."

He paused and took a deep breath. "And a most beautiful bird of prey."

ALSO BY J. PHILIP HORNE

for Adults

The Rescue Nurse - A Michael Grimm Novel, Book 1 (2020)

Pay Dirt - A Michael Grimm Novel, Book 2 (forthcoming)

---

for Younger Readers & the Young at Heart

Joss the Seven - Guild of Sevens, Book 1 (2016)

Guardian Angel - Guild of Sevens, Book 2 (2017)

The Hero Feat of Hannah Helstrom - a Guild of Sevens short story (2017)

The Lodestone (2011)

ABOUT THE AUTHOR

J. Philip Horne probably shouldn't be alive. Born in Florida, he grew up overseas for the most part, spending much of his childhood in Liberia and Micronesia. During those years, he experienced numerous attempts on his life. The wannabe killers included malaria, spinal meningitis, blood poisoning, a staph infection in his heel bone, a close encounter with a green mamba, and other cold-hearted foes.

From his earliest years, his parents read to him fantastical stories from wonderful worlds. Narnia and Middle Earth featured prominently, and had his youth been a generation later, he would have certainly encountered Hogwarts at a young age. Through his teen years he read stories by many other authors and experienced a host of new worlds.

After dabbling in writing for many years, he finally got serious and wrote his first novel in 2011. He has continued to write ever since. For news of upcoming works, please join Mr. Horne's email list at jphiliphorne.com.

Made in the USA
Middletown, DE
29 June 2021